KAW

ROSEVILLE

A Novel of Secrets, Suspicion, and the Cost of Knowing

by Victoria Pitson

First produced in the United Kingdom in 2025 by The Choir Press

Published by Davic Books

Paperback ISBN 978-1-0682662-0-1

Hardback ISBN 978-1-0682662-1-8

EBook ISBN 978-1-0682662-2-5

www.davic.co.uk

DEDICATION

For *David* and *Benjamin*, always.

ACKNOWLEDGEMENTS

I would like to thank Dr Carly Schabowski for her insightful manuscript assessment, Ann-Marie Lowery for her sharp editorial eye, and Rachel Woodman for her guidance and support throughout the publishing process.

CHAPTER ONE

I hauled my luggage down the uneven paved pathway leading to the driveway, where the car was parked in a rather skew-whiff manner. I was about to comment to my friend about the unorthodox attempt at parking when my case suddenly became snagged, jolting my arm and almost pulling it out of its socket. One of the wheels had become stuck in the gap between two of the paving slabs, but with a sharp tug and a few strong words I managed to coax it back on track. Squinting from the glare of the sun, it dawned on me how lucky we were in choosing this particular week to go away. The previous week had been miserable, with a continuous downpour of rain day after day.

I came to the end of the path, drawing alongside the car, and briefly glanced at the front lawn. I was dismayed to see it was really in need of a cut, and considering I was going to be away for a week it didn't bode well what state it would be in when I got back, not to mention the likely disapproval of the neighbours. The majority of my neighbourhood felt like they could be members of some professional gardeners' guild and probably have a shot at a gold award at the Chelsea Flower Show. There was a brief moment when my front garden became a glorious sea of red tulips and would catch the admiration of passers-by. Unfortunately, that moment was short-lived, as once the torrent of rain came crashing down, accompanied by storm force winds, the display was quickly ruined. So, as usual, my garden wasn't quite holding its own.

'I think there should be enough room in the boot for your case to fit,' said Lisa unconvincingly. Lisa opened the boot to reveal that there was a space about half the size of my case on the far right.

'Travelling light then,' I exclaimed sarcastically.

She chuckled. 'Oh, we can make it fit.'

I peered over the parcel shelf to see that the back seat was also crammed with coats, umbrellas and other paraphernalia. I frowned and just couldn't fathom how anyone could load a car with so much stuff just for one person for a week-long break. As Lisa was watching my clearly unimpressed reaction, she looked somewhat sheepish as she tried in vain to make more room in the boot.

'Oh sorry. It honestly didn't seem this much when I was packing it all. I'm glad you are sensible, unlike me, who brings everything but the kitchen sink. Otherwise, we would have to go in two cars!'

Lisa was right. Even though we were the best of friends and had been for a very long time, we were quite different people. I was most definitely the more sensible of the two of us and was much more level-headed. Lisa on the other hand was far wilder and lived entirely for the moment. The fact that Lisa had packed what looked like ten times more than I had was no surprise. Lisa was extremely image-conscious and no doubt packed for every eventuality, whereas I was much more of a minimalist.

To my amazement, after some careful rejigging, Lisa did actually manage to make enough space for my case.

'See, I said it would fit,' she said with that 'I-told-you-so' tone in her voice. I gave a wry smile in response followed by a quick raise of the eyebrows and made my way to the front passenger door.

'So how long do you reckon it will take to get there?' I asked as I prepared to get into the seat.

'A couple of hours maybe,' she said as she firmly slammed the boot down and then in a slightly less audible voice muttered, 'assuming I can find it, that is.'

As I sat down in the seat I closed my eyes and grimaced. It wouldn't be the first time we had been lost together. Forward planning was not Lisa's forte, and neither of us could pretend we had any navigational skills.

'Right then!' she exclaimed excitedly as she plopped herself down into the driver's seat. 'You couldn't just grab my sunglasses from the glove compartment, could you?'

I opened the compartment in front of me and retrieved said sunglasses. A very stylish red-rimmed pair of Ray-Bans, far too trendy and edgy for me. Lisa put the glasses on, had a quick peek in the rear-view mirror, adjusted them accordingly and then turned to me with a broad grin and said, 'Right, ready?'

'Yep, let's do it.'

So here we were; the start of our girly week's holiday. It had come completely out of the blue. Lisa had phoned me up one day to say she had won some competition for a week's holiday in Devon. Apparently, it was a holiday village set in fifty acres of idyllic countryside, and the package that Lisa won included an all-inclusive stay, for two people, in a woodland lodge that even had its own private hot tub. At first, I wasn't convinced, as it all sounded a bit too good to be true.

'So, it's all free?'

'Well, yeh, practically,' she replied. 'I mean, the main stuff is paid for. We might have to pay the odd extra, I suppose. Oh, come on, Em. You gotta say yes. You can't pass up a free holiday!'

The conversation had initially started out like she was an overexcited child, but as it progressed she became more and more irritated at my rather hesitant reaction.

'How did you actually win this holiday?' I asked.

'Oh … I just filled in some puzzle thing from a local paper, sent it in and won.'

I stayed silent as I tried to imagine Lisa even reading a local paper, never mind actually going to the effort of completing some brain teaser page and then posting in the answers.

'Are you sure this isn't some kind of scam?'

Lisa uttered a long disapproving groan. I felt slightly guilty that I was putting such a dampener on something that she had clearly been so excited about and wanted me to share in, but at the same time it just didn't seem to quite add up. Eventually, after some careful persuasion and assurances that it was all above board, I caved in. Although I couldn't help but feel that there was something amiss.

'So you had no problem getting the time off work then?' asked Lisa as she pulled rather abruptly out of the driveway, narrowly missing a post.

'No, although I thought I might, given the rather short notice you gave me.'

Lisa chuckled and pressed the accelerator pedal as we sped off down the road on the start of our journey. I sank slightly deeper into my seat in the knowledge that Lisa's driving was somewhat faster than I was comfortable with and at times could be quite erratic. The first half of the journey was fairly uneventful and straightforward as we travelled along either motorway or main A-roads. We wiled the time away chatting and catching up, and I barely noticed my surroundings or took any real note of the route. Eventually, we exhausted our conversation and fell silent. After a few minutes, Lisa turned the radio on, skipping through a couple of stations before settling on Diana Ross belting out *Chain Reaction*. Personally, I would have preferred one of the other stations that were playing a much more chilled selection of music, but I knew better than to try and overrule her. She then turned the volume up so high I could feel the vibrations from the speaker in the corner down by my feet.

I winced as she sang along at the top of her voice, swaying to the rhythm of the music as she gripped the steering wheel firmly. I realised I might have to suffer in silence for a good couple of hours with this. I decided to try and distract myself by enjoying the country views and so sat staring out of the window looking at some cows grazing in a field. I noticed there were a few lying down in the grass, debunking the theory that rain must be on its way. The weather was glorious, and the forecast was that we were in for a few spectacularly hot and dry days. As I surveyed the view, I noted we were on much quieter and more rural roads. I started to feel nauseous from the constant twisting and turning along the windy narrow roads. I became aware that Lisa was very pensive and repeatedly looking in her rear-view mirror.

'Everything all right?'

At first, she didn't reply, too deep in concentrating on whatever it was that was bothering her. I looked round, between the seats and out through the back window. A red Vauxhall Astra was right up behind us; any closer and it would be in our boot. There were two young men in the front laughing and gesticulating wildly.

'Idiots,' barked Lisa.

I turned back to face the front. 'Why don't you just pull over and let them pass?' I almost pleaded. Lisa shot me a glance and I knew she was far too resolute to even consider that idea. Then suddenly the Astra made its move, pulling right alongside us on the wrong side of the road.

With a look of daggers, Lisa screamed at them, 'You complete idiots!'

I clung to the inner car door handle and braced myself. 'Lisa seriously, just pull over,' I demanded, but Lisa was a very strong-willed and independent individual, and she completely ignored my request. For what felt like an eternity, we were locked side by side. I nervously flicked my attention back and forth. One moment, looking out through the front windscreen, dreading the moment I saw a car coming the other way, faced with another vehicle head-on. The next moment, at Lisa, trying to determine what exactly she was going to do, and then at the guys in the car, who just seemed to be finding it all very exhilarating. To my relief, the Astra finally decided to end what felt like some kind of racing contest and lurched away at an unbelievable speed, disappearing ahead of us round a sharp bend. It was a good few minutes before I started to relax, as I was half expecting to see some carnage round the next corner. I began to loosen my grip on the door handle and finally felt safe enough to let go. My hand ached from where I had been gripping it so tightly for so long. Lisa hadn't murmured a word since her outburst of expletives, and she still looked rattled by the incident. I pondered on whether I should say something or remain silent. I decided it would be safer to stay silent rather than risk upsetting her further. I couldn't decide what best to say. Anyway, I had a habit of making light-hearted comments at not the most appropriate moments and I didn't want to antagonise her.

We continued our journey though the wonderful countryside, neither of us uttering a word for quite a while. Lisa had turned the volume of the radio down a few notches and switched to a station with slightly more tranquil music. After a while, she began to hum along and I could see the tension had lifted and she was in a more affable mood. We approached a crossroads and Lisa stopped to give way. Our path was clear and yet she sat there for a moment contemplating which direction was the right way to go. I could see the slight puzzlement in her eyes as she sat staring at the signage. I looked up and could see a white post with fairly small arrow signs giving the place names followed by their distance in miles. The signs were quite crudely made and were worn by age as well as being partially obscured by brambles and other foliage. Coupled with the fact I was also slightly short-sighted, it meant it was almost impossible to decipher what they said. I screwed my eyes up to try and bring the words into focus.

'I think straight over says Barndale. I have no idea what left is, and right looks like it says Tilfor.' Realising how completely useless my offering of navigational guidance was, I anticipated a sarcastic retort. Instead, Lisa decided to drive straight over the crossroads. I was unclear if her decision was derived from my comment or if it was just pure supposition.

'It's this way,' she replied confidently.

We drove for perhaps another mile and came to a pretty village. It looked fairly substantial, with a couple of pubs, a petrol station and a handful of shops. The pub on the corner looked much more inviting than the other, with hanging baskets overflowing with fuchsias and geraniums and picnic tables set up with sturdy parasols surrounded by a newly painted picket fence. The other looked tired, almost foreboding, and had paintwork peeling off the walls.

'I'm just going to pull in here and get some petrol.'

This came as some relief as I had already noticed the petrol gauge was now well below the quarter, and I was beginning to fear we would run out and become stuck in the middle of nowhere.

'Anything you want while we are here?'

'No, I'm good, thanks.'

'Okey-dokey.'

I waited while Lisa filled the tank, resting my head back against the car seat headrest and momentarily closing my eyes. I could smell the faint hint of petrol fumes and hear the distant roar of a motorbike. I was really starting to hope we were not too far away now. This journey was beginning to give me quite a headache and I still felt nauseous. Suddenly the car door opened and my eyes sprung open to see Lisa standing there with a large bag of jelly babies in her hand.

'Help yourself,' she said as she hurled them on my lap and got back in.

I wasn't sure if I had the stomach for them. Lisa started the engine; I popped a jelly baby into my mouth, rather pleased to find it was a purple blackcurrant one, and we set off on the final leg of the journey.

CHAPTER TWO

'I think it should be along here somewhere,' said Lisa.

I wasn't convinced; we'd done a few U-turns and seemed to be driving round in circles. The original estimate of two hours was far too optimistic.

'Yes, this is it, phew … I was beginning to wonder if we would get there before dark, and I hate driving in the dark.'

I was beginning to wonder if we would make it at all, or if the place even existed. Even with Lisa's confidence and the sign clearly stating that the next right was 'Roseville Holiday Resort', I still wasn't entirely sure. The turning didn't even look like a proper road; it was a dirt track barely wide enough for the car. This did not seem to deter Lisa and she swung into the turning with no hesitation. My uneasiness did not go unnoticed.

'What's up?'

'Are you sure it's down here?' I asked apprehensively as we bumped and jolted along the uneven track.

'Course it is, stop worrying.'

To my relief, the track did eventually transform into a proper tarmacked road although I was still rather perturbed as we approached the main entrance. There was a good two-metre-high steel mesh wire fence surrounding the entire perimeter. In front of us was an automated security gate blocking our access, and to the side was a hut, where a very burly security guard stood in the doorway. He watched us with stern eyes as we stopped right in front of the barrier, making me feel extremely intimidated. I was still not convinced we were in the right place; it gave the impression of being a high-security prison rather than a welcoming place to stay to relax and unwind.

As I kept my eyes fixated on the security guard in anticipation of him apprehending us for trespassing, I did not notice another guy approach the car. Lisa had wound down her window in order to talk with him.

'Hello, ladies, welcome to Roseville Resort,' he said in a strong Devonshire accent.

This guy was the complete polar opposite of the security guard. He was a slender man wearing a double-breasted burgundy waistcoat on top of a crisp lemon yellow shirt, with matching burgundy trousers and a pair of formal black patent leather pointed-toe shoes. He had a gentle and kind appearance and a genuinely welcoming nature.

Lisa showed him all the necessary paperwork, and he gave us our keys and the directions to our lodge. The barrier then lifted and he beckoned for us to drive through. As soon as we were through the gates, the whole atmosphere changed, and any misgivings I originally had began to dissipate.

We drove slowly along the meandering road that would eventually take us to our lodge deep into the heart of the resort. The surroundings were beautifully landscaped, full of topiary and flowers. Across in the distance I could see an area that looked like the main square. It was a large paved area surrounded by several buildings that appeared to be various restaurants and shops, and at the centre there was a water feature with a large fountain. I could see a hive of activity of people bustling about. A few were sat on benches eating ice creams, watching the world go by.

Lisa had to stop briefly to allow a family to cross the road. A young girl who appeared to have only just mastered the art of walking was desperately trying to make her way to the adventure playground. Her mother was frantically trying to grasp the little girl's hand as well as trying to keep an older boy on a scooter in tow. The father lagged behind, paying no attention as he was far too distracted by his mobile phone. The mother raised her hand in recognition to Lisa for kindly stopping as the father just trundled along with his head buried in his phone, completely oblivious to anything around him. I tutted in disapproval at this man's complete ignorance but was then rather amused when he misjudged the kerb and stumbled, just about managing to hang on to his phone as he juggled it from one hand to the other. That seemed to be a wake-up call, as he then put the phone in his back pocket and quickened his pace to catch up with his family. He playfully ruffled his daughter's hair, making her squeal in delight, and my opinion of him softened a little.

As we drove further, the landscape became denser and we were now deep into the forest. Every so often, you would see a small wooden post and attached to that a black metal disc, with white numbering denoting the lodge number.

'This is ours, Number 126,' said Lisa as she pulled into the private driveway attached to our lodge.

'Looks lovely,' I said admiringly.

About ten metres or so from the car I could see our lodge, nestled at the bottom of a gravelled pathway that was lined either side with globe-shaped lights. I was relieved to see it stood alone, unattached, and our nearest neighbour was a long way off, making it unlikely our peace would be disturbed.

We hopped out of the car with excitement and grabbed our luggage. Lisa picked up as many of her items as she could manage, but even with my spare hand to help we still couldn't carry it all in one trip.

'I'll get the rest later,' she said, unconcerned.

We made our way, heavily encumbered, along the path with the crunch of gravel beneath our feet. The lodge sat on stilts, and so there was a wooden slatted walkway starting at ground level from the end of the gravel path, gently sloping up until it reached the height of the decking surrounding the lodge. I was thankful that we had no steps to negotiate; my arms were aching with carrying such a load and I was unsure of my footing.

I got to the top of the walkway first and was glad to release some of the burden on my arms as I placed a couple of items down on the decking. As Lisa approached, she fumbled for the key and promptly dropped it, uttering an expletive as it slipped between the slats of the decking and landed somewhere in the undergrowth beneath the lodge.

'Please tell me that didn't fall through the gap?' I asked in disbelief.

She didn't need to answer as she was already on her hands and knees, peering through the gap it had slipped through.

'Well, I think we can safely say that we can forget about that key,' she finally announced.

'Oh, for God's sake,' I replied incredulously, shaking my head.

'Don't panic, I have another,' she said as she gleefully waved it around in front of my face. 'The guy at the gate gave us one each.'

'Well, in that case, that one is mine and I'll be hanging on to that,' I said, snatching it from her hands. 'Honestly, can't take you anywhere, you're worse than a clumsy child!' And, with that, we both fell about laughing.

We entered the lodge. The entrance hall was quite small and narrow with just some hanging space for a few coats on the wall, but it opened out into a large open-plan living space. The main space was dominated by two large black leather sofas surrounding a large low rectangular coffee table. There was a widescreen TV on the right wall. The focal point was the back wall, which was made up of bi-fold patio glass doors running along almost the entire length. This gave an extensive view of the woodland, and the lodge greatly benefitted from the amount of light it allowed into the room. To the left corner was a kitchenette, and there was a small dining table with two chairs positioned so as to take full advantage of the view. I could see two doors leading off this main room, one on the very left and one on the very right. I assumed these to be the bedrooms, effectively meaning the main room was sandwiched between them.

Lisa had dumped all her belongings in the middle of the floor and was turning the key in the patio door.

'Don't touch that key,' I almost shouted in a panic.

'I'm only opening it. I'll leave it in the keyhole, don't panic,' she giggled.

She folded the doors open in a concertina style, and we both stepped out onto the decking.

'Oh, Em, look at this hot tub.'

Lisa was almost dancing about in delight.

'There's no water in it,' I said, disappointed, as I leant over, peering into it. On closer inspection, I also noticed there was a huge crack running from top to bottom on one side.

'Oh, isn't there? Never mind, I'll let reception know. I am sure they can sort that out easily enough.'

I doubted it was capable of holding any water but I kept quiet. I wasn't a huge fan of hot tubs anyway. I was never convinced of how hygienic they really were.

I leant on the balcony railings and looked out into the distance, admiring the bluebells covering the woodland floor. Just for a moment, I went into a state of daydream, lost in the peace and tranquillity of the place.

'Em, I'm going to take this room, if you don't mind?' said Lisa, jolting me straight back to reality.

I went back in to find Lisa had taken the bedroom off to the right of the main living area. She had collected her things, which she had previously strewn across the floor, and was now beginning to unpack. She looked up with a slight look of embarrassment.

'Are you OK with me taking this one? The other room is more or less the same, other than it only has an ensuite shower room, whereas this one also has a bath. I didn't think you would be too bothered, though?'

'No, that's fine,' I said, although I was slightly irritated by her presumption.

'Are you sure?' she winced. 'I don't mind swapping if you prefer?'

I watched as Lisa proceeded to hang clothes in the wardrobe and fold clothes away into the chest of drawers. The thought of swapping when she had already made herself at home in this room seemed a ridiculous idea.

'No, it's fine, as long as there is a bed and a shower, I'm happy.'

'Good, that's what I thought,' she shouted after me as I left the room to discover what mine was really like.

Lisa was not quite truthful in her assessment of the differences. My room wasn't as big and seemed darker. I guess this was due to this room only having a single patio door out onto the decking area as opposed to the double doors Lisa had and therefore had less light coming in. The ensuite was tiny compared to Lisa's full ensuite bathroom, but it was adequate enough. I decided it really wasn't worth arguing about and started to unpack.

The journey here had felt long and arduous, and I was looking forward to a nice quiet and relaxing evening. My stomach started to growl and I realised we hadn't eaten for quite some time. The only thing I had eaten since lunchtime was a handful of jelly babies in the car on the way down, and they were not going to sustain me.

'Hey, Lisa,' I hollered as I made my way into the living room. Lisa was opening a bottle of white wine that she had retrieved from the fridge and was pouring out two glasses. Great, I thought, just what I need, drinking this early in the evening on an empty stomach. She handed me a glass, which I reluctantly took.

'Cheers,' she said, clinking my glass and then taking a large glug from hers.

'What are we doing about eating?' I said in an exasperated tone. 'I am starving. Shall we look at booking a table in one of the restaurants on the main square?'

'I was thinking exactly the same thing, I've had a quick flick through some of the leaflets on the coffee table and there's quite a choice. Italian, Indian, Mexican ...'

'I really don't mind,' I said, cutting her off mid-sentence. I was so hungry I had little concern over what the cuisine was, just as long as it was edible food.

'Well, I saw there was an American-style grill place. It looks a bit funkier than some of the other places and they serve cocktails!'

'OK, that sounds good,' I replied, although in truth that didn't sound like the quiet evening I was hoping for. Lisa was on the phone in a flash and booked us in for 8pm, giving us about an hour and a half to get ready. And then that's when things started getting really weird ...

CHAPTER THREE

I sat on the sofa waiting patiently for my friend to get ready. I had already showered and changed into something a bit more suitable for an evening out, wearing a simple black tailored pair of trousers with a pretty flower-patterned strappy top and a pair of wedge-heeled sandals. The glass of wine Lisa had poured for me ages ago was sat empty on the coffee table. Lisa had been in earlier for a top-up and had goaded me into having a second glass. At first, I steadfastly refused, but she was persistent and so I relented. Pride beaming from her face from her triumphant victory, she had taken the bottle, as well as her glass, back into her room as I continued to watch the soap opera that I had settled upon earlier after scanning through the endless channel guide. I had never watched it before in my life and in truth I had no real interest in it, but it did help to pass some of the time away.

The end credits started to roll, and I turned the TV off before the end of the signature tune. I sat for a moment wondering how much longer Lisa was going to be. I looked at my watch and was alarmed to see it was now 7.30pm. I stared at the door, contemplating whether to give her a shout and warn her how late it was getting. But as I sat there, I began to notice how deathly silent it was. I strained to listen for any indication of Lisa's movements and gain any clue as to how close she may be to actually being ready. There was nothing; all I could hear was the very faint humming sound of the fridge. For a few minutes I just sat there listening for any sign, but as the time passed I became more bewildered. I moved ever so slightly in the sofa, and the sound of the leather stretching seemed abnormally loud; even the fridge noise now seemed much more amplified. I waited for almost ten minutes before I rose from my seat. I went to the door, which was slightly ajar, and knocked.

'Lisa?' I called out. No answer. 'Lisa,' I said, raising my voice.

I strained to listen again but still could hear nothing. I was becoming concerned.

'Lisa, I'm coming in,' I said, and opened the door wide, stepping just inside the room.

Lisa was not in the room. I immediately turned my attention to the ensuite bathroom and saw the door was wide open. I was panic-stricken and for a moment I froze as I began to fear what I would find in the bathroom. Realising that Lisa might be in danger, I managed to summon the courage to take a look. I cautiously entered the bathroom, but she wasn't in there, either. Initially, I was relieved as I was convinced I was going to find her drowned in the bath or collapsed on the floor, and I had felt overwhelming guilt that I had left it far too long before investigating when I could have potentially saved her.

I was completely bemused and couldn't comprehend where exactly she had gone. Even though I could see from where I was standing that the bath was completely empty and the shower curtain was pinned back, giving no hiding space, I still walked right up to it and took a closer look. I turned back round, facing the bathroom door, where I had entered. It was wide open and right up against the wall, with no chance of anyone hiding behind it, but even so I pulled the door back and checked. I went back into the bedroom and scanned the room, looking for any evidence of where she could possibly be. There was the hairdryer lying on the dresser table which I heard going earlier in the evening as I sat watching the TV. Clothes, which I recognised from our journey down, were slung over a chair in the corner of the room, and on the side table was the bottle of wine and the glass, both of which were empty. There was quite simply nothing that was drawing my attention or giving me any indication of what might have happened to her. It then suddenly dawned on me that she must have stepped outside via her patio doors and my nerves began to settle. But my anxiety soon returned when I tried the doors to find them locked and could clearly see the key was still in the keyhole on the inside. In desperation, I went back into the living room, with no real hope I would find her in there. Twice, I checked the bi-fold doors, but they were locked, key in the keyhole still. I even checked my bedroom and bathroom, but I knew full well she wouldn't be there, either.

'Oh God, where the hell are you?' I shouted.

The front door was locked and I had the only key. I could see it right there on the coffee table where I had left it, alongside my empty glass. I was completely frantic now, desperately racking my brains trying to figure out what could have happened. I came to the conclusion that she just had to be in her bedroom. I'd seen her walk right back in there with a bottle of wine with my own eyes, and she hadn't come back out since. I almost stormed back in, determined she was in there. I painstakingly searched both the bedroom and bathroom, even looking under the bed and inside wardrobes. But all I found in the wardrobe was clothes and a few pairs of shoes, and the only thing the bed was concealing was a few balls of dust. I almost took the patio doors off their hinges where I shook them so hard, convinced they must have been unlocked when, of course, they weren't. Even after all this, I could find no trace of her.

I returned to the lounge and tried to take stock of what was happening, but I was in shock and had lost the ability to make any kind of rational thought. Then suddenly I heard Lisa's voice.

'Right then, Em, we better get going.'

I spun round to see her just coming out of her bedroom into the lounge, fiddling with her phone in one hand and a half-full glass of wine in the other. I stood there, dumbfounded. She looked up from her phone at me and frowned.

'Blimey, Em, you all right?' she asked. 'You look white as a sheet.'

'Where the hell have you been?' I yelled, sounding like a worried-sick parent after their child had come back well after curfew.

She looked up at me, startled by my reaction.

'Sorry, Em,' she said apologetically, 'you know what I'm like, takes me ages to get ready.'

'What?' I yelled.

Lisa looked at me in complete shock, obviously thinking I was overreacting.

'I don't mean the time you took. I mean, literally, where the hell did you go? Physically, where did you go?'

Lisa looked at me, puzzled.

'Umm ... what? What do you mean, where did I physically go?'

She half turned towards her room and weakly pointed, 'In there.'

She was looking at me, quite concerned now, and I could tell she was thinking I had completely lost my mind.

'No, you weren't in there,' I said firmly. 'I checked. I checked everywhere, in fact. Christ, I even looked under your bed!'

She laughed almost nervously, as if she couldn't quite tell if I was joking and this was some kind of wind-up. She placed her glass on the coffee table, so as to free up a hand and then placed it round my shoulders.

'Oh, Em, come on,' she said reassuringly, 'it's been a long day, you've had a bit to drink, and we haven't eaten for an absolute age. It's probably all got a bit too much and you've got a bit confused.'

I looked at her in horror, stunned by her easy dismissal of something that was so serious and had rocked me to the core.

'You were not in that room,' I said, pointing angrily in the direction of her bedroom. 'I saw you, Lisa. I bloody well saw you come in here, top up the wine and then go back in. At no point did you come back out. You just disappeared!'

I was practically shaking I was so distraught. Lisa looked really worried.

'Em, I really don't know what to say. I was getting ready in the room. I didn't go anywhere. I was probably in the bathroom.'

'No, you weren't in the bathroom,' I said resolutely.

'Well,' she hesitated as she tried to find a plausible solution, 'you probably nodded off on the sofa and then … I don't know … maybe I came back through. I can't remember my exact movements. Or maybe you dreamt it.'

Lisa's phone, which she was still holding in her hand, then started ringing. She looked down to see who was calling and looked confused.

'Sorry, I'm going to have to take this,' she said, sounding relieved at the interruption and then silently mouthed, 'it's my mum,' as she went back into the bedroom, closing the door behind her. Exasperated, I slumped back onto the sofa, just sitting there in a confused state. I could hear Lisa talking on the phone in what sounded quite a serious tone, but she was talking in too low a voice to hear any actual words. I began to calm down and tried to logically rationalise what had happened. Had I really fallen asleep and dreamt the whole thing? No, I was adamant that I had been fully conscious the whole time. I wasn't in the habit of just nodding off on the sofa during the day and, in any case, any dreams I had were not this realistic, and I could barely remember them. I was certainly not able to recall them in so much detail. I concluded it was definitely not a dream; Lisa really did disappear for those few moments, but I could not work out how or why it happened.

As I sat there, my eyes became transfixed on the glass of wine that Lisa had placed on the table just after she had made her miraculous reappearance. The glass was half full, and yet when I looked in her room, the bottle and the glass had both been empty. How could that be? Surely, that was the same glass.

Eventually, Lisa finished her phone conversation and came back into the room. I'd lost all concept of time, although I was fairly sure we must be late for our dinner reservation by now.

'How you feeling, Em? OK now?' she asked gently.

I wasn't sure how to reply because I wasn't actually sure how I felt.

'Umm, I-I-I'm OK,' I stuttered, giving her a perplexed look.

'Good, because we really do need to go. I am not sure how long they will hold our table for and we are quite late.'

I watched as Lisa went to pick up the main door key from the coffee table, but just before she did, she gulped down the rest of the wine that remained in her glass.

'Don't want to waste any!' she giggled.

'Did you open another bottle of wine?'

'God, no, I'm not that bad,' she said, as if she was quite taken aback by the suggestion. 'You coming?' she urged, and headed towards the door, and I obediently followed.

CHAPTER FOUR

We were very late for our dinner reservation, but the restaurant did not seem at all bothered and had happily held the table for us. Somehow, we actually had an enjoyable meal, and reasonable normality was restored. I was in a much more relaxed state, undoubtedly helped along by the alcohol we had consumed, but I was still preoccupied by the event and at times my mind wandered, thinking about it over and over again. There were several times during the meal I almost broached the subject, but Lisa seemed hell-bent on having a damn good night, and I was fearful she was beginning to think I was delusional. So instead I chose not to mention anything about it and gave my best efforts to enjoying the evening.

We'd both just polished off a slice of New York cheesecake each, and Lisa was trying to catch the waiter's attention to get the bill. Dinner and the bottle of wine we had was all included as part of the inclusive deal, but apparently the shots of tequila we had were classed as additional extras.

'Shall we move over to the bar area and grab some cocktails?' asked Lisa, once we'd settled the bill. There was a large section separate from the main restaurant area with comfy seating, a pool table, several TVs showing extreme sports and the main bar. I was already feeling quite drunk, and the thought of having a cocktail just didn't seem like a good idea.

I breathed out a long slow sigh. 'I suppose so,' I said unenthusiastically.

Lisa didn't seem to notice my unmoved response and was out of her seat in an instant and off selecting her preferred seat. She picked a table in a secluded corner, placing her bag in one of the two armchairs and her phone on the table. I hesitantly got up, walked over slightly unsteadily from the effects of the alcohol, and flopped out in the opposite armchair.

Lisa was fumbling in her bag for her purse. 'Right, I'll get the first round. What do you fancy?'

I winced at the words 'first round', suggesting this wouldn't be our last drink of the night.

'Oh, I don't know, whatever you're having,' I said, instantly regretting it.

Lisa smiled mischievously at me and set off for the bar.

I settled back into the chair and began to watch a couple of young guys playing on the pool table. They didn't seem very competitive, and it amused me to watch their antics and teasing of each other whenever one of them missed their shot. Eventually, I grew bored of watching them so looked over in the direction of the bar to see what was taking Lisa so long to get the drinks. She was stood at the bar, almost leaning over it, having what looked to be quite an intense conversation with the barman, and there was no sign of any drinks being poured. At first, I thought maybe there was a problem, but as I continued to watch it didn't appear like a heated exchange; in fact, I began to wonder if they actually knew each other. The barman then clocked me watching them and he immediately changed his demeanour, abruptly ending their conversation and suddenly busying himself retrieving the cocktail glasses. I watched as he poured the different liquids into the drinks mixer and then started to shake them up.

Suddenly I was made to jump as Lisa's phone started vibrating on the table. Distracted, I averted my eyes from the bar and watched as it continued to reverberate. The display had lit up and I could see the words 'Jahl calling'. I looked quizzically at the name, as it seemed quite unusual and I had never come across it before. The phone ceased vibrating and the display went off just as Lisa returned to the table with the drinks.

'Everything OK?' I asked.

'Yeh, fine. There was quite a bit of choice, I couldn't decide! I got us a Blue Lagoon in the end. Hope that's OK?'

'Did you know the barman?' I asked, ignoring the choice of cocktail.

'No,' she said, sounding surprised. 'How would I know the barman? Why on earth would you think I know him?'

'Just when you were up there and talking to him, it seemed like you knew him.'

She raised her eyebrows at me in astonishment. I became aware that I was starting to sound paranoid, so I quickly changed the subject.

'Oh, by the way, your phone went while you were at the bar.'

'Oh, did it?' She picked up the phone, scrolling through the records to see who called. 'Oh. It's my mum again. I'll call her later.'

Initially, I was a bit put out that she had clearly lied to me. Lisa and I had always had a close and trusting relationship, often confiding in each other about quite personal matters. I wondered why she had chosen to lie about whoever this 'Jahl' was who had called. I could only assume it was perhaps a new boyfriend that she wasn't ready to tell me about yet. Although this seemed unlikely, as this was usually one of our hot topics and was certainly a subject Lisa was always keen to share details about.

'I don't believe it,' Lisa said, incensed, as she looked over at the same young men I had been watching earlier playing pool. They were just racking up the balls for a new game, still larking about with each other, but I couldn't see what Lisa was so irate about. Without any warning, she stood up and marched over to them and aggressively shouted, 'Oi, you two.'

Alarmed, I quickly rose to my feet and then cautiously manoeuvred myself over to them.

'Think it's funny, do you, trying to run me off the road?'

Suddenly it clicked; these were the same two guys in the Astra. I hadn't recognised them from earlier although now I could clearly see it was them. Judging by the looks on their faces, they had now recognised us too.

'Chill out, it was just a bit of a laugh.'

Lisa was full of rage. 'You're a complete moron, you could have killed us.'

At this point, I stepped in, placing myself between my friend and the two guys like a referee separating two fighters in a boxing ring.

'Hey, let's just all calm down,' although Lisa was the only person not calm here. Lisa threw me a hard look and for a moment I feared I might be next in the firing line.

'Look, seriously, we were just messing about. Hey, let me buy you ladies a drink as a peace offering.'

Lisa's eyes widened. 'You can stick your sodding drinks where the sun don't shine, you complete imbeciles,' and to my relief turned her back on them and stormed off. They shrugged their shoulders and went back to playing their pool game while I was left standing there in limbo, feeling incredibly uncomfortable.

Half an hour it took me to find Lisa. I wrongly assumed she'd walked off in a huff to the toilets and would return to the same seats. Luckily, the barman had noticed the kerfuffle and kindly informed me she had in fact left the building. By the time I had realised this, she had now a good few minutes' head start on me, and by the time I had stepped out the main entrance and back onto the main square, I couldn't see any sign of her. Frustratingly, I couldn't get any signal on my mobile so couldn't call her either to find out where she had gone. I was about to give up the ghost and head back to our lodge, when I noticed her sat on one of the benches talking on her phone. As I headed over in her direction, she spotted me and gave me a nod in recognition. I sat down alongside her and waited for her to finish her call.

'Yeh, OK, Mum, see you in a week or so. OK, bye. Yeh, bye.' She flicked her eyes up at me. 'OK, bye then, Mum,' and finally ended the call. 'Why you frowning at me?' Lisa asked, bemused.

'You've got a signal.' I was fairly sure we were on the same network, unless Lisa had recently changed. 'What network are you on?'

'Orange.'

'Yeh, that's what I thought, me too. I can't get a signal, though.'

'Can't you?'

'Don't you think that's a bit weird?'

'Yeh, it is a bit.' Then after musing it over for a while, she offered, 'Cheap phone, probably,' and laughed. That to me seemed a weak explanation. Admittedly, Lisa's phone would have cost more than mine as she always had to have the top-of-the-range model; however, mine was by no means cheap, just more modestly priced, and I didn't generally experience this problem.

'Right,' said Lisa emphatically, 'the night is still young. Let's find somewhere to have a drink. Not going back in there, though, where those idiots are.' And, with that, we headed off for the final fling of the night.

CHAPTER FIVE

I woke with my head throbbing and an excessive thirst. The room was spinning and I had to really concentrate and focus on the clock to determine the time, as it seemed to be jumping all over the place on the bedside table. It read 13.33 and I groaned at the thought that I had slept in so long and already missed half of the day. I lay there for a while, not even sure I had enough energy to get up as my body felt so weak. Eventually, I managed to sit up and swing my legs round so I was sat on the edge of the bed. The motion of sitting up made me feel nauseous, and I dared not move any further in case I was physically sick. I waited until the sickness passed before I attempted venturing to the bathroom. I looked at myself in the mirror, pale and bedraggled, and told myself I'm never drinking again.

I managed to freshen myself up a bit and look marginally presentable, throwing on the most comfortable clothing I could find: a plain black vest top with grey jogging bottoms. I tottered into the main living area to find Lisa sat at the kitchen table drinking a coffee and reading a women's magazine.

'Oh God, look at you, you look rough.'

'Thanks. I feel like I've been hit by a bus or something. God, my head hurts.'

'There's some paracetamol on the side. I've had to take some too.'

'Thanks,' I said gratefully.

'I popped out this morning and picked up a few things. So there is orange juice and bread and a few other bits and pieces. Help yourself.'

I poured myself a pint of water and gulped the whole lot down in one go along with a couple of tablets. I then poured a second glass and was about to sit down beside Lisa at the kitchen table when she suddenly yelled at me.

'Don't sit there!'

I jumped out of my skin and almost dropped the glass.

'I went to sit on that earlier and almost fell off. The legs are wonky.'

Everything was feeling a bit wonky to me this morning, but I chose a different seat just in case.

Lisa continued reading her magazine but, occasionally, between a turn of a page, she glanced at me and smirked. The pint of water I had drunk had not even remotely stopped the extreme thirst I was feeling. I could feel it swishing around in my stomach, and it almost made me retch. I put both elbows on the table, dropped my head into my hands, and closed my eyes. I could feel the room spinning around me and my head was still pounding.

'I was thinking I might pop out for some lunch. I guess you don't fancy joining me?'

'No, I think I'll pass,' I moaned.

'Well, you ought to try and have something. You need to line that stomach of yours.'

I peered over my hands and watched as she proceeded to make me some toast. I was envious of how chirpy she seemed to be in comparison to how awful I felt.

'How is it that I feel like death warmed up and you are right as rain?'

'Because I can take my drink and you are a lightweight.'

Lisa reclaimed her seat back at the table and carried on reading her magazine in between conversing with me.

'Some night, hey?' she sniggered.

I struggled to try and remember exactly how the night had gone.

'Well, I remember having to step in to prevent you from punching those guys who almost ran us off the road, and then we sat outside for a bit and then …'

I tried to recall the events that followed as I pushed the toast around the plate, unable to face actually eating it.

'And then we went to that disco place and danced the night away,' said Lisa, completing the sentence.

I took a slurp of my water, still trying to rack my brains. I remembered going there; Lisa was desperate to go and I tried my best to persuade her we should go somewhere quieter and more chilled. But, as usual, I lost the argument and got dragged into going. I remembered the music was too loud for me and I wasn't overcome with the genre as it was too cheesy for my liking. But then after that, the memories became vague and it was all very hazy. There was dancing and definitely more drinking, and I seemed to remember chatting to various people, but I could only recall odd snippets of the evening. They were just small flashbacks of images of the night, and I couldn't really piece them together or even work out what order they happened in. I certainly couldn't remember how it ended and coming back to the lodge.

'I am not sure I can really remember much of it,' I said, embarrassed.

'Trust me, it was a good night.'

'Well, it may have been a good night, but it's a bloody awful morning.'

Lisa looked at her watch. 'Afraid to say we are well into the afternoon now. You don't mind if I nip out for some lunch, do you? I shan't be too long. Maybe we can do something later. Something gentle perhaps,' she said, chuckling.

I nodded and Lisa left me to nurse my hangover.

After a few hours, I started to feel relatively human again, at least to the point where I could function without feeling sick and I was no longer gasping with thirst. I'd even managed to eat the toast, although it had felt like a mammoth task. I sat outside for a while, enjoying the peace and thinking back to when Lisa had mysteriously vanished only to reappear later in just as mysterious circumstances. It still bothered me and made me feel very uneasy. No matter how many times I played it over in my head, I couldn't come up with a viable explanation. The more I thought about it, the more paranoid I became, and I decided I shouldn't sit any longer stewing over it but should go for a walk to try and push it out of my mind.

'Damn,' I muttered as I failed to find the key to the main door of the lodge. I realised that Lisa must have taken our one and only key, and I wasn't prepared to leave the lodge unlocked while it was unattended. I grabbed my phone to call her but I still had no signal. I slumped down on the sofa, annoyed that I would have to wait until

Lisa got back before I was free to leave. I just sat staring down at the floor, sulking like a child. I clutched at my aching left arm and began rubbing it in an attempt to try to relieve the pain. It had been causing me some grief throughout the day, but it was becoming noticeably worse. I couldn't find any evidence of any bruising, or damage of any kind, so I wasn't sure why it was aching so much. I guessed I had fallen at some point during the night in my drunken stupor and imagined myself keeling over as I tried to negotiate my way back to the lodge. I cursed Lisa for losing the other key and making me feel like a prisoner but, rather than be defeated, I decided to try and retrieve the lost key.

I stepped out onto the main front decking and gently lowered myself down onto the wooden slats. My head was still delicate and so even a slight movement of the head felt more like a jolt. It took me a while to locate it. I had to move several times to a different area before I found the right slats to look through and actually be able to see it. I felt elated when I discovered it, as if I'd found a solid gold ring. I soon realised that finding it was probably the easier task; trying to actually retrieve it was going to be more challenging.

My first thought was to find something long and thin that I could use to poke through the gap and hook it out with, but after a brief search of the house I couldn't find anything remotely likely to be able to perform that task. In the end, I decided my best bet was to try and find a way to actually get underneath the raised platform. I judged the lodge to be sat just high enough off the ground to make it possible for me to crawl underneath, but even just trying to find an opening big enough between the wooden stilts the lodge sat on was problematic. I was almost resolved to giving in but then decided to give it one more go. My persistence paid off and I managed to find an opening just big enough for me to crawl under. Initially, I had to stay down on my belly and slide myself along, but the further in I went, the more the gap between the ground and the floor of the lodge widened, and I was able to scramble around on my hands and knees. I retrieved the key and began to wonder if all this effort was really worth it. The likelihood was Lisa would return just as I was clambering out under the lodge and she would find the whole escapade hilarious.

I took a momentary breather as I contemplated which would be the easiest way out. Should I try turning myself around and going forwards or just back myself out? I decided that turning myself around would be a better option, and so I started to rotate myself around on all fours. I got halfway through my manoeuvre when I had to stop as a bolt of pain ran through my arm, the same one that had been causing me trouble all day. I lifted it off the ground to relieve the pressure and instead placed all my weight onto the remaining good arm. I rested for a while, waiting for the pain to subside, feeling quite dejected by how weak my body was feeling and the ludicrous situation I was in. So much for a relaxing break to rejuvenate the mind, body and soul. I felt like I'd aged about fifty years and I could very well be losing my mind.

Just as I was about to swivel and complete the remaining part of my manoeuvre, something caught my eye. At first, I didn't dare to believe what I was seeing, and the more I stared at it, the more churning I felt in the pit of my stomach. The lodge was not completely on stilts and raised off the ground level as it appeared to be from the roadside. Only from this concealed position, right underneath it, did it become clear that at one end of the lodge there was a section that extended from the lodge's floor right down into the ground level and looked to continue underground. The area from where this concealed section protruded was right underneath the bedroom that Lisa occupied and revealed to me a very plausible solution as to how Lisa had performed her supposed vanishing act. I was overcome with complete horror as I came to the realisation that the paranoia I had been suffering from was fully justified and that the sincerity of my best friend was now very much in doubt.

My mind was racing and I couldn't comprehend what could be going on. Lisa had been my best friend for over ten years now. We first met at university as first-year students sharing the same halls of residence. We hit it off almost from the very beginning and soon became as thick as thieves, and we'd been close friends ever since. The thought that Lisa was now deceiving me was unthinkable and for what possible reason was completely mind-boggling. I decided that trying to work through the ramifications of this discovery while I was on all fours, underneath a building and in some physical discomfort, was not the most ideal place to be. Ignoring the pain still throbbing away in my arm, I managed to rotate myself round so I was facing the right way to be able to move forward rather than back my way out. I crawled as far as I could until I was forced once again to drop flat and slide myself along the last part of the course. Just as I reached the opening and was pulling myself out from under the building, I could see Lisa returning up the path towards our lodge. Without any conscious thought, I immediately ducked back down and slid back under so as to stay hidden. Lisa didn't seem to have spotted me, and I felt huge relief as I watched her walk up the ramp and back into our lodge. I was surprised at my reaction of feeling so fearful towards her and I wondered if I was overreacting. I mean, what had I really discovered, possibly some hidden room or passage that Lisa knew about? Maybe she was just playing some practical joke on me and it wasn't as sinister as I was believing it to be. I lay still, not entirely sure what my next move should be. Eventually, I decided I should pursue my original plan of going for a walk to clear my head. Hopefully, it would calm me down, allowing me to think things through clearly and rationally and come to a sensible conclusion.

CHAPTER SIX

The sun had dipped behind a cloud and there was a slight breeze, but it still felt warm and pleasant to walk in. I had been walking for half an hour, following a designated trail through the woodland and eventually stumbling upon an ornamental garden pond. I sat on one of the benches conveniently placed alongside the water's edge and watched the koi nibbling away at the leaves of some vibrant lemon-coloured water lilies. Disturbingly, I did notice that in one far corner of the pond there were several dead fish floating about. As the water lapped at the edges, it pushed the fish against the sides as if they were trying to escape. I quickly turned my attention back to the original and far more pleasant scene of the koi with the water lilies and remained staring at them for a while as I sat mulling things over. Were things really as sinister and peculiar as they seemed or was I just blowing things all out of proportion and envisioning the worst? But as I sat there, thinking back on everything that had happened since we had left my house to come here, it was plain to me that something untoward was going on. There were far too many oddities occurring to just explain them away. What I couldn't get my head around, nor accept, was that Lisa was somehow a part of it. The burning question now was what was I going to do from here on in? I decided not to confront Lisa about it, at least not for now. She was clearly deceiving me, although for what reason was a complete mystery, and so how could I trust anything she now told me?

I felt very uneasy about the prospect of spending any more time here; the demeanour of the place had never felt right from the moment we arrived and given what had happened over the last couple of days, I was not sure I really felt that safe here. I wasn't entirely convinced that I now felt safe around Lisa, all though the thought of Lisa harming me seemed absurd. However, it was going to be difficult to just up and leave without raising suspicion and causing a fuss, not to mention how awkward it was going to be to travel back. I had been reliant on Lisa driving us here and therefore I had no immediate form of transport to get back in.

In the end, I concluded I should stay put for now and just try and keep my head down. I could feign illness and retire to my room for the night, avoiding the need to engage too much with Lisa and raising any suspicion. I was no master of deception and I was sure she would see right through me if I was forced to converse too much. In the morning, after giving my excuses to Lisa, I would look to arrange a taxi to the nearest train station and make my escape.

Just then, I heard some voices in the distance. I could see a family making their way towards the pond and as they got closer I realised it was the same family we were forced to stop in the car for on our arrival here while they crossed the road. The father this time had hold of both his children, one in each hand, as they walked right up to the water's edge. The mother was a few paces behind, overburdened with a child's rucksack, a bottle of water, some children's toys as well as her own handbag. Before reaching her family, who were now engrossed in watching the colourful fish swimming about, the bottle of water slid out from her grasp and in her attempt to catch it she managed to drop everything else she was carrying. I could see the look of exasperation in her face, and as the rest of her family were seemingly too distracted to notice, I felt obliged to help.

'Here, let me help pick these up for you,' I said as I approached her and bent down to retrieve the bottle.

'Oh, that's very kind, thank you.'

'That's OK. You look a bit overloaded.'

'Well, it's nice someone noticed,' as she glanced over at her family, who were still in complete oblivion to her difficulties. They had now walked further round the pond, where there was a gentle cascading waterfall surrounded by colourful irises.

She'd placed all the items on the bench that I had been sitting on and was now trying to repack the rucksack so the extra toys and bottle she had been carrying would also now fit. I sat back down on the bench, but at the far end so as to give her the necessary room she needed, and watched as she reorganised everything. I judged her to be about the same age as me, which meant she must have had her first child in her early twenties. She looked extremely tired and worn out, as if she was running on empty. After successfully repacking everything, she sat down on the bench with me and watched her family from afar.

'It's nice to just sit down for five minutes,' she said. 'I love my children and wouldn't swap them for the world, but boy, are they draining.'

I smiled and said, 'They do look quite energetic,' as I watched them both jumping up and down and running about in excitement.

'Are you here with any family or friends?' she asked.

'Yeh, my friend. Just come down for a jolly girl's week away really. Nice to have a break from work.'

'That is nice, I'm jealous. I can't remember the last time I got to have a relaxing weekend away with one of my girlfriends and no demanding kids.'

'Well, if it makes you feel any better, I'm not sure I would describe my break so far as very relaxing.'

'Oh?' she said, intrigued.

'It's a long story, but let's just say it's had some quite intense moments. Not helped by the fact that I must have gone a bit overboard last night and am feeling a little the worse for wear.'

'Oh, you too?' She sounded almost relieved that she had found a fellow sufferer with whom she was able to share her story.

'I have felt rough all day, like I have had the worst hangover ever. Although I can't understand why; I only had two small glasses of wine with my dinner last night. I'm not really a big drinker, so it doesn't take that much to get me drunk, but even so, I can't believe that amount would make me feel that bad. I can't even remember the last part of the evening. I think I can vaguely remember my husband helping me to the bedroom. Then I must have fallen asleep. A heavy sleep at that. I didn't wake till gone midday and felt absolutely awful. I've been struggling all day. Luckily, my husband has been really good and has been mainly looking after the kids. I feel a bit guilty, but I don't know why, as nine times out of ten it's usually me looking after them.'

As she was describing her unpleasant experience, sounding not too dissimilar to my own, I curiously noticed that she was rubbing her left arm.

'Sore arm?'

She looked a bit surprised at my question, as if she hadn't realised she was actually rubbing it, and immediately stopped.

'Yes,' she said, frowning, 'I'm not sure why it's hurting so much. I can't remember knocking it or anything. It's actually quite painful. You'd think I'd remember what might have caused it.'

Since going for my walk and sitting on the bench enjoying the calm surroundings, I'd become a lot less het up. But now I felt the wave of panic rising again.

I didn't say anything to begin with. I thought she might think I was completely crazy if I revealed that I also had an unexplainable painful left arm. We'd only been chatting for a few minutes, I barely knew her, and in fact I didn't even know her name. But for some reason I felt at ease with her and so I confessed.

'That's really weird. I woke up today with a really painful arm too.'

She looked at me in astonishment as I continued, 'And although I had a fair bit to drink last night, I can't remember most of the tail end of it, either, and I also woke up sometime after midday.'

She leant back against the bench and her face paled. She then leant in closer towards me and whispered, 'Don't you think this whole place is a bit weird?'

'Very,' I agreed.

Then just as I was about to divulge everything strange that had happened to me, her children came bounding over, with her husband in hot pursuit.

'Mummy!' shrieked the little girl, running towards her, arms outstretched.

Her mother picked her up onto her lap and gave her a loving cuddle.

'Daddy said we can have ice cream!'

'Did he now?' she said, giving her husband a disapproving look.

'Yeh, well, we are on holiday,' he replied, and gave me a cheeky wink.

'Oh, come on then,' she said, rather reluctantly. I was disheartened to think that our conversation was now terminated and we would be denied the chance to share our stories and thoughts.

But as they were about to leave, she hesitated, and I got the impression she too wanted to talk more on the subject.

'John? Are you OK to look after the kids for a bit tonight, after they have gone to bed, so I can pop out for a quick drink with ...' She tailed off as she realised she didn't know my name.

'Emma,' I quickly added.

John looked quite surprised at his wife's request, and I guessed that it would seem a bit strange going for a drink with someone you only met a few minutes ago and wasn't even on first-name terms with.

Nonetheless, after some thought, he shrugged his shoulders and agreed.

'Yeh, OK. There's a film on tonight I wouldn't mind watching anyway, and I doubt you would like it.'

We arranged to meet at the fountain, on the main square at 7pm, after her children were tucked up in bed, and I was desperate to tell her everything.

CHAPTER SEVEN

I'd walked back up to our lodge to kill the last couple of hours off before I was due to meet my new friend. I entered in trepidation, but thankfully Lisa was not there. I threw on something more appropriate to wear for going out in, rather than remain in my simple jogging bottoms and T-shirt. Realising that I still had some time before the rendezvous and with Lisa absent, curiosity got the better of me and I decided to seize the opportunity to search the property for any hidden opening that might allow access to a secret passage or room. I was on tenterhooks the whole time, expecting Lisa to catch me in the act. Several times I thought I heard something that made me jump and rush back into the living area to avoid getting caught, but they were false alarms. Sure enough, after scrutinising every inch of wall and floor in Lisa's bedroom, I found it. On one of the walls was a full-length mirror that ran from just below ceiling height to just above the skirting board. Running down one side of the frame I found five latches. When these latches were lifted, the mirror swung open like a door and revealed a cavity with just enough room for a person to stand upright in. Even though I had already suspected that there was something concealed in this room, I was still not prepared for it. I stood rooted to the spot, staring in complete disbelief into the void in the wall. I dared not believe what I was looking at. I stepped into the gap and once inside I could barely breathe. I felt claustrophobic from being confined in such a small space. There was only bare walls around me, so I looked down at the floor and saw I was standing directly on a trapdoor. I spent several minutes trying to open it, but I could not lift it. It was awkward due to the lack of space in the cavity. I had to carefully straddle the trapdoor in order to ensure I wasn't preventing it from opening simply by me standing on it; nonetheless, I still couldn't get it open. I gave up, partially because I was worried Lisa would return any minute now and also because I was in danger of being late for the 7pm meeting. In all honesty, even if I had managed to lift the trapdoor, I was not convinced I would have gone any further anyway. Venturing down into some dark unknown secret tunnel or room, not having a clue what was down there, didn't seem like a good idea. The real fear, though, was whether or not I could get back out.

I stepped back out into the bedroom and put the mirror back in its normal place, ensuring the latches were securely fastened, and made my way out of the bedroom. Just as I reached the bedroom doorway, I turned and took one last look at the mirror. It looked just like an ordinary mirror; there was nothing I could see that gave away its true purpose. I was fairly sure that Lisa would not have just happened on discovering it to be a door, which meant she must have already known or been informed about it. I felt sickened by the thought and so hurried off, making my way to the fountain on the main square.

The square seemed quieter than it was last night, maybe because it was earlier. I perched on a bench placed just in front of the low wall that surrounded the fountain and waited. I kept my eyes peeled the whole time looking out for her. I felt quite conspicuous, and there were a couple of moments when I felt like I was being watched, but I decided that my heightened emotions were probably just fuelling my paranoia. At one point, a vehicle suddenly entered the square, which put me even more on edge. Considering this was a pedestrian paved area and the vehicle was being driven at quite a speed, it seemed very out of place. I watched inquisitively as to its intentions. It was a half-bed truck and I could see it was carrying metal barriers and warning cones. In the blink of an eye, two workmen jumped out and began to cordon off an area round the edge of a building. Once the barrier was in place, they left as hurriedly as they had arrived.

I studied the building they had now surrounded with bright orange cones and metal fencing, completely ruining the look of the frontage, and noticed that part of the building looked damaged and was in danger of falling away. I was beginning to wonder how safe these buildings actually were as I cast my eye across several other buildings and noticed that wasn't the only one suffering from degradation. After twenty minutes of waiting and no sign of her, I became very anxious indeed. I started to worry that maybe there was another fountain around here somewhere and I was at the wrong one. I scanned the square and I couldn't even see any other fountain, so it had to be this one. After another twenty minutes had passed, I was fairly certain she would not be turning up. Maybe she was just too tired, or the kids had played up, or maybe even her husband had stopped her from going. He didn't seem too happy about the idea, but then it was probably not unjust of him to think that. He may after all just be concerned about his wife meeting up with a complete stranger all on her own, in an unfamiliar place, at night.

'Hey, how's it going?'

I almost jumped out of my skin. After getting over the initial shock that someone had snuck up on me unawares, I then rolled my eyes when I saw who it was.

'Oh, it's you,' I said, disappointed.

He smiled as he rolled up a cigarette and sat down beside me.

'Where's your friend?' I asked. 'Driving around trying to see who he can run off the road next?'

He smiled again then lit his cigarette and took a drag.

'And where's *your* friend?'

I didn't answer. I didn't actually know where Lisa was, but I didn't reply out of spite rather than lack of knowledge.

He took another couple of drags and after puffing out the smoke asked, 'So can I buy you that drink now?'

I raised my eyebrows at his brazenness.

'You know, the peace offering I offered yesterday, to you and your uptight friend.'

I huffed and refused to answer him.

'Well, suit yourself.'

He threw his cigarette end on the floor and stamped it out. Then got up and went to start to walk off.

'Wait,' I blurted out. It came out a bit too desperately sounding, so I quickly changed the tone to sound less bothered.

'Yeh, why not? Looks like my friend isn't coming and I'm thirsty.'

I was surprised how disconcerted I felt at the thought he was just going to walk away from me. The sensible side of me told me he was trouble; someone who could have such little regard for someone's safety and literally put our lives at risk was the sort of person not to mix with. But I couldn't help but find him alluring. He was strong, confident and very handsome. Physically, he was well toned and nicely tanned and, above all, he had a charming smile. I felt flattered that he was paying me attention and was interested enough in me to buy me a drink, even with the tension between us.

Three hours went by in the blink of an eye. We chatted away with ease and I found him truly mesmerising to listen to. My initial judgement of him was well off target and I had massively underestimated him. He was not the uneducated, good-for-nothing clown I thought him to be. He was clearly a free spirit and someone who had a rogue streak, but he was far more intelligent than I envisaged. In fact, he seemed wise beyond his years. He was well travelled and had experienced many cultures, and I listened intently to the fascinating stories he had to tell. I was embarrassed whenever he asked questions about me, as my life seemed quite boring in comparison.

His name was Sam and he was twenty-five years old, slightly younger than myself. I learnt that he had left school at sixteen with nine A-grade GCSEs, but he preferred life in the outdoors and couldn't face spending time stuck studying in a college. From what he told me, it sounded like he had a hard job sticking at anything, switching from one job to another, always outside labouring-type jobs, with plenty of travelling escapades mixed in. Still, he didn't talk of it with any regret, so obviously that lifestyle particularly suited him. Apparently, he had only recently come back from six months of backpacking round Thailand and had now just started working in a boatyard in Cornwall. A lot of his family were based in Cornwall, and he was living with one of his half-brothers right on the coast.

In contrast, I didn't have any real interesting stories to tell him, and our backgrounds were quite different. I'd stayed in education right up to university, studying a degree in Business Studies. After graduating, I worked in hospitality, mainly on the front desk in a hotel in Bath. I'd never been abroad; the furthest I had ever travelled was Scotland and even then I only just went over the border. While he had a large family, including half-siblings, many still living in Cornwall, I had no blood family at all. Well, none that I was aware of. He was surprised to hear I was orphaned as a baby and had spent a lot of my childhood in a children's home, and he continually pressed me for more details. At first, I was rather coy about it, but gradually as I grew to like him more and more, I began to open up.

I was embarrassed to tell him I wasn't adopted until I was seven. That was quite a late age to be adopted, and I always felt embarrassed to admit that it took that long for someone to willingly adopt me. I never really understood what it was about me that people didn't like, but whatever the reason, I was always overlooked, and I felt forever rejected. Sam however wasn't fazed by it, and he listened intently as I explained about the family I was adopted by.

'So do you still live with them or do you have your own place?' he asked.

I noticed we were now the only ones in the bar, and the staff were starting to clear the tables around us.

'Do you think they are closing up and waiting for us to leave?'

'Nah. They'll soon chuck us out if they want us to go.'

I felt quite uncomfortable as the only customers remaining and felt sure we were getting the odd glare to hint we were outstaying our welcome. Sam was not in the least bit bothered and started rolling another cigarette, half looking at me expectantly for my reply.

I hesitated, feeling awkward explaining that my adopted parents were both now dead.

I took a deep breath and explained.

I told him how they died in a car crash when I was seventeen. I lived with my adoptive brother for a short while until I went to university in Bristol. Then when I graduated, I came back to Bath. My parents had left me one of their holiday-let cottages in their will, so after I graduated I moved in there and had lived there ever since.

'So your parents were into holiday lets and stuff? Is that how you got into hotel work?'

'Yes. Sort of.' This seemed too complicated to explain, especially as we were on the verge of being kicked out.

'My grandfather owned a hotel which he ran for most of his life. Towards the end, as he started to struggle with age, my father gave up his job and joined the business until he eventually inherited it. He bought several holiday cottages along the way and my brother also joined the business, with me helping out a bit in holidays and stuff. Then when my parents died, they left me one of the cottages and the rest to my brother.'

'That doesn't sound like a very fair split.'

It was a fair remark. In monetary terms, I was left a much smaller proportion. However, it was no real surprise. I was well provided for when it came to being fed, clothed, sheltered and educated. However, I was shown little love or given much attention by either of my parents. That was all reserved for my brother. I often felt detached from family life as if I didn't really fit in, and I wondered why my parents even chose to adopt me in the first place.

'Well, they'd also left me some money to cover my university expenses,' I replied as a weak defence.

'So the hotel you work in is the same hotel? The one your brother now owns?'

'Yep. After I graduated, I wasn't really sure what I wanted to do. My brother was having a few staffing issues, so I helped out. It was meant to be a temporary thing, but I don't know, time dragged on, I was quite enjoying the work and the people I worked with, and I'm still there, like ...'

I broke off while I tried to calculate how many years later that would make it.

'Uh ... well ... it's 2003 now, isn't it. So ... yeh ... that's six years. No, wait. Yeh, six years later.'

Embarrassed at my poor attempt at some simple mathematics, I was mighty relieved when a staff member interrupted us before Sam got the chance to make fun of me.

'Right, folks, really sorry but we are closing up now.'

Sam looked annoyed with the staff member and for a minute I thought he was going to argue with him, but I think he may have sensed my anguish and managed to refrain himself.

Instead, he downed the last of his pint and we left.

'So which lodge are you in? I'll walk you back,' he said, offering me his arm.

I linked mine in his and we walked back together.

By now, it was approaching midnight. There were still a few people out in the main square, but once we left the vicinity it was very quiet. It was a warm and clear night, with an abundance of stars in the sky accompanied by the sound of crickets.

'So, you never did tell me where your friend was tonight,' said Sam.

'No,' I retorted, 'and you didn't tell me where *your* friend was, either.'

Sam smiled at me, amused. He really did have such an enchanting smile.

'I reckon you two had an argument and she stormed off in a huff.'

'You reckon, do you?'

'I do.'

'Why? Is that what happened between you and your crazy mad driver friend?'

He chuckled, clearly enjoying my banter.

'Nope. I don't actually know where he is. I haven't seen him all day, well, not since breakfast. He can't be far, though. His car is still parked up outside our lodge. He's probably back there now, wondering where I am.'

Finally, we arrived at the end of the gravel path of the lodge I was staying at with Lisa. I was disappointed the walk had come to an end so soon. It felt far shorter than earlier when I had walked it on my own. The evening had flown by and a bond had already formed between us. I felt very comfortable and safe in his presence, and I was beginning to regret not mentioning anything about my strange experiences and suspicions with the place.

'Looks like your friend is home.'

I looked in the direction Sam was pointing and could clearly see Lisa sat on the sofa watching TV. She had the lights on but had not drawn the curtains.

There was an uncomfortable moment as I tried to figure out how to confide in him. But I couldn't find the words of how to even start the conversation. So instead I just thanked him for a lovely evening, bid him goodnight and we parted.

'Who was that?' enquired Lisa as I came through the door. She had spied us talking through the window.

'That was Sam.'

'Well, look at you. Managed to pull already? We've only been here five minutes. You hussy, you. I thought you were too hungover to go out?'

'Yeh, well, I recovered,' I joked, almost forgetting the person I was talking to right now had been deceiving me.

'So are you seeing him tomorrow?'

I frowned as I realised we hadn't arranged anything. 'No.'

'Good. I've booked us into a spa session tomorrow. Starts at eleven, got an hour massage and a half-hour facial and then lunch at one-thirty. How does that sound? Good, eh?'

'Yeh, great,' I replied, contemplating what excuse I could come up with to avoid going. If I had realised, I could have lied and said I was meeting Sam.

'Don't sound too enthused.'

I gave a wry smile and went to bed.

It took me a long time to go to sleep. I lay there in the dark, with my hands behind my head and my elbows pointing outwards. I was staring up at the ceiling, but it was too dark to really see anything. I was thinking back over my evening with Sam and musing over how ironic it was that only a day ago I had labelled him as a complete idiot, and now here I was yearning for the chance to see him again. My mood soon turned more sombre, though, when I started to think about everything else. What was I going to do? I was fairly adamant earlier that I was going to leave first thing in the morning. But that was before I met Sam; now I felt a bit differently. Also, my curiosity was getting the better of me, and I was keen to see if I could find the other woman who had hinted at also having suspicions about the place. I really wanted to know her story. I decided to wait and see how I felt in the morning. With hindsight, I probably should have left there and then while I still had the chance.

CHAPTER EIGHT

I was awake early the next morning. I showered, skipped breakfast and left a note on the kitchen table for Lisa to say I would meet her at the spa at eleven.

I'd decided that I wasn't going to run off and make my escape from this place just yet. I had a renewed sense of confidence and I was less fearful about the place. After all, nothing bad had actually happened, just a few bizarre moments. Admittedly, Lisa's trust had been thrown into question, but even then I wasn't sure ten years of friendship could be written off just because she had hidden from me for a short period in some secret room. In any case, I felt like I had a couple of allies here now and I was keen to find both of them.

I headed to the main reception. It was still very early, and there wasn't a soul about. There was a damp fog lingering in the air, and it was only just beginning to get light. The atmosphere was quite eerie and it made a shiver run right through me.

I was relieved to reach the main building where the reception was and hoped that they could help me find my new friends.

'Hello, madam, how may I help you?'

I recognised the strong Devonshire accent and the burgundy outfit as belonging to the same man who had first greeted us when we arrived at the resort. It was strange, though. I recalled at that time finding him friendly and very personable, and yet now I found him slightly sinister and false.

'Hi. I'm trying to find a friend of mine that is staying here. Well, two friends actually. But I don't know which lodge they are in. Well, they're not together, they're two separate friends. So it's two different lodges I am trying to locate. I was hoping you might be able to locate them for me?'

He gave me quite a frosty look, unnerving me slightly.

'I'm afraid I can't just give out people's lodge numbers. We have to respect people's personal information and privacy, you understand?'

'Yes, of course,' I replied, feeling rather ruffled by his tone. 'Perhaps you could call their lodge for me and leave a message?' I asked, unwilling to give up that easily.

He gave an affirmative nod and readied himself at the PC's keyboard which was in front of him.

'Name?'

'Sam.'

He looked up from his keyboard with a scornful look.

'Um. Sorry, I don't know his surname. He is with another male friend and they have a red Astra.'

He leant back away from the keyboard, and I could see his displeasure at the lack of information I was providing him with.

'They're in their mid-twenties,' I quickly added, hoping the extra information might help.

'Madam, I need a surname. I can't do a search based on a forename or the colour of the car they are driving.'

I was quite taken aback by his reaction. Maybe this wasn't the same guy who had welcomed us to the resort after all.

'Yeh, of course, sorry.'

I was feeling quite dejected now and also beginning to realise how ridiculous I was sounding. Suddenly realising I knew even less about my female friend I was also trying to locate, I didn't dare tell him I didn't even know her first name, never mind her surname.

Instead, I asked, 'How many lodges are there?'

'Two hundred and fifty.'

'Have you got a map I could have of the resort?'

He just stared at me, causing me to feel very ill at ease, and I thought he was going to give me my marching orders. Without saying a word, he handed me a leaflet that outlined the map of the entire resort and clearly marked where all the lodges were located and their corresponding lodge numbers.

'And a pencil?' I asked with a weak smile, praying that I hadn't pushed my luck too far.

He handed me a pencil from behind the desk.

'Thanks.'

'Have a nice day,' he said, grimacing, and I took my cue to leave.

I stepped back outside, trying to calculate how long it would take to go around two hundred and fifty lodges.

It was too early to start knocking on people's doors now, though. I decided 9am was a reasonable time to start. Annoyingly, that would only give me two hours before I was supposed to be meeting Lisa for our spa session. Nowhere near enough time to get round probably even a quarter of them.

I made my way back to the main square to see if I could find somewhere to get some breakfast before starting out on my search mission. Everything was shut; it was still too early. I huffed in annoyance and sat down on the same bench from last night when I first met Sam. I shivered from the cold and berated myself for not bringing a coat. I'd been fooled into thinking I didn't need one as the weather had been so warm lately, but now the temperature had taken a sudden nosedive.

Eventually, there began to be some activity. A café just across the way had pulled up their shutters and it looked like they were about to open, so I made my way over.

'Morning,' said the lady as she held the door open for me.

'Morning,' I replied, and seated myself at a small round table in the window. It had a plastic red and white chequered table cover with a small vase of pink carnation flowers placed in the middle.

'Can I get you tea or coffee?'

'Tea, thanks.'

As she disappeared back behind the counter to make my drink, I reached for the menu standing on the table behind the flower pot. However, in the time it took her to make the tea and bring it to my table, I had barely even scanned it. There was more activity in the square now it was a bit later in the morning, and I had been distracted anytime I saw someone walk past outside. I was hoping I might spot Sam or the other woman I was trying to find.

'What would you like to order for breakfast?' she asked, pen and pad at the ready.

Caught off guard, I quickly glanced at the menu and picked the first thing I saw.

'Toasted teacake, please.'

Forgetting that I was actually trying to kill some time, hunger overtook me and I wolfed down the teacake. I ordered another tea and drunk it deliberately slowly, trying to bide my time, but gradually the café started to fill up and I was acutely aware I was taking up a table for potential other paying customers. Feeling too uncomfortable to stall any longer, I paid my bill and left.

A glance at my watch told me it was only 8.30am, but I was running out of patience and so decided to start earlier than first planned. I would take a slow walk to the first lodge.

After knocking on nearly thirty lodge doors, of which the majority of occupants were not suitably impressed at being disturbed, I seriously began to doubt if this was such a good idea. I returned to the bench in the main square, which was now starting to feel like my own personal seat. It was now mid-morning and there were plenty of people about, so I sat there people watching and abandoned my mission.

My heart skipped a beat and my stomach fluttered as I spotted Sam walking across the square.

'Sam,' I yelled, but he didn't hear me.

I jumped up and jogged over to him.

'Hey, Sam,' I said, placing a hand delicately on his shoulder.

'Hey,' he replied, appearing genuinely pleased to see me. 'Fancy some breakfast?'

'Yeh, sure.'

'Great. There's a café just over there,' he said, referring to the café where I had already recently had breakfast.

The café was very full now. We took the only table that was free, and it just happened to be the same table I had sat at earlier.

'Back so soon?' said the waitress as she came to take our order.

I could feel the heat rising to my face.

'I'll just have a tea, thanks,' I said, ignoring her remark. I could see the confusion across Sam's face.

'Can I have the bacon roll and a black coffee?'

'Certainly,' she said, and gave me a quick glance that looked apologetic, as if she realised she had caused me embarrassment.

Sam was looking at me questioningly.

'Have you already eaten?'

'Umm ... y-y-yes, I have actually,' I stuttered, feeling ashamed that I was making him feel awkward.

'Oh sorry, you should have said.'

I gave a childish nervous laugh and told him not to worry. Thankfully, it didn't take us long to get over the awkward moment and we soon started fervently chatting.

'So where's your friend?' he asked as he took a large bite out of his bacon roll. Some grease trickled out of the end of the roll as he bit down on it and dribbled over his hand. I quickly passed him a napkin before it dripped any where else.

'I'm meeting her later. We've got a spa session booked.'

'You are still on talking terms then. I thought maybe you'd fallen out.'

'No, we haven't fallen out, not as such.'

He raised his eyebrows at my remark as he stuffed the last bit of his roll into his mouth.

'Well, it's all a bit weird. I'm not really sure what to make of it all.'

He looked at me, amused, clearly not realising how serious I was being and how much I had been affected by recent events.

Suddenly he changed his expression, probably because of my annoyed reaction.

'Why, what's happened?'

I didn't feel comfortable explaining the scenario in close proximity to so many people. The tables were quite tightly packed, and even whispers would probably be overheard. So we left the café and went for a walk, where I revealed the whole story to him. For the most part, I babbled incessantly, relieved to finally share my story with someone. Only occasionally did Sam manage to get a word in to ask the odd question. When I finally finished, my throat felt sore from talking so much. Worryingly, he didn't actually say anything once I had stopped talking, and I wondered if he thought I was deluded.

'So what do you think, do you think I'm going nuts?'

He sniggered. A response that did not fill me with much confidence.

He sat on a bench at the side of the pathway we were walking down. I sat next to him, perched right on the edge of the seat, angled towards him, expectantly waiting for a proper response.

He folded his arms, leant back into the seat and began his appraisal.

'No. I don't think you're nuts. I agree it does sound a bit weird.'

I waited to hear the rest of his monologue, but there was none forthcoming.

'Is that it? After all I have told you, that's all you've got to say?'

I sank back into the seat, thoroughly exasperated.

'What?' he chuckled, throwing his hands up in the air. 'I agree with you. You're not crazy and it is weird.'

Unimpressed, I gave him a glare, but I soon buckled under his charms as he grinned back at me, and I couldn't prevent myself from grinning back.

'Oh crap, what time is it?' I quickly looked at my watch and saw it was a little after 10.30am. 'I've got to go. I'm supposed to be meeting Lisa for this spa session.'

Sam nodded.

'Perhaps we can meet later?' he asked as I set off at a fast pace up the path.

'Sure, meet you in the square at our usual bench around seven,' I shouted back over my shoulder, and dashed off.

CHAPTER NINE

'Geez, I thought you weren't coming.'

The clock in the spa waiting area near reception read just a little after 11am. Lisa was sat in a bathrobe and slippers filling in a health questionnaire form.

I sat alongside her and gave her an apologetic look.

'Yeh, sorry. I completely lost track of time.' I was exhausted and sweating quite heavily.

The walk that Sam and I had gone on took us a little further away from our lodge than I realised. I had to practically sprint back to quickly grab my stuff and then run all the way to the spa.

The lady on reception approached me and gave me a disapproving look. I felt extremely embarrassed with my dishevelled appearance and the fact I was late.

'Hi,' I said, as jovial and friendly as I could muster. 'Sorry I am a bit late.'

'No problem,' she said, smiling rather insincerely, and handed me a soft white fluffy bathrobe and matching slippers. 'If you'd like to change, then when you are ready pop back out here and take a seat. We've got you booked in for a full body massage.'

'OK, thanks.'

'The changing rooms are this way,' she said, leading me over to a door marked with a pink coloured 'F'.

'I'll see you in a bit,' I whispered to Lisa as I got up to follow the staff member.

'OK. Enjoy.'

Once I had got changed and come back out into reception, Lisa had already gone for her treatment. I was feeling flustered and quite stressed. Due to my lateness, I had felt hurried into getting changed as quickly as possible, and this had made the task seemingly harder than it should have been. I had wrestled with trying to get a tightly fitting swimsuit on, become seemingly baffled on how to actually do up a bathrobe and had completely forgotten all about the slippers and left them in the changing room. It wasn't until I was seated in reception and saw another lady waiting for her spa session, dressed in the full attire, that I realised I didn't have them on. When the receptionist came over to hand me the health form to fill in, I noticed her give a cursory glance towards my bare feet. She said nothing, probably giving me up as a lost cause.

I dutifully filled in the paperwork and placed the clipboard and pen on a side table. I was feeling quite thirsty, no doubt dehydrated from where I had sweated it all out from all the running I had done to get here. I spotted a drinks dispenser in the corner, but just as I was about to get up to walk over there, the receptionist came over.

'OK, if you'd like to come this way for your treatment?' I didn't have the gall to say actually I was dying of thirst and could really do with a drink first, so instead I obediently followed.

On entering the treatment room, I was struck on how immediately calming it felt. The décor was sumptuous, the lighting was soft and there was soothing music playing in the background.

The masseuse gave me a warm smile and welcomed me in. She instructed me to remove my robe, roll down the top half of my swimwear and lie face down on the treatment bed. There was a deep burgundy blanket draped over the bed for me to slip under to cover my modesty. She then left the room to give me a few minutes to do as she said, promising she would return shortly. I found it amusing that I had valiantly struggled to put everything on as quickly as I could and now here she was telling me to practically take everything off.

I did as I was instructed and was now lying face down on the bed with my face placed in the breath hole, looking down at the floor underneath. I squirmed a few times, trying to reposition myself to find a more comfortable position. Eventually, the masseuse knocked on the door, indicating she was about to enter, and so I had to settle on the position I was in.

'Come in,' I said, not sure that was the expected response. It felt strange I was giving the masseuse permission to enter her own treatment room.

'Comfortable?' she asked as she lowered the blanket further down my body, exposing my shoulders and back.

'Yes,' I fibbed. I wasn't sure if my head was a bit too low down in the face hole. I could feel a little pressure on my throat and I started to worry I was restricting my breathing. I also couldn't work out what to do with my arms. They were hanging loosely down either side of the table, but they felt uncomfortable and heavy and were starting to make my shoulders ache.

My attention was soon diverted as she placed a scented candle giving off a very powerful aroma right under the breath hole.

'Take three deep breaths.'

I could see the flickering of the wick emitting a gentle vapour as I took a timid first breath.

'OK, and now this time take a long, deep breath,' she encouraged.

I took a long, slow and deep breath, inhaling the scented air into my lungs, through my nose. On the third breath, my nose starting to tingle and I felt light-headed.

I ignored the strange sensations, deciding they were all part and parcel of a relaxing spa treatment.

Taking the candle away, she went over to a preparation area over on the other side of the room. I briefly lifted my head up and angled it slightly in her direction. She was washing her hands in a small ceramic basin sunk into the worktop and I could see the candle, now extinguished, just alongside with a clear glass beaker placed over it.

My neck was aching from trying to hold it up at an acute angle, so I resumed my position with my head back down in the breath hole.

The minutes ticked by and I began to wonder when my actual massage would begin. The masseuse was still over at the preparation area and I could hear her opening and shutting various cupboards and shuffling about. Then I heard the door open and someone else enter the room. The calm and tranquil ambience was slowly being eroded. I went to lift my head again to see what was going on, but for some reason I didn't have the strength to lift it. Suddenly I started feeling very woozy, and although I could hear the masseuse and whoever else had entered the room in conversation, it sounded muffled. I had never had a treatment before so I wasn't sure exactly what to expect, but this didn't feel right at all. Relaxation was obviously the primary goal, but rather than feeling relaxed, it was more akin to having all the strength drained from my body and my senses slowly taken away from me. Too weak to move, I tried to speak out, but the effort to talk was too great. All I could do was lie there, in a confused state, straining to listen to what was going on around me. The sounds were distorted now, like I was under water, and so I couldn't distinguish any meaningful words.

In the next instance, I was being hauled over onto my back. My body was so weak I was unable to put up any kind of resistance. My eyes darted around the room as I tried to determine what was happening, but everything was blurry and I couldn't focus on anything.

There seemed to be several people in the room now, in white gowns, but I couldn't be sure how many as all I could really make out was rough shapes. My hearing had now deteriorated so badly all I could hear was a continuous buzzing sound.

Gradually, my eyesight failed completely, and there was only black and the buzzing sound in my ears. I knew I was in real trouble, and that this might be the end.

CHAPTER TEN

Chink.
Crunch, crunch. Crunch.
Chink. Chink.
Was I dreaming or were those sounds real?
Crunch, crunch. Crunch.
Chink.

I battled to rouse myself from the extreme depths of sleep. I seemed so far, far away, and I had to fight hard to try and bring myself back into the real world.

Eventually, I won the battle and woke.

I was lying flat on my back in a bed. As my eyes adjusted and came back into full focus, I realised I was in my own bed, in my own home. I lay still, confused. How could this be?

Expecting to be incapacitated, I was surprised to find I was actually able to sit up, my strength seemingly restored. I looked down at what I was wearing. I had my red tartan pyjamas on. I looked around the room and everything looked just as I had left it, with everything in its rightful place. I slowly got to my feet and walked to the window. I pulled back the curtains and looked out onto my street. Dawn was just breaking and the milkman was making his deliveries.

I staggered backwards and sat back down on the bed, bewildered. For all intents and purposes, it felt just like any ordinary morning. I felt normal, I looked normal and everything around me was normal.

After several minutes of just sitting, I finally pulled myself together. I got up and opened my wardrobe to find all my clothes hanging as I would expect. I noticed that items I had taken with me on my excursion with Lisa were now also hanging in the wardrobe. I touched one of the tops hanging on a wooden hanger. It was the very same flower-patterned strappy top I wore on our first night away when Lisa performed her disappearing act and this whole saga started. The top appeared freshly laundered. Confused, I closed the wardrobe. With my hand still resting on the wardrobe door, I caught sight out of the corner of my eye of several pairs of shoes neatly lined up. The pair of wedge-heeled sandals I had also worn on our first night out alongside a pair of trainers and some black ankle pixie boots I had also taken. I stood there, my eyes fixated on the neat line of shoes. I rarely brought my shoes into my bedroom. Normally, I would kick them off the moment I got through the front door and leave them more or less in a heap, rather than an organised line-up. The realisation then suddenly dawned on me that maybe someone else had placed the shoes in this way and that meant someone else had been in my house, in fact, that someone might still be in my house.

Alarmed by the thought, I suddenly felt very vulnerable and scared. My eyes widened. I looked at my bedroom door; it was slightly ajar. I crept towards the door and put my ear to the gap, straining to listen for any sound. There was nothing but silence. I listened for a few more minutes, but still there was no sound. I summoned enough courage to open the door, tiptoe across the landing and slowly sneak down the stairs, listening the whole time for any signs of an intruder. Once downstairs, I investigated each room in turn until eventually I was satisfied that there was no one in the house except myself.

Breathing a sigh of relief, I made my way back upstairs and changed out of my tartan pyjamas and into a pair of blue denim jeans and a cream crew-neck long-sleeved ribbed top. My stomach rumbled, but for now I chose to ignore my hunger. I had more pressing things to deal with right now. I got down on my knees and looked under the bed to find the suitcase I had taken with me on our trip was stowed away under the bed. I slid the suitcase out, unzipped the main pocket and lifted the lid open. It was empty. Zipping it back up again, I pushed it back under the bed then reached across to my trainers and slipped them on. This time, I hurried down the stairs in search of my mobile. I spied my handbag slung across the back of a kitchen chair. Inside the bag I found my mobile, along with my purse and my set of keys. The mobile was flat. I found my charger lying around on one of the kitchen sides and so plugged my mobile in and left it to charge. In the meantime, I rifled through my purse and handbag to see if there was any evidence or clues to my trip away, but I found nothing unusual to speak of. I flittered around the house, room to room in a subdued state, not really sure what I was looking for or the real purpose of going into those rooms. While in the lounge, I noticed through the window my next-door neighbour tending her front garden. Betty was a small plump lady and a complete battleaxe. Mostly, I tried to avoid her, although my attempts were generally futile. She always seemed to catch me as I was coming or going from the house, and she had an uncanny knack for always bumping into me at the local shops.

I opened the front door and stepped out into my front garden. Betty had her back to me and was hunched over, fiddling with some pot of flowers.

'Hi,' I said, trying to catch her attention.

'Oh, good God!' She jumped at the sound of my voice and placed her hand over her heart, as if to try and calm its beating. 'You trying to give an old lady a heart attack, sneaking up on me like that?'

'Sorry,' I said, wincing at her scolding.

'Well, as you're here, you can make yourself useful and help me move this pot.'

That was typical of Betty; she didn't ask. She just told, well, more like ordered.

For a while, I thought it was just me she spoke to in that way, but it turned out she didn't discriminate. She was impolite and demanding to everyone. Her overbearing nature meant she had fallen out of favour with many in the neighbourhood, and she only received occasional visitors. But there were some of us who still maintained a relationship with her and helped her out when needed. She was an elderly lady living alone and her physicality had waned over the years, so there were times when she relied on the goodwill of her neighbours for help. However, the limits of this goodwill were often tested, as she rarely showed any appreciation.

'Well. Are you going to help or not?'

'Sure,' I said, trying desperately to disguise a grimace.

I walked out of my garden and round to hers. The pot was large and made of stone. It weighed a ton. I struggled to move it even a few inches.

'Where do you want this exactly?' I said, praying it wasn't going to be any significant distance.

She pointed to a stone slab just to the right side of her front door. I looked in dismay; it was a good four or five metres away.

I heaved and strained and huffed and puffed, trying to move this lead weight across her garden. I chose to ignore her comment about me 'ripping up her lawn' as I wriggled the pot about, trying to slide it into position. Eventually, I got it into place and gingerly stood upright again. Thankfully, my back had survived the ordeal.

Betty was scrutinising its position. 'No, that's not right. I need it swivelled round.'

'Seriously?' I moaned, astonished at the audacity of the woman.

'I need that lion facing outwards to the street.'

She was referring to the carvings around the pot. There were various designs of different creatures etched into it. Why the lion had to be facing in a different direction was lost on me but I daren't argue. Swivelling the pot around was going to be far less trouble than debating the point with Betty.

I bent back down over the pot, placing both hands either side round the rim in preparation to twist it round. But before I did, I looked back up to Betty, who was now standing over me, monitoring my every movement, ready to reprimand me should I make the wrong move.

'What day is it?' I asked.

'What?' she shouted back.

'What day is it?'

'Oh, I don't know, dear. Every day is the same day to me.' She sounded annoyed, obviously finding the question completely irrelevant.

'Now can we get this turned round?' she snapped.

I did as she said, gave a weak smile and made my way back up her path. As I reached the gate, she shouted back to me.

'Wednesday.'

I turned round and looked squarely at her.

'Wednesday?'

'Yes, that's what I said. Wednesday.'

'Wednesday the what?'

'What?'

'Do you know the exact date?'

She gave me a dismissive wave of the hand and went back indoors.

'Twenty-eighth.'

I looked round to see the postman was now making his rounds and must have overheard the conversation.

'Thanks.'

He smiled as he walked past me to take a bundle of letters to Betty's letter box.

'Of May?'

There was a long pause. I felt embarrassed at my question. To lose track of what day of the week it was or the exact date is plausible. To not know the month is much less understandable.

'Twenty-eighth of May, yes.'

'OK, thanks.'

Now back in the house, sat at the kitchen table, I calculated I had somehow lost eight whole days. Lisa and I had embarked on our trip early Saturday afternoon, thirteen days ago. The last thing I remember from that trip was when I was barely conscious, lying on a spa bed. Since that moment, I could recall no memory at all, until the moment I woke up in my own house on a Wednesday morning, just over a week later.

My mobile phone, which was now able to power up since it had some charge, revealed I had neither received or made any phone calls nor sent or received any texts since that very Saturday we left. I found that highly unusual, expecting at least a phone call or message from work to find out why I had not come in. I was due to return on Monday, two days ago, although it was possible records could have been deleted.

I got up from my seat at the kitchen table and went into the hallway, where my landline phone was fixed to the wall. I grabbed the phone receiver off its hook and dialled the number for recalling the last incoming number. Once again, no calls received since I had left for the trip. I dialled my work number and waited patiently for someone to answer, although I had no idea what I was going to say.

'Good morning, Sapphire Hotel. How may I help you?'

'Hi, is that Jess?'

'Uh, yes it is,' she replied, slightly taken aback.

'Hi, Jess, it's Emma.'

'Oh sorry, Em, didn't recognise your voice. How are you feeling?' She sounded genuinely concerned.

I hesitated and there was an awkward pause as I tried to figure out what to say.

'Um … Yes, I am feeling much better now, thanks.'

'That's great news. Are you coming back in tomorrow?'

'Yes. I'll be back tomorrow,' I replied, without even thinking.

'Brilliant. Tom will be relieved. He has been a bit stressed out struggling to cover staff going on leave. We've had a few off sick this week. Must be something going around.'

I imagined my brother dashing around the place in a whirling frenzy. He was a stress freak at the best of times, and I expect this would have been a monumental disaster for him. He had already laid the guilt on when I asked for a week's holiday, citing the difficulties of coping when he already had other staff on leave that week.

'Did you have a good hols? You didn't get ill while you were away, did you?'

'Yes, hols was good, thanks. No, I wasn't ill until after.'

I felt a terrible guilt for lying, but then I wasn't entirely sure what the truth was. It seemed easier to just give the expected answer rather than the absurd and extremely vague alternative.

'Oh good, well, you can tell me all about it when you are in tomorrow. See you then. Bye.'

'Bye.'

I replaced the receiver back on its hook and gave a sigh. Jess was a very excitable and talkative person. She liked nothing more than a good old gossip and catch-up on everything and anything. She would witter away about things that really did not interest me and went into far too much detail. She could also become very tiresome with her constant bombardment of questions as she tried to prise more details from you if you were less than forthcoming. Returning to work tomorrow, after a week's hols and several days sick, would mean Jess would be in full swing, and I shuddered at the thought.

My stomach growled and I could no longer ignore my hunger. I grabbed a packet of crisps from the cupboard, not my usual choice for breakfast, but there wasn't much else given I had run my stocks low, knowing I would be away for a while. I washed it down with a glass of water and then considered what to do next. I was so confused; the world around me was acting and functioning like normal and yet to me things seemed surreal. I suddenly felt very alone, unsure if there was anyone I felt I could really talk to about it. Under normal circumstances, Lisa would be the first person I would naturally turn to confide in. However, that was clearly not an option. I had no family I could turn to. I only had my brother and we were not very close. He only maintained a civilised relationship with me as a moral obligation. Apart from Lisa, I didn't have any other real close friends. I had a few casual friends I would happily socialise with, but they were not on the kind of friendship level I would feel comfortable talking about personal or intimate details with. I did consider phoning the authorities, but that didn't feel like a viable option, either. My story would seem so vague and I wasn't sure would be believed. In any case, I wasn't sure what exactly I would be reporting. That I had experienced some unusual things over the past few days and lost a few days of my memory? I would sound like some kind of nutcase and in need of consulting a doctor. They would likely put it down to a young naive female enjoying her holiday a bit too much and falling into a drunken stupor.

My mind then turned to Sam. I wondered where he was now and if I would be able to trace him. He was the only one true person I felt I could trust and talk to candidly. I felt a pang of real desire to see him and yet it seemed odd I should feel like this as my time with him had been so brief and short-lived. I contemplated jumping in the car and driving straight down to Cornwall in search of him, but locating him on the limited information I had could prove a massive task, and if he wasn't in Cornwall it could prove nigh on impossible.

I felt overwhelmed and incapable of making a decision. I began to ferociously rub my fingers back and forth across my forehead as if I was giving myself an intensive head massage in the hope it would encourage the answer to pop out. I juggled the various options around in my head and internally debated what I should do, until I finally landed on a decision. I hastily grabbed my phone, keys and handbag; too afraid if I didn't move quickly I would have second thoughts.

I had barely locked the front door behind me before I was accosted by my neighbour Betty.

'Oh good, I was hoping I would bump into you.'

I gave a wry grin. 'Hello again,' I said, unenthused, anticipating her making her next demand.

'My bulb's gone in my kitchen and I can't see a damn thing. I can't reach to put a new one in, and I refuse to get up on a chair. I've got no sense of balance and I'd fall off and break my hip.'

I was about to explain that actually I was on my way out and maybe I could come round later to do it, but she was already making her way back into her house.

I gave a deep sigh and gently shook my head. For all the strange goings-on recently, Betty was acting exactly how Betty always acted, and for that I was surprisingly grateful.

She was now stood in the doorway, looking at me impatiently as she held the door open. I quickly walked down my pathway, out of my gate and round into her garden. As annoyed as I was at being detained, there was a chance I might be able to use this moment to glean some useful information out of my nosy neighbour, whose prying eyes may have seen something.

'So which bulb do you need changing?' I asked as I passed by her and into her house.

'The kitchen. I already said it was the kitchen,' she snapped back.

I manoeuvred one of her kitchen chairs into place and gingerly stood on it. I wasn't convinced it would take my weight as it looked ancient and not in the best condition. As I unscrewed the light bulb, I could hear the joints of the chair creaking under my weight and it rocked slightly where one of the legs didn't quite touch the floor. Betty snatched the light bulb from me and thrust a new one at me.

'Betty, this isn't going to fit.'

'What?' she barked back.

'This is a bayonet fitting. I need a screw-type one.'

She looked at me, perplexed, and then started rummaging through her kitchen drawer.

I stepped off the chair and waited, watching her sifting through various different bulbs and other odds and ends, muttering to herself all the while.

'So, Betty, you haven't seen any recent comings or goings at my house by any chance, have you?'

'What?' She was still determinedly rifling through the drawer and didn't even look up at me.

'Anything out of the ordinary, maybe?'

This time, she stopped and looked me straight in the eye.

'What are you wittering on about? Can you come and have a look and see if this screw thingy is in here. I can't see one.'

I took a few minutes sorting through all the different light bulbs of various wattage and shapes and sizes, but there was none that would fit.

'Doesn't look like you've got one that will fit.'

'Well, that's just great,' she moaned. 'I suppose now I will just have to stumble around in the pitch black.'

I let out a slight chuckle, amused by her overreaction at what I classed as a small inconvenience but which Betty was treating like the end of the world. The look of disdain across her face quickly wiped the smirk off my face, and I immediately altered my attitude to a more serious tone.

'I'll pick you one up while I'm out and bring it round later. In the meantime, have you got a spare lamp I could set up to give you a little light?'

'There's one in the bedroom, on the bedside table. You can use that,' she replied more affably.

I decided this was likely to be the best mood I could catch her in so tried my line of questioning again.

'So did you see anything odd at my house recently?'

'Odd? What do you mean odd? I haven't seen anything. What do you think I do, stand at the window all day?'

I tried not to give any outward reaction as, yes, I did imagine that she spent a great deal of time looking out the window spying on her neighbours.

'You woke me up, though, when you came back last night. Slamming the car doors as your friends had to carry you in. It's disgusting you youngsters drinking yourselves into oblivion like that.'

'Friends? There were several of them? How many? Did you see who they were, what they looked like?'

'Oh, dear God. You don't even know who brought you home? What kind of a state is that to get into for a young lady? You'll find yourself in real trouble one day.'

Unperturbed by the lecture, I pressed again. 'Did you see them? How many?'

'Three, I think. No, wait, might be four. I think the driver stayed in the car.'

'What kind of car was it?'

'Oh jeez, I don't know. A big one, estate-type thing.'

My heart was beginning to race as Betty slowly but surely began to spill out the information.

'One of them was that girl that comes round here sometimes.'

I raised my eyes; she had to be talking about Lisa.

'You know? The one that came here the other day when you went off on your holiday. The one that thinks she's a goddamn racing driver.'

I nodded. 'Yes, I know. You mean Lisa,' and with a sarcastic tone added, 'my best friend.'

CHAPTER ELEVEN

I was shaking so much as I rattled the letter box that I had to have a second attempt. The first was far too weak and would not have made a noise loud enough for Lisa to hear that I was at her front door. The door opened and Lisa looked startled to see me.

'Hi,' she said, surprised.

'Hi,' I replied abruptly, and just stood firmly looking at her.

She hesitated for a moment and I could see she was sensing my hostility.

'Sorry, what am I doing? Leaving you stood on the doorway. Come in, come in. I was just a bit surprised to see you. I wasn't expecting you.'

She stood aside and frantically gestured me in. Then she leant to give me a welcoming kiss on the cheek which I almost baulked at. I couldn't tell if Lisa had missed my reluctance or had chosen to ignore it. Either way, she firmly planted the kiss on my cheek, took my coat and offered me to sit down on her couch.

'So how are you?'

I didn't answer; I was trying to stay calm but inside I was raging. Lisa had sat down alongside me but she seemed unrelaxed and fidgety.

'Do you want a drink? Let me put the kettle on.'

She jumped up and went to the kitchen. I got the impression she was relieved to leave the room.

'You don't take sugar, right?'

Her head popped round the door as she waited for my reply.

'What time did you drop me off last night?'

The question had clearly rattled her. Her expression changed from a smiley friendly face to a deep frown.

'Sorry?'

'What time did you drop me off last night?'

'Last night?'

The kettle clicked as it reached boiling point.

Lisa disappeared back into the kitchen, and I could hear her making the tea. First, the water glugging into the cups followed by the opening and closing of the fridge as the milk was added and then the sound of a teaspoon clinking against the cup as the tea was being stirred. There was a long pause and I imagined her stood there staring into the cups, fretting about how she was going to handle this. Finally, she re-entered the room and placed two plain white mugs down on the coffee table.

'There you go.'

There was an awkward silence and Lisa reached for her mug, took a sip and then kept firmly hold of it as if for comfort.

'So, how are you?' she asked.

I repeated my question slowly and accentuating the words.

'What time did you drop me off last night?'

She laughed back nervously and I could see she was in real discomfort.

'I tell you what, perhaps this is an easier question for you. What exactly happened on our holiday? What happened to me?'

Lisa turned as white as a sheet, and I thought for a moment she would faint. She put her mug down and composed herself.

'Holiday? I don't understand what you are saying, Emma. You're not making any sense. Are you OK?'

I stared at her, flabbergasted.

'Lisa, for God's sake. Don't play dumb and just pretend it never happened. You picked me up a week before Saturday and we went away on holiday to Devon. We were there a few days. Some really weird stuff happened, stuff mainly centred around you, and then I fell into some kind of unconscious state. No, actually, I was put into some kind of unconscious state.'

Lisa's eyes were wide and she looked fairly terrified.

'And then suddenly I find myself returned to my own house, several days later. I have no idea how or why it has all happened. I do know, however, that you are somehow part of it.'

As I said the last sentence, my voice began to wobble and tears came to my eyes. My initial rage had waned and I was now overcome with sadness. Sadness that I had lost my best friend.

'Oh, Emma. I don't know what it is you're saying. We didn't go on any holiday to Devon. The last holiday we went on was last year when we went to the Lake District. Remember?'

I looked at her in horror. I was speechless. I literally couldn't physically say anything.

'Emma. I think you need to see someone. A doctor. You need to see your doctor.' She placed her arms around my shoulders and added, 'You might be having a mental breakdown or something.'

I recoiled from her grasp, dumbfounded by what she was saying. I hadn't been sure what to expect when I came here to confront her about it, but I certainly did not expect her to react by pretending it never happened and that I was suffering from some mental disorder.

'What?' I screamed. 'My neighbour saw you, Lisa. She saw you pick me up to take us on hols. In fact, she saw you drop me off last night. Well, carry me in, I think were her words.'

'What, that batty old woman that lives next door to you?' Lisa had now got much more emotional and was bordering on angry. 'You believe what she says over me?'

'She saw you.'

'No, she didn't. She's a decrepit old woman. She can't see bugger all.' Then in a softer tone, said, 'Emma, you need to see a doctor. Seriously, you need to see a doctor now. Something is not right.'

'So you are saying the memory I have of us going away to Devon is all complete nonsense? My neighbour's corroborating story can't be believed because she's too old to be trusted and basically I'm just going mad?'

I didn't wait for a reply. I didn't know what was going on, but I could tell Lisa was just covering up something and I was not going to get anywhere staying here. So I left. I left with Lisa shouting after me, all the way to my car, until I slammed my door shut and could no longer hear her. I saw her walking down her path and then running after the car as I pulled away until I was round the corner, out of sight. As I drove down the road, I gently sobbed, knowing that our friendship was over. By the time I got home and pulled up on the drive, I had got the tears out of my system and had a renewed sense of determination that I was not going mad. Something was going on, and I was going to find out exactly what it was.

CHAPTER TWELVE

The next day, I decided to go to work. After coming back from Lisa's house the previous day, I had spent many hours trying to locate the holiday resort with the intention to revisit it. I'd scoured the internet, rang countless Devon holiday agents and searched my home from top to bottom looking for any kind of inkling. But I found absolutely nothing. There was not one piece of evidence to even prove its existence, never mind identify where its exact location was. My key witness was flatly denying any knowledge of it, and anyone else whom I had met while there I had no real idea how to contact. So when I woke the next morning, it felt a very dubious decision travelling all the way to Devon with so little to go on. I had nothing more than the memories that resided in my head, and I had nothing and no one to back any of it up. The only shred of possible evidence I had to support my story came from Betty, but even that was only a tiny glimmer. The reliability of that evidence was debatable. Betty was extremely nosy and kept her ear to the ground. Unfortunately, Betty's eyesight and hearing had deteriorated with age, and she could be rather presumptuous and sometimes make wrongful assumptions. To make matters worse, Betty and I were not currently on the best of terms. I had completely forgotten to pick up the light bulb I had promised and so when I had returned from Lisa's without it, Betty had given me a few sharp words and I had retaliated with a few of my own. Going to work seemed like the only thing for me to do, if only to try and get some normality back in my life. It would be the weekend soon and I generally only worked during the week, so it would be more prudent to continue my investigation then.

The car took a bit of persuasion to start. It took several turns of the key before the engine spluttered into action. I revved the engine a few times and thankfully it seemed like it was now running OK, presumably just cold from not being started for a while. As I sat on the driveway, waiting a few minutes to instil enough confidence that it would not conk out on me, I could see Betty's curtains twitching. I imagined her stood there scowling at me and probably uttering scathing remarks. I sneered at the absurdity that something as insignificant as a forgotten light bulb could cause such a fuss but did give myself a cursory reminder that I really ought to pick one up and end the farce.

The drive to work was the usual mundane commute. It took about forty minutes to drive there, most of which felt like it was spent waiting at traffic lights or sat at a junction waiting for a big enough gap in the traffic to slip into. When I did finally arrive at work, I could see Harry was on the ride-on lawn mower, cutting the hotel's front lawns. As I approached along the impressive driveway, gradually driving closer to the hotel's main entrance, Harry gave me a friendly wave. I waved back, although too late for him to see, as he had already turned his attention back to his mower.

I parked the car up in the staff car park which was a simple tarmacked area tucked away from the main hotel frontage behind a large red brick wall. As I stepped out of the car and locked the door, I took a moment to brace myself for the inevitable onslaught that was about to ensue. This time of year was a particularly busy period for the hotel and things could get quite hectic. I only hoped that my brother's temperament had not reached levels of a blind state of panic; otherwise, the day could get quite unbearable.

I made my way round to the front entrance and, as I did so, looked back across the lawns to try and gain Harry's attention, but he was facing in the wrong direction and moving away from me as he mowed the next parallel line. Harry was one of the few people here who I genuinely liked talking to and spending time with. He was an unassuming man, a few years older than me, and although I wouldn't describe him as shy or averse to conversation, he did tend to keep himself to himself. He was the head gardener and kept the hotel gardens in pristine condition. He had a couple of young lads working for him who very much looked up to him and deservedly gave him the greatest respect. Due to his job role, he naturally spent most of his time outside, rarely venturing inside the hotel and therefore unfortunately our paths seldom seemed to cross.

I skipped up the stone steps, passing the grand Georgian-style pillars, and entered cheerfully through the hotel doors. I don't think anyone actually noticed my arrival, for it was bedlam. Stefan, the hotel porter, who had only arrived from Poland to start his new job the week before I went away with Lisa, was being reprimanded by my brother. Jess was behind reception looking incredibly hassled, hastily searching through mounds of paperwork, and Maisie was frantically polishing the staircase balustrades at such a speed she was almost tripping over her own feet as she made her way up the stairs.

'Emma, thank God you're finally back.'

Tom had finished berating Stefan, who was now scurrying off down the hotel corridor with his tail between his legs, and turned his attention to me.

'Hi,' I whimpered, waiting for the barrage of orders and demands.

'I need you to help Jess behind reception right away. We've got a coachload turning up any minute for a two-day conference, and they all need to be checked in before the conference starts at 9am.'

I could see the beads of sweat across his forehead and he was red with rage.

'Jess, where the hell is Amelia? She is supposed to be getting the conference room ready for them.'

Jess was so engrossed in the paperwork she barely registered Tom yelling at her.

'Jess?' Tom yelled.

'Huh?' said a half-hearted Jess. Just then, the phone rang and immediately Jess switched into front desk mode.

'Good morning, Sapphire Hotel. How may I help you?'

Jess gave Tom a shrug of the shoulders and pointed to the phone, intimating her attention was needed elsewhere.

Tom stormed off in a very distressed state, and I worried he was on the verge of exploding. As he walked off with his back turned, Jess stared hard after him. She then looked over at me and gave a flick of the eyes which I returned with a knowing smile.

Underwhelmed by my welcome back to work, I stepped behind the counter ready to take on reception duties, knowing that it would not be long before it felt as if I had never even been away. Normally,

I would find this a rather depressing thought but given recent circumstances maybe this was more favourable.

'Hey, welcome back.' Jess finished the telephone call and gave an overzealous squeeze of my shoulders.

'Thanks,' I said uncomfortably, still feeling the tension in my shoulders where she had squeezed so hard.

'So how was it? Can't believe you got so ill after. Amelia said you sounded really rough when you phoned in sick. She was convinced it was all self-inflicted. It wasn't self-inflicted, was it? I told Amelia I doubted it was, but she seemed adamant. But you did have a good holiday, right?'

Jess barely stopped for breath as she babbled away, and as I tried to digest her ramblings I could see the coach pulling up in front of the hotel doors.

'Uh, looks like the coach has just arrived,' I said, relieved at being saved from answering, well, at least for now. I was sure once they had dispersed and everything had quietened down, Jess would be pestering me again with twenty questions.

'Great. Let the mayhem commence,' replied Jess in an unjoyful tone.

Men and women, of a diverse age range, all smartly dressed, filed one by one off the coach and quickly filled every available inch of space of the reception area. At first, the prospect looked quite daunting, but Jess and I soon got into our stride. One by one, we went through the formal process of check-in and directed them towards the conference room, until eventually we had cleared reception and the din had subdued.

'And all is calm again,' said Jess as the last delegate disappeared through the double doors, off to join his fellow colleagues. Moments later, the double doors flung open again as Amelia came stomping through. She was wearing a stunning red dress, showing off plenty of leg, accentuated by very high-heeled black shoes, huffing and puffing as she clutched at her clipboard.

'Can't stop, very busy,' said Amelia, raising her hand, directing us not to dare interrupt.

'Stuck-up cow,' murmured Jess as Amelia was strutting off down the corridor.

I smiled at what I considered a fairly accurate description. Amelia thought herself far above most people and was someone I only tolerated and where possible avoided. My smile quickly disappeared as Amelia suddenly stopped in her tracks and turned round to face us, and I feared she had heard Jess's derogatory comment.

'Good to see you finally back, Emma.'

'Thanks,' I replied apathetically. The tone in her voice suggested a ticking-off for not coming back sooner rather than a genuine welcome back.

'Oh God, I thought she'd actually heard me then,' said Jess with a nervous laugh. 'Anyway, come on. Tell me all about your hols. I bet you had a right laugh, two single girlies away. Did you meet any nice fellas?'

I gave her a disapproving frown, but I found my mind wandering, thinking back to Sam.

'Oh, you did meet someone, didn't you? I can tell!'

'What? What you talking about? How can you tell?'

'What was his name? What was he like? Come on, spill the beans.'

'No. I didn't meet, well, I did meet someone …'

'I knew it!'

'No, not like that. I met Sam and we had a few drinks but that was it. I got ill and the holiday ended abruptly.'

'Oh God. Sorry, I didn't realise your holiday was cut short. What happened? Did you get a virus or something?'

'Yeh. Something like that.'

'So did you get Sam's number? Where does he live? What's he like?'

Already, I was finding the questions draining, and I could feel a headache coming on.

'No, no number. I think he lives in Cornwall, boat building. He's a nice guy. We got on well.'

'Oh, that's such a shame.' Jess sounded distraught and typically overdramatic. 'So, do you think it is likely you will see him again?'

'Don't know. Probably not.'

'Oh …' cooed Jess. 'Well, plenty more fish in the sea,' she said, perking up and giving me a wink.

Suddenly Amelia was storming back towards reception. I heard her approach before I actually set eyes on her, as was often the case, with the heavy clip-clop of her heels. I took a breath and contemplated which was the lesser of the two evils – the wrath of Amelia or constant interrogation by Jess.

'Emma, where's Harry?' she squawked. 'You're going to have to go and get him. He'll have to come in and take over some maintenance duties. God, this place is falling apart. The conference room is practically in pitch black, all the lights have gone. I've got guests complaining left, right and centre about broken TVs and everything else under the sun you can think of.'

My mind drifted slightly as I imagined Harry's reaction when I told him of Amelia's demands. I could guarantee he would not be happy. For one, he was not a fan of Amelia and would not appreciate her bossing him around, and he was often irritated by having to carry out duties beyond his normal remit.

'Emma,' Amelia hollered. 'Can you please go and get Harry?' she said, exasperated, and sounding like she was at the end of her tether.

'Sure.'

I hurriedly left reception and slipped quietly out of the main front door in search of Harry. It was a relief to escape both Amelia and Jess, and I wondered how long I could get away with hiding out here, away from the mayhem. I looked out across the neatly striped lawns. Harry was nowhere in sight and I could not hear the engine of the mower. Clearly, he had finished long ago. The grounds of the hotel were quite extensive, so it was not always easy to locate him. As I stood contemplating which area to start my search, I heard the faint murmur of a strimmer, so I followed the sound until I finally found him.

'Hi, Harry,' I shouted as I tried to compete with the noise of the machinery.

Harry looked up with a look of annoyance at being disturbed, but then when he realised it was me, it was quickly replaced with a smile and he immediately cut the engine on the strimmer.

'Hi, Emma. How are you?'

'Very good, thanks. And you?'

'Yes, not too bad.' There was a slight pause as he looked down to the ground, and I wondered if he was about to start the strimmer back up again. Instead, he lifted his gaze back up and caught my stare.

'How was your holiday?'

'Umm,' I stuttered, as I tilted my head to one side trying to think of a suitable answer. I found it difficult to give just the customary positive remark to a question I knew was being asked sincerely.

'So-so.'

Harry's brow furrowed, but I knew he was too polite to probe me further.

'Now don't shoot the messenger, but you're wanted to do some chores inside the hotel. Amelia's doing her usual drama queen routine. Apparently, everything is just falling apart.'

The expression on Harry's face immediately dropped, and I felt bad for clearly ruining his day.

'Well, I guess that's the end of the strimming then. Of course, later she'll be complaining the garden looks a mess. Bloody woman.'

I grimaced apologetically at his reaction and felt incredible guilt, even though it was completely unwarranted.

I sensed that Harry noticed my unease as he quickly changed his tune.

'I'm just going to pop this strimmer back in the shed. I won't be long.'

'I'll come with you. I could do with stretching my legs and, to be honest, I am in no rush to get back.'

He looked genuinely pleased that I offered to accompany him, which was a relief as I was slightly embarrassed I had been so forward in my suggestion.

Harry's shed was positioned at the far side of the hotel grounds near to the garden veg plot that supplied seasonal produce for the hotel kitchen. It was sufficient distance away from where any guests would venture, which suited Harry as he was not keen on mingling with guests. In fact, sometimes I wasn't sure he liked mingling with anyone.

As we walked the distance to his shed, he pointed out some of the new beds he had planted for the summer, reeling off all the Latin names of various species of plants. I was always amazed how he could remember them all or even pronounce some of them. I would accuse him of making half of it up in the knowledge that he knew I was hopeless at naming any, apart from the very common flowers.

'Right, here we are.'

I smiled as we entered what Harry referred to as a shed but what I would call a workshop. It was bigger than any room in my house, holding an array of tools and machinery, workbench and several racks of shelving. I sat in the chair at his desk while he found a spare space on one of the racks to house the strimmer.

'So have I missed anything while I was away?' I asked curiously.

'No, not really. Same as always.'

I smiled, knowing that Harry was not the best person to ask to find out about any comings or goings or interesting gossip.

'So, what is it Amelia wants me to do exactly?'

'Not too sure. She mentioned lights not working.'

'Well, she can change a light bulb, can't she?'

'Maybe a broken TV as well?'

'Great.'

This only seemed to add to his woes, making me slightly regret adding the last statement.

'OK,' he said with very little enthusiasm. 'Best get this over with.'

I got up out of the chair and gave Harry a nudge with my elbow, accompanied by a cheeky grin.

He raised his eyebrows and gave me a weak smile, and then we made our way back to the main hotel.

All was quiet when we got to the main reception area. Only Jess was about, manning the front desk.

'Hi, Harry,' said Jess cheerfully as we walked in. 'You managed to find him OK then?'

'Yeh, not too hard to find today.' Her comment made me feel a bit conscience-stricken. Sometimes, when I was sent to locate him, usually to run some errand for either Amelia or Tom, I had a tendency of over-exaggerating how long it actually took me to find him. Sometimes, I managed to find him quite quickly, but instead of us heading straight back to the hotel, we would walk round the garden and Harry would show me some plant or other he had been cultivating, or perhaps his latest vegetable crop he had successfully grown.

'I think Amelia is in the conference room, Harry. She's stressing out because a lot of the lights are not working and apparently the delegates are getting a bit tetchy.'

'Right, OK.'

Just as Harry was walking off down the corridor towards the conference room, I suddenly had a thought.

'Harry?'

He stopped in his tracks and looked back over his shoulder.

'I know you're probably going to be rushed off your feet, but if you do happen to have a spare light bulb going, one that's a screw type, fairly bright one, 100 watt maybe. I'd appreciate it, but don't worry if not.'

He gave an affirmative nod and carried on his way, disappearing through the double doors.

The rest of the day dragged on. Apart from the initial morning rush, there wasn't too much else to deal with for myself or Jess, apart from the usual humdrum of reception duties. There were times during the day when I slipped into a daydream thinking back to the previous week or so, and I decided I would attempt this coming weekend to locate the resort. However, that plan of action was quickly dispelled once Tom had caught me five minutes before I was about to finish my shift and leave for the day.

'Em, I need you to work this weekend.'

'Really?' I replied, whining like a child.

'Yes. Really. Is that a problem?'

I gave Tom a sulky stare. 'Well, I was thinking of going away this weekend actually.'

He looked aghast and I knew what was coming.

'Emma, you've just had nearly two weeks off! These are our busiest months. I'm struggling for staff as it is.'

'Yes, OK, fine,' I relented. 'I can do this weekend.' I decided to let slide the fact that I was actually ill for part of those two weeks.

As Tom was staring at me wide-eyed and Jess was shrinking in the corner of reception, trying her best to avoid Tom's eyeline, Harry quietly slipped into reception. He strode up to the desk and placed a light bulb down on it.

'This any good?'

You could have cut the atmosphere with a knife it was so tense, but either Harry hadn't noticed or he had chosen to ignore it. Knowing Harry, it was probably the latter.

'Yeh, that's great. Thanks, Harry.'

'No problem,' and with that he left through the front entrance, giving Tom only a momentary glance as he passed by.

Tom just stood stock-still, staring now at the light bulb, looking quite confused.

'OK, I'm off, see you tomorrow,' I said hastily, grabbing the light bulb on my way before Tom had the chance to say anything else.

'Yeh, see you, Em,' replied Jess.

I sighed with relief as I escaped through the door, clutching at the light bulb, which was beginning to feel like the bane of my life.

CHAPTER THIRTEEN

I didn't get chance to even knock on the door, as Betty must have seen me coming and had already opened it before I got there. I was feeling sheepish as I entered, not quite sure what Betty's reaction would be. I decided to let sleeping dogs lie and act as if our last heated encounter had never occurred.

'Hi, Betty. I remembered that light bulb,' I said, waving it around.

There was an unnerving long delay before Betty actually said anything.

'Good. Come in.' It was a very blunt reply and I waited in anticipation for the follow-up of sarcastic comments. To my surprise, none came, and instead she offered me a cup of tea. I was taken off guard at her offer of hospitality. Sensing that Betty had mistaken my silence for shunning her, I quickly accepted her offer.

'Oh yes. That would be lovely.'

Betty said nothing, but her glower at least lessened. While she made the tea, I replaced the light bulb for her, neither of us speaking as we did so. I sat at the kitchen table. The atmosphere felt a little tense, but I began to wonder if the offer of tea was Betty's attempt at an apology for our earlier falling-out.

I watched her as she placed a round mat on the table and stood on it a bone china teapot adorned with pink flowers and purple butterflies and with wisps of steam coming out of the spout. Alongside, she placed a sugar bowl and milk jug, all of the same set, followed by a teacup and saucer for us each. As she placed two silver teaspoons down on the table, she caught me smiling at the rigmarole she was going through, just making tea.

'I bet you don't normally drink tea out of a proper teacup?'

'No. I just normally chuck a teabag in a mug.'

Betty screwed her face up in disapproval and looked almost revolted by my reply.

'Urgh. Doesn't taste the same out of a mug,' she said as she poured me a cup. 'Help yourself to sugar.'

'I'm fine, no sugar for me,' watching with alarm as she dropped three heaped teaspoons of sugar into her own cup.

'So back to work today, was it?'

'Yeh,' I replied sullenly.

'That good, eh?'

'Amazing,' I said sarcastically.

'You'll have to book up your next holiday with your friend, have something to look forward to.'

I shuddered at the thought.

'Well, I don't know about that. I think I'm done with holidays with my friend. In fact, I think I'm done with my friend. Holiday on my own might be safer.'

I'm not sure why, but for some reason I had turned off any filter between what I was thinking and what I was actually saying. Betty didn't seem particularly fazed by it, and strangely I didn't regret being so honest in front of her.

'Oh. I thought you two were best friends.'

'Yep. I thought so too.'

'Jeez. You must have had some falling-out. Over a man, was it?'

I gave a disapproving frown. Lisa and I had very different tastes in men and that would never be an issue.

'No.'

'Money, then,' she said with strong certainty.

'Nope.'

'Well, whatever it is, you need to think very hard about whether it is really worth falling out about. Good friends are hard to come by, and you might live to regret it.'

I looked deep into Betty's eyes and could see a slight glisten. I wondered if she was talking from experience.

'I'm not sure this is something I could forgive. It's a trust issue. Although even though I know she's lying, I'm not quite sure of the reasons why. I think it makes it worse as you have no way of justifying it.'

'Well, it's your choice. But don't say I didn't warn you, that one day in the future, you may look back and realise you threw something valuable away for nothing.'

She took a sip from her tea and then added, 'Or apples.'

'Or what?'

Just as I was seriously listening to Betty and thinking how I should maybe heed her wise words, she suddenly threw in an odd ball.

'Apples,' she repeated more loudly and clearly.

'Yeh. I thought that's what you said. Apples?'

For one brief moment, Betty had completely changed my perception of her from some eccentric, annoying and rude woman to someone who might actually be worth listening to. Eccentric had made a comeback, and I was sure it wouldn't be long until annoying and rude was back in play.

'I threw away something valuable for apples,' she said, as if that was some rational explanation.

'OK,' I said, baffled. 'Do you want to elaborate?'

Betty took another sip of tea and then began her story.

'Elsie was a good friend of mine. We did lots of things together. Went to dancing halls, theatre, shopping; I could go on. One day, in the late summer, I went to her house. I had turned up unannounced and she didn't seem overly impressed. We chatted for a bit but she seemed moody and very frosty towards me and I was a bit put out. I only stayed for a short while, but just before I left I asked her if I could have some apples. She had a large mature Bramley apple tree in her garden and every year she gave me a great big bag of apples, usually without me even asking. We went outside and I could see the tree was ripe with fruit. It was laden with hundreds of apples, and many of the branches were in easy reach from the ground. Elsie picked up two apples from the ground – both were bruised, one had an insect in it – and just handed them to me. I couldn't believe it. Hundreds of lovely apples hanging on the tree and she handed me two windfalls that looked practically rotten. Well, I made my feelings known, threw the apples back on the ground and walked off. That was thirty years ago. I've never eaten an apple in all those years, and I shan't up until the day I die.'

I sat back in shock. I wasn't quite sure what to say.

'Have you not seen her since then? Thirty years because of a couple of rotten apples?'

I could see the beginnings of tears welling up in her eyes, but she cleared her throat and maintained her composure.

'Well, I saw her today, in a manner of speaking. I catch the 10am bus every Thursday that stops near the cemetery, where I visit her grave and tell her about the mainly crazy goings-on in the world.'

Suddenly I began to realise that the story wasn't quite as I first thought, and I listened as she continued.

'You see, what I failed to realise that day was my friend wasn't annoyed with me turning up unannounced nor was she being rude. She was just suffering with shock, having received the news only moments before I arrived that she had an aggressive tumour. Inoperable.'

Her voice began to wobble and I could now feel my eyes welling up.

'We didn't speak for three whole weeks after the apple incident, until my stubbornness wore off and I finally came to my senses. Two days too late. She'd already died. I did make the funeral.'

Betty stood up and began to clear the table. I could see she no longer wanted to talk about it and needed to take her mind back off it and busy herself. As she picked up my cup, she leant towards me and looked hard into my eyes.

'Just be sure, whatever it is, is it really worth it? Do you really know the whole story?'

As Betty washed up the crockery, I thought long and hard about what she said. It was upsetting. No. I didn't know the whole story. I didn't even know the half of it.

CHAPTER FOURTEEN

Three months slid by and I became no closer to knowing what happened. Lisa and I were no longer in touch. She had tried contacting me a few times in the first few weeks, but I ignored all her texts and calls. On one occasion, she came to my house, but I hid upstairs and watched as she left from behind a curtain. Eventually, she just stopped trying.

I managed only two separate weekend trips to Devon as I was having to work so many extra shifts at the hotel, which either robbed me of available time or meant I was just too exhausted from the long hours. Both times I did manage to travel, the trips proved unfruitful. I had no idea if I was even close to the vicinity, and nothing I saw was recognisable to our previous travel there. I asked a few locals in various pubs and shops, but no one had any clue what I was referring to. I became frustrated at the lack of any forthcoming information. It was like the place had disappeared off the face of the earth. I did not, however, lose my determination to uncover the truth. At least now, with the summer holiday period coming to an end, I would have more time to devote to my quest.

Tom had agreed to give me a long weekend off and I jumped at the opportunity to take another trip out, hoping it would be third time lucky. I had kept a notebook where I jotted down as much information as I could about everything I did know. The front page was entitled 'Roseville Resort', and inside it contained dates, names of people I met, any memories of details I could remember and any scant piece of information that might pertain to a clue or vital piece of evidence. I thumbed through the pages until I reached the page entitled 'Location' to see if I could glean anything from it to give me an idea on where I might try looking next. The county of Devon was emblazoned along the first line. I had drawn a box round it several times, so the line was now quite thick. Even though the page was full of writing, this was the only real conclusive piece of information I had. Most of the rest was just scribbles of indeterminable information. I had tried to recall any place names that we had come across along the journey to give some clue as to the area we were in or roads that we drove down, but I couldn't really remember anything definite. I had relied on Lisa to work out the route, and I had simply just been the passenger, along for the ride.

Under the 'County of Devon' box I had drawn a crossroads with a sign. I clearly remembered us stopping for a while at a crossroads not far from the resort while we tried to establish the direction. I even remembered the sign; I just couldn't remember what was written on it. I had made several attempts at writing down what I thought the place names were, but I had put a line through each entry. According to my Devon map, which I had picked up from a corner shop in Devon on one of my earlier trips down there, none of those places existed. Further down the page, I'd written down 'Stopped at village nearby with garage and two pubs'. I shook my head at the sentence. How much vaguer could I be? That probably described hundreds of little villages and towns. Once again, I couldn't recall any names. I didn't even have a slight inkling as to what the pubs might be called. I despaired at how useless I had been at taking notice of my surroundings and wondered how much I missed in life as I wandered around apparently with blinkers on. I slammed the notebook shut and threw it across the room in a temper. I would do just as well to drop a pin on a map and see where it landed in order to pick my next location to search.

I looked out the lounge window and could see Betty making her way back down the road towards her house. As it was late morning on a Thursday, I guessed she was coming back from visiting the cemetery. It was funny; in all the years I had lived next door to her, I had never noticed her Thursday morning routine until she had told me her story. Another stark reminder on how blinkered I was to the world around me. Although, in all fairness, I would very often be working during that time.

Feeling despondent at not having any real concrete idea on where I should visit next in search of the elusive resort, I decided that maybe I should wait until the morning before actually travelling down. That would ease the pressure on making my choice of where to go, give me the rest of the day to decide, and maybe after a good night's sleep I would feel more invigorated. I would leave early hours to avoid any traffic and then have a good two full days down there. It would then give me plenty of time to leisurely drive back on the Sunday, ready to return to work the next day.

I picked my notebook back up and placed it on the coffee table. I decided to make myself a cup of tea and then try looking through it again.

Just as I was walking through to the kitchen, the doorbell rang. I heaved a sigh, thinking it was most likely to be Betty, and I really wasn't in the right frame of mind to talk to her. I went to the door, but as I looked through the glazed pane I could see the outline of the person, and it wasn't Betty, far too tall for a start and clearly a man. I opened the door and froze when I saw who was standing in front of me. I dared not believe my eyes.

'Hi,' he said casually.

'Oh my God. Sam, I can't believe it's you.'

We both stood there for a minute just gazing at each other, Sam seemingly giving me the time to digest that it was actually him. Finally, I spoke.

'Come in, come in.' I wanted to hug him as he came in and stood in the hallway, if only just to reaffirm he was real.

'Are you all right? How did you find me? I still can't believe you're actually here.'

He smiled. 'Yeh, I'm fine. You took a bit of tracking down, but I got there eventually. There are a lot of hotels in Bath, you know?'

'Well, come in, come and sit down. Oh God, we've got so much to catch up on.'

I'd got over the initial shock and was now really excited. This was unbelievable. So much time had passed with not a whiff of any kind of tangible piece of information to even prove that the place existed, and now here was a piece of very strong evidence that had just walked right into my house.

We both sat down on the sofa, Sam resting back and stretching out his legs, while I sat right on the edge of the seat in complete wonderment. He gave a yawn and then noticed my notebook on the coffee table. He picked it up and started flicking through it. I watched as he turned to the 'People' page with his name top of the list, the only one underlined and with stars around it. I felt incredibly embarrassed as I saw he was amused to see his name highlighted and I could feel myself blushing.

Sam closed the book and put it back on the coffee table.

'So do you remember that place?' I asked curiously.

He nodded. 'Sure do.'

'And you remember me being there?'

'Well, of course I do. That's why I'm here.'

I could feel myself blushing again, feeling silly for asking the obvious, but it had all been so strange that you could never be too sure.

'So what happened? Did you stay for the whole week? Was everything normal?'

Sam exhaled deeply. 'Well, where do I start?

'I didn't actually remember anything about it until much later, not until after my accident.'

'Accident?'

'Yeh, it's OK. I'm fully recovered now,' he said, reassuring me, and then continued. 'So, basically, my mate Blake kept hassling me about this holiday we went on. I didn't have a clue what he was going on about. I thought he was high on drugs or something. But he was insistent. He kept saying that we went away to this holiday resort but they did something to him and he wanted to go back there and find out what it was they were really doing. He seemed to think the holiday resort was some kind of cover for something more sinister. Like I said, I thought he was on drugs and hallucinating. I mean, it wasn't unheard-of for him to pop the odd E pill on a night out. Perhaps he'd gone for something a bit harder this time.'

I flinched at the comment of drug taking, worried that Sam might also be into drugs.

'Anyway, he was adamant he was going to drive there to discover the truth. In the end, I agreed to go with him. I still thought he was completely off his rocker, but I couldn't let him go on his own. I was worried what he might do. He was really agitated, almost manic.'

Sam paused as he took a breath and stared out the window. I waited for what felt like an eternity to find out what happened next.

'We didn't get very far. Blake was always a boy racer, but this was the fastest and most aggressive I had ever seen him drive. He took a corner way too fast. I'm not entirely sure what happened but we definitely flipped, maybe more than once, careering off the road, down an embankment, hitting something – a stone wall, I think.'

'Oh God,' I said, putting my hands over my mouth, shocked by his description of what sounded like a very bad crash.

'I was in hospital for over two months, six weeks of that in a coma. Apparently, Blake died at the scene.'

'I'm so sorry.' It was heart-wrenching to listen to, and a lump came to my throat when I realised how close Sam had been to also losing his life.

'It took me a while to recover but as well as successfully regaining my strength, I also regained memories. I started to remember the holiday and I realised that everything Blake had told me was true. I was so angry with myself that I hadn't believed him. Then I was angry with Blake for driving like a lunatic. I was angry for a while, but I got over it. Once I was back on my feet, I tried to find the place myself. But I couldn't find it. So then I thought I would come and find you. I remembered you telling me you worked in a fairly posh hotel in Bath. So I just kept going to all the hotels, asking for Emma. I knew you worked in reception and I knew your brother owned the hotel. Finally, I found Sapphire Hotel. Hey presto. I met someone called Jess, who seemed to know who I was and happily gave me your address. And so here I am.'

'Yeh, I bet she did.' I imagined how over the moon Jess would have been to meet him, and now I knew I would be in for a torrid Monday when I returned to work.

'I can't tell you how glad I am that you are here. It's been awful. I was beginning to actually doubt myself and think maybe I was losing my mind. Do you remember I went for a spa treatment?'

'Yes. That was the last time I saw you. I couldn't find you after that.'

'Yeh, well. They did something to me. I think I inhaled some kind of substance that knocked me completely unconscious. When I came to, I was in my own house, but it was eight days later. I don't remember what happened in that time. Then Lisa, the friend I went with, she denied knowing anything about it.'

I stopped abruptly. I suddenly realised that maybe she wasn't lying to me. Maybe she couldn't remember anything about it, just like Sam couldn't, well, at least not until much later, after his accident. I sank back into the sofa with Betty's words echoing in my ear: *Do you really know the whole story*?

'What?' asked Sam as I stalled.

'I was just thinking. Maybe, I've got some of this wrong. When I confronted Lisa about it, I was sure she knew about it, was involved somehow in it and that she was lying to me. Now, after what you've just said, I'm wondering if actually she just really couldn't remember.'

'What happened after you confronted her?'

'That was it. We haven't spoken since.'

Sam looked at me in surprise as I began to fear that this was my interpretation of the apple story.

'So what happened after I left for the spa?' I quickly asked, keen to move away from talking about Lisa.

'Not much. I went to meet you at the bench later as we arranged, but you didn't show. I thought maybe you'd stood me up, had a better offer. Just dossed around for a day or two after, with Blake. Thought I might bump into you, but didn't. Blake then disappeared. For a while, I didn't really take too much notice as it wasn't unusual for us to do things separately. But then he was gone for ages, and when he never came back that night or returned in the morning, I got worried. Then I began to wonder about you, and so I came looking for you both. I couldn't find either of you, though. The last thing I really remember was being at the main reception talking to a guy in a burgundy outfit. I was basically reporting you both missing, but he was really unhelpful, almost dismissive, and practically threw me out. I remember being manhandled, but I can't recall what happened after that. And obviously I didn't actually remember any of this until long after my accident.'

In some ways, it was such a relief to hear Sam telling me all this. At least now I knew I wasn't going crazy, but then it also made me feel very funny inside as now I knew something sinister had happened.

'I'm going to put the kettle on. Do you want anything?'

'Coffee, please?'

I made us both a drink and settled back down on the sofa. Sam was now standing up near the window, looking back over my notebook.

'So did you ever try to find the place again?' he asked.

'Yes, twice. Couldn't find it. I was going to go again tomorrow actually. I was just trying to decide where to try next.'

'Can I come?'

'Yes. That would be great.'

We spent the rest of the afternoon chatting, both choosing to avoid the elephant in the room. I made us a simple spaghetti bolognese for dinner and it wasn't until the evening that we eventually discussed Roseville Resort again and agreed on a location to search for it together. I made up the bed in the spare room and we said our good nights. I was hopeful that tomorrow might finally bring some answers.

I awoke suddenly in the early hours of the morning to hear Sam shouting outside at someone.

Startled, I quickly got up, put my dressing gown on, slipped on my slippers and dashed down the stairs. The front door was wide open and Sam was just making his way back in.

'What's going on?' I urgently asked.

'Someone was prowling around out here. I was in the kitchen getting a glass of water and I could hear the gravel crunching and someone near the front door. I didn't get here quick enough. They were running off up the road by the time I got here and then jumped on a motorbike that sped off.'

My stomach turned as I felt terrified that someone was probably trying to enter my property and there was no telling what they might have planned on doing.

Sam closed the door but, as he did so, an envelope was revealed on the carpet. Presumably, it had been pushed through the letter box by the prowler. I picked it up and slowly opened it. Inside was a piece of paper with a typewritten note. My heart rate quickened and I felt light-headed as I read the contents.

'Well, what does it say?'

I looked at Sam with a very confused expression then reread the note, but this time aloud.

'There is an address in London and then it says meet us here if you want to discover the truth.'

Sam gave me a puzzled look.

'The truth? About Roseville Resort? Well, I guess that changes our plans then. Is that all it says?'

I looked back down at the note. There was still one word that I hadn't yet read out, and it was this word that I found the most chilling.

'No. At the bottom of the note, in capital letters, it says JAHL.'

'What? What does that mean?'

I stared at the note then eventually replied, 'It means that perhaps I didn't judge Lisa so harshly after all.'

CHAPTER FIFTEEN

After our disturbance, I was unable to get back to sleep, so we set off early that morning, destined for an address in Marylebone, London. I'd called a taxi to pick us up and take us straight to the station. We'd made no real plans other than to go straight to this address. I was keen to make a reservation at a hotel for at least the one night, but Sam was of the opinion we should wait and see. I felt uncomfortable with Sam's blasé approach and would have preferred to have at least some base at which to seek refuge in a city I deemed immense and daunting. When I pointed out my concerns, Sam laughed and reminded me that London was 'pretty big' and would have countless hotels to choose from if we decided to stay. So, against my better judgement, I just stuffed a few things into a holdall and hoped once we got there it really would be that simple.

Sam prodded me in the ribs, disturbing me from my daydream.

I lifted my head from the train window and turned to look at him.

'Madam, would you like anything from the snack trolley?'

'Oh sorry, no, I'm fine, thanks.'

The thought of eating was too much to bear. I was filled with trepidation and beginning to wonder if this was such a good idea. Sam clearly didn't share my anxiety as he was happily tucking into a sandwich and his seat tray was laden with a packet of crisps and a chocolate bar along with a coffee.

'You sure? You haven't eaten anything yet.'

'I'm fine. I don't think I could face eating anything.'

I turned my head away and placed it in its original resting place back on the train window.

Sam gave me another prod in the ribs, harder this time.

'Ow. Will you stop doing that. It hurts.'

He grinned as he placed the empty sandwich container on the seat tray and proceeded to unwrap his chocolate bar.

'Stop fretting, will you.'

'I'm not fretting.'

Again, I turned away, although this time I kept my head upright as I stared out of the window. I was expecting another jab in the ribs but none came. I turned my head back in Sam's direction.

'Do you think we are doing the right thing?'

Sam was on the last bite of his chocolate bar and was screwing the wrapper up into a little ball. I had to wait for him to finish his mouthful before he could answer.

'What, going to this address in London?'

'Yeh, I mean, are we being a bit rash, stupid even?'

'Em, look, we had to go. This thing is driving us both nuts and consuming our lives. We don't really know anything about what is going on. This is the only thing we have to go on.'

'Yeh, but it might be dangerous. We don't know who this person is who's asking us to meet them. They might be an axe murderer, for all we know.'

'Well, yeh, they could be, or they might actually be able to help us. I mean, if they are an axe murderer, I'm not sure why they would go to the trouble of pushing a note through your door rather than just hack you up there and then.'

'I don't know how you can be so calm and easy-going about it all.'

'I'm just trying to be positive. Trouble with you is, you just assume everything is bad and only see negatives.'

'I don't,' I retorted, taking offence. 'I am just more careful and like to take things more responsibly. We're not all risk-takers looking for a thrill.'

'Sometimes in life, you have to take some risks. Otherwise, you get stuck in a rut. What would you have rather done? Stay at home? Ignore the note?'

'We could have stuck with the original plan and gone to Devon to look for the resort again.'

'What, and that's not taking a risk? I doubt we would have even found it based on other attempts, but even if we had, maybe your axe murderer is actually there. Have you forgotten the experience you had there?'

He had a point, annoyingly, so I had no real comeback.

'Look, Em, it will be fine. We had to come. There is no way either of us could have just ignored the note. It would have niggled away at our minds. We'll still go to Devon, just not this weekend. OK?'

'OK.'

The lady who'd wheeled the snack tray down was back but this time with a black bin bag in hand. Sam placed his rubbish in the sack, returned the seat tray back against the seat and brushed a few crumbs off his lap. People were now starting to get up and get their belongings together as we approached the station. The train began to slow and I could see lines of people on the station platform waiting to catch the train we were about to get off. I grabbed my holdall and went to sling it over my shoulder, but Sam took it off me and carried it instead. I smiled at his gentlemanly behaviour and was glad he was accompanying me. I felt much safer by his side. I blindly followed him as he jumped down from the carriage train and then weaved his way through the endless crowds of people. I was relieved when we came into open air and had left the hordes of people behind. Sam had stopped and placed my holdall on the pavement between his feet. I caught up with him as I was a few paces behind and took a deep breath to recover, but the atmosphere felt heavy and dusty as I inhaled the polluted air. Sam lit a cigarette and I raised an eyebrow. He put the cigarette to his mouth, using only his lips to hold it, and then pulled a street map from his back pocket.

'OK. We are here and this is where we need to get to.'

I watched as he pointed to our location and our destination and tried to calculate how far apart they were. Sam took a few drags of his cigarette before throwing it on the pavement and stamping it out.

'Right, let's go,' he said, picking the holdall up and heading off down the road.

'Hang on,' but he chose to ignore me and just kept walking.

'Sam! Wait.'

He turned for a moment to face me, still walking, but now backwards.

'What?'

'Are we walking there? What about a taxi?'

He looked as if I had made an outrageous suggestion, turned back in the direction he had set out and picked up the pace. Disgruntled, I shook my head and reluctantly followed.

After an hour, with a few wrong turns, we finally found the address. Standing on the pavement, I looked up at the imposing red-brick Victorian building. Sam had lit another cigarette and puffed on it while he watched me try to summon the courage to ring the apartment's door intercom. I looked at him with questioning eyes, as if seeking his seal of approval. He inclined his head towards the door, encouraging me to approach it. I timidly stepped forward through the wrought iron gates and up the stone steps. I hovered my finger over the 'Flat 3' button on the intercom, not quite daring to actually press it. Before I had chance to even consider if I would choose to follow through with it, Sam was pushing my finger down with his and the deed was done.

'Hello?' said a young-sounding female over the intercom.

I froze at the sound of her voice while I temporarily lost mine.

'Hello,' I finally replied, regaining my composure. 'I'm looking for Jahl? I was given this address for him.'

There was no reply and I looked at Sam worrisomely. He frowned, but just then the door emanated a buzzing sound and there was a sudden click. Sam tried the door and it opened and he entered. I nervously followed, wondering what we were both walking into, praying it wasn't a trap.

CHAPTER SIXTEEN

On our first encounter with Patricia, the voice over the intercom, and her fellow flatmates, Danny and Greg, there was an edginess to the atmosphere as we all tried to suss each other out. However, it soon became apparent that they were just as wary of us as we were of them.

After a few tense moments, I could feel myself start to relax as I realised they were no threat to us, and I felt more inclined to think that maybe we were all on the same side.

Danny, who seemed to be the most confident of the group, had made the initial introductions and assured us they were friendly and not intending to cause us any trouble. Apparently, they were a group of five university friends all living together, two of whom were out at the moment.

The flat was large, with a big open-plan living area with high ceilings, and was furnished to a high modern standard. Patricia went to get us all a drink while we all sat ourselves down at the big dining-room table. Danny and Greg sat one side and Sam and I sat opposite.

Danny opened the conversation.

'So, where do we start? I guess you have about a million questions.'

'Where is Jahl?'

Danny looked taken aback, maybe not anticipating that as my very first question.

Greg answered instead.

'Jahl is not a person.'

Now I was taken aback. I had taken it as a given that Jahl was a 'somebody'. I presupposed the idea to the extent that I had even conjured an image of what he looked like.

Sam interjected. 'Well, what is it then?'

Patricia returned with a tray of cold drinks and distributed them. She then sat at the head of the table and shifted her gaze nervously between us, looking unsure of what had been said.

'Jahl is a project,' said Greg.

'A project?' said Sam, almost laughing with absurdity.

Greg gave Sam a hostile look that made me feel I needed to take back over the questioning.

'What kind of project? A uni project?'

'No. A government project.'

Sam looked perplexed and I was beginning to wonder if I would be better off not asking any more questions and just staying in the dark.

Danny decided to take over the reins.

'Look. This is going to be a bit hard for you to take in and probably quite a shock for you. Jahl was a government project initially set up in the mid-seventies. A project that you were part of, well, still are a part of.'

'What?' I almost choked. 'A project about what exactly?'

Danny got up and disappeared into another room. Greg looked shifty and Patricia looked nervy and was finding it difficult to give me any eye contact. Eventually, Danny returned with a document in his hand which he placed on the table in front of me before returning to his seat. Everyone sat in silence while they waited for me to read it.

I peered only at the front cover, fearing it to be a poisoned chalice that would bring me harm if I touched it. I could see the document was entitled, in big bold letters, 'The JAHL Project (Phase 2)'.

It looked official, with a government logo and the words 'Highly Classified' stamped on both the header and footer. No one breathed a word while I stared blankly at it. I felt very strange and suddenly became very aware of my own heartbeat, which had now quickened. I turned the page, opened the document and began to read.

I studied the contents of the pages for what was probably only a few minutes but I'm sure to everyone else felt like an eternity. I had to reread several sections over and over because I was having difficulty digesting its meaning. However, the more I read back over it, the more I took in, and the thought of what it could mean horrified me.

I looked back up and could see everyone watching me intently, waiting for my reaction. Sam had got up from the table and had now perched himself on a window sill. He was looking at me with concerned eyes.

Directing my next few words at Danny, I finally spoke.

'JAHL is an acronym.'

Danny nodded and as he did so he seemed almost remorseful.

'It stands for "The Jointure of Alien matter with Human Life",' I added.

'Yes,' confirmed Danny.

'It stands for what?' Sam had now risen from the window sill, walked back over to us and was now looking over my shoulder at the document.

Sam had sounded like he was having great difficulty believing the words I had uttered and needed to see them for himself. I watched his eyes darting back and forth across the pages and could see his eyebrows furrowing deeper, the more he read. I wondered if he had noticed my name written in the list of names on the page entitled 'Subjects'.

'I recognise this name on the list, Blake Riley. Why is his name here? Are you seriously suggesting he is part of this project as well? There is no way Blake would have any connection to government rubbish.'

I'd completely forgotten all about Blake and did not notice his name listed as I had been so fixated on mine. I estimated there to be maybe twenty-five or so names, and rather than being in one continuous list they were instead split up into three groups: A, B and C. Mine and Blake's were both listed under Group A, and I wondered what that signified.

'The names written in those lists are not associated with the government,' replied Danny. 'They were the people that were selected as subjects for the experiments.'

I began to feel very weak, as if I was about to faint. It may have been because I hadn't eaten for quite a while, but I suspected it was more to do with the terrifying thought that I was part of a government experiment. Even more terrifying was that I was beginning to conclude that there was the suggestion I had some alien blood or parts inside me.

'So, hang on,' Sam said, sounding maddened, 'are you actually saying that Blake had something alien added to him?'

'Well, we don't know exactly. We just know there was a government project in the seventies that took human subjects and injected ... something ... into their bloodstream. Blake was one of them,' Danny paused and looked at me with an apologetic look, 'and you as well, Emma.'

I covered my face with my hands to momentarily block it all out. I took a deep breath and re-emerged to find everyone staring back at me. No one said a word; they all seemed to be waiting on me to say something.

Finally, Sam broke the silence.

'I think you are all a bunch of nutters. You expect us to believe that there is some government conspiracy going on involving aliens from outer space?'

No answer was forthcoming.

'Emma,' Sam snapped at me, 'you are seriously not buying into this nonsense?'

I was frozen to the spot, and Sam was glaring at me as if I had lost my mind.

Greg was quick to wade in and try and rescue the situation. He directed his comment towards me, and I felt like he was pleading with me.

'The document does refer to the word alien in the acronym, yes, and does describe the experiment as injecting alien matter, but the word alien can take on several meanings. It doesn't necessarily mean extra-terrestrial.'

'What else can it mean?' I asked, very confused.

Greg hesitated and was fumbling to find the words.

'Well, it can mean a foreign object.'

I gave him an unsatisfied frown.

'Something that doesn't naturally belong to the person or thing,' he added.

'So you see,' said Greg, 'it is only suggesting the experiment involved injecting humans with something not natural to the human body. It doesn't mean it was extra-terrestrial related.'

If Greg's explanation to try and steer it away from the extra-terrestrial was supposed to make me feel better and somehow lessen the blow, it was not working.

'We should still be open to the possibility, though,' Danny added, with a hint of excitement in his voice.

Greg shot Danny a very harsh look and was clearly annoyed with his comment.

'Come on, Danny. We've talked about this before. There is nothing to confirm it is referring to that. It is inferred only by the name in the acronym and a person's own interpretation of the word.'

'True. But it's still a possibility.'

'But unlikely,' said Greg authoritatively. 'It is much more likely that it is an artificially produced drug of some sort.'

I got the distinct impression Danny wanted to fight his corner, but with the numbers against him and probably not wanting to upset me any further, he kept his mouth shut.

Regardless of the true meaning of the word alien, the mere suggestion that something unnatural was coursing through my veins was enough to make me feel terrified.

'I'm sorry, I need some air,' I barely managed to communicate back. I headed for the exit, fearing that my legs could buckle at any point. Thankfully, they held.

I only made it as far as the corner of the road before I had to sit down before I fell down. It was an uncomfortable seat, a low concrete wall outside someone's house. Sam had followed and sat down beside me.

'Are you OK?' he asked.

'No! They are saying I am part of an experiment! That I have been injected with ... well, I don't know what. I don't even want to contemplate what it is.'

'I don't think they know what it is, either,' offered Sam as some kind of solace, 'and that's if you believe any of this to be true, of course.'

'Do you believe them?'

Sam shrugged. 'My initial reaction was no. Not a word. But then this is sounding all a bit too familiar. It was not so long ago that I accused Blake of being some kind of crackpot and completely dismissing what I thought was just crazy talk. So maybe I should be more open-minded. What about you?'

'I thought maybe we had stumbled across some weird paranormal investigative group. Under normal circumstances,

I would think they were crazy and run a mile, but things have become far from normal for me lately and I'm starting to think maybe they do know something.'

'Do you want to go back in there? We can always just leave here, go back to the original plan and look for Roseville.'

While Sam's suggestion of leaving sounded the sensible option, I couldn't help but think I needed to go back and listen to more of what Danny and Greg had to say.

'I think we need to go back and find out more.' I sighed heavily while questioning my own sanity regarding such a dubious decision. 'I know it sounds far-fetched but some of what they say does fit. I am sure I was drugged at the spa when I was at Roseville, and I am starting to think I may have been given an injection a few days earlier.'

I still had etched in my memory the moment when I was crouched down searching for a key to the lodge at Roseville with a very sore arm and my encounter with the woman on the bench who had also been suffering with the same complaint.

'Although I can't bear to think that I was injected with something all those years ago, I am not sure I can fully rule it out based on what has happened to me recently.'

Sam pondered on it for a moment and looked like he could see I had a point.

'Hmm ... and me forgetting about my trip with Blake to Roseville was probably due to some drug they administered.'

'Exactly. Also, they knew about the name JAHL. How would they have known about that name? And the document they showed had Blake's name on it as well as mine. I am not sure they had even made any connection between his name and you. It was you who mentioned him.'

Sam thought about it for a while and then, after much discussion and a lot of mustering of courage on my part, together we agreed we should go back.

Danny looked mighty relieved that we had decided to return. He let Patricia welcome me back in while he stood back and gave me some breathing space.

She managed to coax me to sit back down at the table and I could see the document was still resting there from when I had previously left it. Greg and Danny watched nervously on as I stared vacantly around the room, transferring my gaze from person to person. Two new faces had joined us.

Patricia had obviously sensed my confusion about who these two people were and so quickly introduced them.

'This is Teddy. He's a research student at the university, studying for a PhD. In computers or something like that.'

Teddy was a peculiar-looking individual; he was tall and thin, with long straw-like hair, and wore thick black-rimmed glasses.

'Hi,' he said nervously, with an awkward wave of the hand, 'it's actually Artificial Intelligence. I originally studied Computer Engineering for my degree but I've gone on to specialise in AI.'

Patricia then introduced me to Fiona, who immediately struck me as looking like a librarian. She too wore glasses but with a cord attached to the glasses frame and then wrapped around her neck. She had shiny long black hair and was small in stature. As it turned out, she was an English graduate also now studying for a PhD and did, in fact, work part time at the British Library.

'Well, as lovely as all these niceties we are having are, I think maybe we should get back to some more vital questions that we have for you,' Sam pressed, looking at me expectantly.

'Of course, fire away,' replied Danny as he took a seat at the opposite end of the table from me. Greg gingerly took a seat next to me, smiling nervously, while Sam took his perch back on the window sill and watched over the proceedings.

I tried to gather my thoughts and focus on what I wanted to ask first, but I had so many questions I wasn't sure where to start. As a distraction, I aimlessly twiddled with the document in front of me with the word JAHL staring ominously back at me. Eventually, my brain kicked into gear and I had my first question.

'How did you find out about this JAHL project?' It seemed a pertinent enough question.

Danny looked at Greg and asked him, 'Do you want to explain?'

Greg let out a puff of air as if he was being given a tall order.

'I used to work as a software developer for the government. Enrolled on their graduate programme right after I got my degree from uni.'

Sam squirmed at the mention of working for the government and I sensed his mistrust.

'I *used* to work for them and for less than a year before they fired me,' emphasised Greg strongly.

That seemed to lessen the blow for Sam, although I got the distinct impression he was not a fan of Greg. Undeterred by Sam's reaction, he continued.

'There was a guy there, Charlie, much more senior than me, who was assigned as my mentor. We got on quite well and sometimes we used to go out drinking after work. Charlie was quite a talkative chap and once he'd sunk a few pints he would become very chatty. Sometimes he would, well, talk a bit too freely and divulge more information than he should. I never really knew exactly what his job role was there, but he must have been privy to quite classified information. Anyway, one night, he started talking about my interests in conspiracy theories. We'd talked many times in the past about the subject. He knew that I spent many hours of my spare time doing research on theories like the moon landing being faked and places like Area 52. He usually spoke light-heartedly about it, but this particular night it was different. He was much more interested, much more serious, and that's when I first learnt about the JAHL project.'

I was about to ask my second question, but Greg was now in full flow and launched straight into explaining the conversation he had that night and several conversations that followed over the next few weeks. There was a lot of detail and much of it went in one ear and straight out the other. I was still reeling from the news that I was part of these experiments, and so I found it quite hard to focus on what he was saying most of the time. However, I did manage to pick up the gist, and it was enough to make me feel like my whole world was beginning to crash down around me.

I was born in 1975, the same year that the JAHL project was selecting their test subjects. According to Greg, government drug experiments had occurred many years before, decades, in fact. He muttered something about CIA's secret LSD experiments going as far back as the fifties. He also referred to the Porton Down government facility, a name that was vaguely familiar to me. According to Greg, who seemed to be quite the expert, it was a highly top-secret lab that had been running human experiments as long ago as 1916.

The JAHL project, as far as Greg was aware, was an attempt to enhance humans in some way. He admitted there was little evidence on the actual specifics although he offered resistance to disease or poison or increased strength as possible suggestions. Apparently, twenty-eight subjects, all of whom were under three months old, had been specifically selected due to their circumstances. They were basically all parentless, either orphaned, unwanted or given up for adoption. In our early years, we were all raised in our own community, away from the outside world, under the guise of a government-run facility that housed and provided all amenities to its employees within the complex. Its true purpose was a closely guarded secret. But the experiment lasted less than three years, until it was deemed a failure and eventually abandoned and the subjects were released back into the real world to live normal lives. Now, some twenty-eight years after the initial project was started, it was being resurrected and Phase 2 was now in action.

By the time Greg had finished talking, any other questions I may have had were long forgotten. I was starting to feel very queasy, and so I asked to use the bathroom. Patricia instinctively got up to help me out of my seat, taking my arm and leading me to their bathroom.

'Are you OK? You look very pale.'

'I just need a minute,' I answered as I tottered into the bathroom and locked the door behind me. I splashed cold water over my face to try and revive myself. I presumed my trip to Roseville was somehow linked to this Phase 2, and I shuddered at the thought of what that entailed.

When I finally re-emerged, Patricia was still hovering at the bathroom door and looked mighty relieved to see me. Everyone else, apart from Sam, who had maintained his position at the window, was still gathered around the main table in deep discussion.

'You OK?' asked Sam.

I gave an affirmative nod, although I was not sure how OK I really was. OK in the sense I was alive and breathing at least. I managed to sit myself back down at the table. At least those few minutes away by myself had allowed me to regain some of my composure. Strangely, I realised that I was beginning to feel more at ease with these people; almost a relief to have found them. After all, they were providing me with more answers in just one day than I had managed to find out in all these past months.

'OK. OK.' Sam, who had been relatively quiet since his previous outburst, had suddenly reawakened and was back to demanding more answers. 'So you seem to know quite a bit about this JAHL project. But how much do you know about us? I mean, which one of you scared the hell out of us and poked that note through the door? Had you been following us?'

'Oh yea, sorry about that,' apologised Danny, 'we genuinely didn't mean to scare you. It wasn't actually one of us. We asked a friend in Bath to deliver the note to Emma on our behalf.'

'So you have other friends across the country that know about JAHL?'

'No. No,' interjected Greg, almost as if scolding Sam. 'It's just us five, seriously it's only us. There are twenty-eight names on the list scattered all over the country, and trying to locate them all and find out about them is difficult. We have limited resources. So where we can, we have called on the odd friend to do us a favour, usually in return for a favour, and carry out a reconnaissance mission. But we don't give any major details away; they don't know anything about the project. To them, it was just a note to hand-deliver. Although they got a bit of a scare when you chased them down the road.'

Sam and Greg both stared hard at each other, and I could feel the tension between them and was worried they both might be gunning for a fight. In an attempt to divert their attention, I quickly started asking more questions.

'So now you've found us and we are here. What is it you want from us?'

'We are just trying to find out the truth about the JAHL project,' said Danny. 'Look, we didn't start out specifically looking at this. We were already a group of friends sharing an interest in government cover-ups and we had already done much research on the subject. We just happened to stumble across this and it has intrigued us. Slowly but surely, we have started to unravel a hidden government secret and now it is like an addiction. We cannot stop until we have uncovered the whole truth. Obviously, with you being one of the subjects of the original experiment, we are naturally interested in you.'

'Well, I am not sure I can tell you a lot. Until today, I didn't know anything about this JAHL project, never mind that I was involved in it.'

Danny screwed his eyes up in puzzlement, as if he didn't quite believe me.

'But you know something about it. I mean, you've been looking for the government complex and you know of Lisa's involvement.'

I was stunned to hear him mention Lisa's name and his reference to me searching for Roseville Resort, which Danny seemed to think was a government facility of some sort.

'How do you know about Lisa? What do you mean by searching for this complex you keep mentioning? You mean Roseville Resort? How do you know I have been looking for it?'

'Well, like I said, we have spent a lot of hours researching, and part of that research has been focused on you.'

'So, you've been following me?'

'Not exactly. We've been monitoring some of your internet activities and phone calls.'

Danny looked at me awkwardly, and I sensed his feeling of shame.

'So you don't know where Roseville, or this government facility as you call it, is, either?'

'Unfortunately, no. Not yet at least, but we hope to find it. Maybe with your help, together we can find it.'

It was then that I realised this could be my best chance at finding Roseville and that perhaps we should team up.

I nodded, much to Danny's delight.

'So how much do you know? Do you remember going to the actual complex?'

I looked at Sam to check that he was OK for me to answer. He nodded his head in affirmation.

'Like I said, before coming here, I didn't really know a lot. Yes, I do remember going to the complex. Although I didn't know it was a government complex. I went under the pretence that it was a holiday retreat. I was supposed to be going away for a relaxing break with my friend Lisa.'

'Judging by your internet search history and the calls we traced that you made to holiday reps, you think it is somewhere in Devon?'

I was slightly indignant at the thought of being watched but kept my feelings to myself.

'That's right. So far, though, I have found no trace of it.'

'Can you remember what happened while you were there?'

'I can only remember the first few days. The last thing I remember was having a spa treatment. But they made me inhale the aromatic scent of a candle that must have contained some drug and knocked me unconscious. When I came round I was in my bed at home, eight days later.'

'And the few days you can remember, do you recall anything suspicious or strange happening?'

'Oh God, yes. There were plenty of strange things going on.'

Both Danny's and Greg's eyes lit up with excitement, and I could see they were eager to hear what I had experienced.

Sam and I remained in the apartment for the rest of the day and well into the evening. I relayed the entire story of my visit to Roseville Resort and everything of significance that happened thereafter. Sam chipped in with his side of the story, telling them all about his experience of his stay with Blake and how Blake had come to die in a car accident. Danny and Greg occasionally interrupted with a question, but for the main part, myself and Sam did practically all the talking. Teddy and Fiona listened intently but never uttered a word, and I almost forgot they were even there. Patricia was less interested in our story and preferred to busy herself playing hostess. She kept us fed and watered throughout, making the drinks, ordering takeaway pizza and clearing up after us all. I got the distinct impression that she was not quite such an avid fan of their research and appeared like the outsider of the group.

By the time dusk started to fall, my throat was sore from all the talking and I was feeling physically exhausted. I could no longer stifle my yawns and obviously it had been noticed.

'It's been a long day, maybe we should call it a night,' said Danny, who was also looking very tired.

'Yes, OK,' I readily agreed.

‘You are welcome to stay here,’ offered Danny. ‘The sofas convert to a bed.’

‘No, it’s fine,’ Sam replied hastily, ‘we’ll stay in a hotel. I think I saw a Travelodge not far from here.’

‘Oh. OK,’ said Danny, sounding offended. ‘Yeh, there are several hotels in the vicinity.’

I was relieved that Sam had refused their offer. It had taken a lot for me to reach this level of trust; staying with them seemed a step too far.

We said our goodbyes and agreed to reconvene at their apartment in the morning to discuss our next course of action.

As we stepped out onto the street, searching for our bed for the night, I began to wonder what was flowing through my veins, and the thought sent a shiver right through my spine.

CHAPTER SEVENTEEN

I sat watching the rain cascading down the window, following the intricate path the droplets chose to take. I had eaten a couple of rounds of toast, which was more than enough to satisfy my hunger, and was now nursing a cold cup of tea. Sam had already devoured a huge plate of cooked breakfast and was now munching his way through a Danish pastry. Considering the circumstances, I had managed a reasonably good night's sleep and was feeling relatively human again. We had shared the one hotel room for the night, at Sam's insistence, citing cost savings as the reason. I made sure the receptionist knew it was to be a twin room.

'Ready for today?' asked Sam, breaking my concentration and causing me to lose the trace of the droplet I was following.

I took a moment to consider my response. I felt sure I would wake up this morning, bottle it and run straight back home. For some unfathomable reason, the opposite was true. I was actually feeling quite positive and determined to see this through.

'I think so. Ready as I'll ever be.'

'May as well get fuelled up before we go,' stated Sam as he rose from his seat. 'Do you want anything?'

'No, I'm good.'

I sniggered as Sam made his way to the breakfast buffet, quite amazed at the quantity he could eat.

He returned with his umpteenth pastry and slumped himself down into his seat.

'I don't know how you can eat so much.'

He gave me one of his charming smirks and as I watched him munching, I felt great warmth and a deep realisation that I held a strong affinity towards him.

I took the last sip of my tea, forgetting it was stone cold, and grimaced at the taste. I placed the cup on the table.

'We ought to get over to Danny's and co. soon.'

Sam nodded as he put the last piece in his mouth and wiped away the last remnant of crumbs.

'You sure you are OK to do this?'

I wasn't a hundred per cent sure; in fact, I wasn't even close, but it was beginning to feel as if I had little choice. I was in too deep now and this was the only way I could see to find out more about what had happened to me at Roseville.

'Yes.'

'OK then. Let's go,' he said with vigour, and so we made our way out of the hotel and back towards the flat.

Much to my annoyance, it was still raining outside, although only lightly. Luckily, I had brought a coat with a hood and so was at least able to keep the rain off my head and hopefully prevent myself looking like a drowned rat when we arrived. Sam only had a jacket and so had simply pulled the collar up and scrunched his neck up towards his ears to prevent the water gliding down the back of his neck. We spoke little during the short walk there as we were both concentrating solely on getting to our destination as quickly as possible and limiting our chances of getting too wet.

Sam buzzed on the intercom and the door almost immediately clicked open. Sam hesitated for a moment, taken unawares by the lack of any voice coming over the intercom. Just then, the heavens opened, and so we both quickly dived through the door to escape the downpour.

Patricia welcomed us in and I was instantly hit with the smell of bacon. Greg was in the kitchen cooking the breakfast, Fiona was making tea and coffee, and Danny and Teddy were at the table poring over large sheets of paper spread across the table.

'Morning,' said Danny and Teddy in unison.

'Do you want a bacon sarnie?' asked Greg, briefly looking up from his frying pan.

'Love one,' answered Sam unequivocally.

'I'm fine, thanks,' I replied, and stared hard at Sam as I added I had already eaten plenty at the hotel. Sam gave me a pout and joined Greg in the kitchen area. I was surprised at Sam acting so amicably with Greg but then realised it was the offer of free food that had likely softened his mood.

I sat myself down with Danny and Teddy, curious to see what they were looking at. The large spread of papers appeared to be maps of some sort and, as I looked closer, I could see they were very detailed and specifically of the county of Devon. They had been heavily marked with red pen, crosses, dotted lines showing boundaries, some parts circled; all clearly marked to indicate something of significant importance.

'We thought we would focus on trying to locate the government complex, or what you refer to as Roseville Resort,' said Danny as he watched me trying to decipher the maps. I nodded, although I wondered how realistic actually finding it was. Maybe with all this extra resource, it was now becoming more of a possibility.

We spent the next couple of hours studying the maps and pulling together all the information that we could muster. It was clear that the group was relying heavily on me providing the extra missing details that would finally unlock the mystery as to its exact location. The disappointment was clear to see on all their faces as it became evident that I was not able to provide them with anything of much use. Sam was also of no use as it transpired that he too had taken little notice of the route. Moreover, he had drunken copious amounts of alcohol before they had even left and then continued to top up his alcohol levels from a hip flask while en route. He fully admitted that his sense of awareness, along with his vision, was at best blurry and that by the time they were within the vicinity of the complex he had fallen sound asleep. I was hanging my head in shame as it became apparent that the two people who had actually been there and would be best placed to know where it might be were contributing absolutely nothing to the fact-finding mission.

Danny, however, was undeterred and still placed his faith in me being the key to solving the puzzle.

'Look, our best clue is the crossroads sign that Emma saw. If we can work out what was on that sign then we are surely going to have a very good idea of roughly where it is.'

Suddenly all eyes were on me, and I felt the pressure as they waited for me to give them an answer.

I was hunched forward, elbows on the table, with my hands clasped together like I was praying to some god. I had only a vague recollection of the crossroads and at this rate only divine intervention was going to help me remember anything useful. With my hands still clasped, I banged my thumbs on my forehead as I racked my brains trying to remember even any remote detail, but all that accomplished was a slight soreness in the centre of my forehead.

'I'm sorry, but I just can't remember anything much about it. Even in the few days after, I couldn't remember much. That was months ago, so I'm not going to have any chance now of remembering anything.'

'Well, what can you remember? Maybe something will just give us that vital clue.'

I wasn't sure if I felt admiration for Danny's optimism or sorrow for his desperation, but either way his persistence made me feel obliged to help.

'Well, I remember it was white with arrow-shaped pointers. It was almost impossible to read what was written on them. The arrows were tiny; there was stuff growing over it. My eyes aren't that great at reading from a distance. Even someone with twenty-twenty vision would probably struggle.'

I shuffled awkwardly in my seat, knowing how ridiculously unhelpful I was sounding. My Roseville Resort notebook was on the table, although blatantly cast aside as a less valuable resource than the mountains of paperwork and books the rest of the group had to offer. I reached across for it, sliding it out from where it was half hidden under some other paperwork.

'I did make an attempt to write down names of what I thought was written on them,' showing Teddy and Danny the relevant page.

'They're all crossed out?' queried Teddy.

'Well, I know. That's because I don't think any of them are right. Look, at the time, I just didn't think it was something I would need to remember, so I didn't place any importance on storing it away in my memory banks.'

I was starting to sound rather cross; not directed towards anyone in the room, more at the failure of my memory.

'But you did actually look at the sign and consciously read it?' asked Danny sternly.

'Yes.'

'Good. Then we have something.'

'We do?' I said, feeling very perplexed.

'You've read the sign, you know what it says and it's likely that somewhere it is recorded in your memory. You just can't recall it. All we need to do is unlock that memory.'

'OK,' I replied nervously, 'and how do we do that?' I had visions of some hideous contraption probing my brain, trying to extract it.

Danny looked straight at Patricia, who had joined us at the table a while ago but had so far remained silent.

'Oh no. Danny, I am not sure that is a good idea.'

I had no idea what they were talking about, but Patricia's reaction did not fill me with delight.

'I'm still in training. I am not qualified and there are strict protocols about practising outside of proper supervision.'

Danny huffed as if her argument was just a pathetic excuse and then asked, 'Emma, how would you feel about undergoing hypnosis to try and unlock this memory?'

Patricia, it turned out, was a student at the UK College of Hypnosis and Hypnotherapy. Danny believed that Patricia could get me to remember while placing me under hypnosis. I wasn't sure I was that keen on the idea, particularly as Patricia harboured some doubt, which hardly instilled me with much confidence.

'So, you're not actually qualified to hypnotise somebody?' I nervously asked.

'No. I should really only do it under qualified supervision.'

'But you know how to hypnotise someone?' asked Sam, who had now joined us from the kitchen area after scoffing his bacon sandwich. I noted the eagerness in his voice and felt rather unsettled by it. It was only yesterday he was calling them all nutters, and yet now he seemed quite at home with them.

'Yes.'

'And you have actually hypnotised someone before? Successfully?' Again, Sam sounded far too eager.

'Yes. Several times.'

'Well, I think we should give it a go,' said Sam, extremely positive, much to the delight of Danny.

'Whoa, whoa, hang on a minute,' I interjected, taken aback by Sam volunteering me for something that sounded potentially dangerous and possibly not entirely legal.

'Oh, come on, Em, we've got to try, we are running out of options here. It'll be fine, she's done it before.'

I screwed up my face, feeling scorned. By this point, everyone seemed to be gathered round the table. Even Fiona, who I'd perceived as someone normally lacking in emotion, now too had eagerness in her eyes. I was feeling considerably outnumbered and as if I had little choice.

I focused my attention back to Patricia. 'You're happy you can do this?'

I detected a slight hesitation, but she eventually nodded in confirmation.

'OK,' I agreed, although much against my better judgement.

I was sat in a comfortable armchair; all was quiet apart from the gentle voice of Patricia sitting alongside me on the sofa. In a soft and soothing tone, she spoke to me, asking me to cast my mind back to the day I travelled down with Lisa on our way to our holiday break. My body felt extremely relaxed, heavy even, and I felt a heightened sense of awareness and my mind was highly focused. The event was unfolding before me, almost like a dream, although I was not asleep.

'Now, Emma, you and Lisa are sitting at the crossroads, trying to decide which way to go. You can see a sign. It is white, with little arrows. Can you see the sign?'

'Yes, I can see it.'

'Now read what it says written on the little white arrows. Tell me, what does it say?'

'It's hard to read. There's brambles growing over it, obscuring it.'

'Look closer, you can just make out what it says. Tell me, what does it say?'

'Barndale. It says Barndale for straight over.'

'And left? What does it say for left?'

'I don't know. I can't see.'

'OK, what about right? Can you see the sign for the right turn?'

'Yes.'

'What does it say, Emma?'

'Tilfor.'

'So it says Barndale for straight on, and Tilfor for right?'

'Yes, I think so.'

'OK, Emma. So now you've read the sign, you are going to continue on the journey. Which way did you take at the crossroads?'

'We went straight on.'

'That's great, Emma. You have done really well. That is the end of the exercise now, so you can start to bring yourself back into the room.'

I began to come out of the trance, suddenly becoming aware of my surroundings, and Patricia's voice no longer sounded as gentle and calming as before.

'OK, Emma? You feeling OK?'

'Yes. Actually I do.'

Everyone was looking at me; some looking relieved, some looking quite amazed, and Danny looking ecstatic.

'I remembered. I actually remembered what it said. Barndale and Tilfor. Patricia, that's amazing. How did you do that?'

She smiled and then winked at Danny, who gave her the thumbs-up.

My memory recall had injected energy into the group, and suddenly people started busying themselves. Fiona was knee-deep in books; Danny, Greg and Sam were practically sprawled across the table as they painstakingly searched the maps, while Teddy was sat at the computer furiously typing away.

Patricia and I were sat in the lounge area. I'd been specifically ordered to rest and have some tea and not overexert myself. I wasn't sure if this was a genuine case of care for my welfare or just because they felt they already had enough people on the job and didn't want too many cooks spoiling the broth. At first, it was fine; Patricia and I spoke easily and freely with each other and I was glad of her company. After a while, I began to grow restless, and so I ventured over to the table to see how much progress had been made.

Sam was hunched over, engrossed in some specific area on a map. I placed my hand on his shoulder.

'How is it going? Find anything?'

Sam didn't answer, still deeply engrossed in what he was looking at. Greg was sat opposite, fixated on the same point of the map and deep in concentration. Teddy was still typing away at the computer, and I wondered how smoke wasn't pouring off the keyboard given the rate he was typing at, while Fiona and Danny were sat on the floor surrounded by a sea of books.

'Sam? Have you found anything?' I said, trying again to gain his attention.

'Umm. Hey?' He replied this time, actually turning round to look at me. I sensed he hadn't appreciated being disturbed at that point.

'Not really, no,' and then just went back to staring at the map.

'We are struggling to find any of the places you named,' said Greg, sounding quite dejected.

Sam got up from his seat, stretched and let out a long yawn. I could see that he had lost interest and had had enough.

'I'm going out to get some fresh air,' Sam announced. 'This is starting to do my head in.'

'OK, it's done,' said a euphoric Teddy. Danny immediately got up from the floor, almost tripping over some books in the excitement.

'Brilliant.'

'Have we got something?' I questioned, once again not following what was happening.

'Not yet. But hopefully soon,' replied Danny in his usual buoyant and positive mood.

'I've written an AI program,' explained Teddy, 'that is going to trawl through every possible place name until it hopefully makes a match with the names you have given us.'

'OK,' I said, not entirely convinced, 'and how long will that take?'

'Impossible to say. It could be a few hours or it could be a few days, or it could be never.'

'Emma, are you coming or staying here?' Sam had his coat on and was now halfway out the front door. My moment of triumph when I had actually remembered what was written on the sign was now long gone. Instead, I felt demoralised by the whole thing.

'To be honest, Emma, there is not much more we can do until this program has run,' said Greg. 'Why don't you and Sam call it a day and meet us again tomorrow? Hopefully, by then, we will have some answers.'

'OK,' I agreed. 'We'll catch up again tomorrow.' Sam needed no other encouragement to go and was out of the door in a shot. I trudged out, following behind him, feeling rather disheartened that another day had passed without us knowing where this damn place was. I just hoped that Teddy's computer program could actually find what we were looking for, as I was beginning to feel sick of wasting life continually searching for answers.

CHAPTER EIGHTEEN

Sam buzzed the intercom as I stood alongside feeling a curious sense of déjà vu.

There was no answer but we heard the door click and so entered. I was praying that Teddy's computer program had completed and successfully made a match, but in truth I wasn't feeling too positive. As we stepped through the door, I secretly crossed my fingers behind my back, purposely ensuring Sam would not see, as I knew he would only tease me.

'Morning,' said a very exuberant Danny. I could tell immediately that they must have found something. Teddy turned round to look back at us from his computer with a huge beaming smile.

'We've got a match,' he yelled with delight, looking mighty proud of himself.

'Have you?' I said, not daring to believe it. When Teddy had given me his very loose estimation of how long it might take, I was resigned to thinking the 'never' part of it was the most likely outcome.

I walked up to the back of Teddy's chair and looked over his shoulder. The computer screen read 'closest partial match found', which didn't sound quite the confirmation I was expecting.

'Only partial, not exact?' I questioned, with disappointment blatantly in my voice.

'Ah yes, so our first run didn't return us with any matches. The parameters we set up were quite specific. We checked for an exact match on the two place names you gave us with an assumption they were within a ten-mile proximity to each other and existed in the county of Devon. For the next run, we widened the criteria. We allowed a greater tolerance on the name matching, so it didn't have to be an exact match but had to be reasonably close. This second run gave us a match. OK, so it's only partial, but it's too much of a coincidence that two names very similar to what you gave us exist close to each other in Devon.'

'Look, if you come here, I can show you,' beckoned Danny, who was now over at the table where the maps were still laid out from the day before. He pointed to an area in the north of the county. I had to screw my eyes up to read the names.

'See. There is this one here, Bamdale, and a village only three miles away called Tifford.'

Sam fell about laughing. 'So not only do you have the worst memory on record, you also have crap eyesight.'

'Hey,' I said, stopping him from making any more unfair accusations, 'says the guy who got so drunk he probably wouldn't have even noticed if the signpost had smacked him straight on the forehead.' Sam laughed harder and I couldn't resist retaliating further. 'In fact, you could have been flown to the moon and back and you would have been too paralytic to notice.'

'OK, calm down.'

'Well, I wasn't that far away. Bamdale, Barndale. Tilford, Tifford. I mean, what's the difference?' I protested, struggling to hide my smirk.

'Several bloody letters, difference enough to throw us right off the scent. Lucky for us, we have our own little Einstein here.' Sam patted Teddy on the back, who beamed an even bigger smile, wholly pleased with receiving recognition for his efforts.

'OK, guys,' said Danny in a serious tone, keen for us to quit the banter and get back on track. 'Using the detailed maps Fiona has provided us with, we can see there was a government installation just here, only a few miles from Bamdale.'

Danny pointed to a section on the map with red dashed lines marking out a reasonable-sized rectangular shape. I noticed that there was barely anything inside the boundary lines of the rectangle. It mainly consisted of just wide-open space except for the odd small building, and peculiarly there were no roads leading to it.

'It doesn't look like much. Most of it looks like ...' I paused as I tried to fathom what the empty space could be '... fields or wasteland or something.' It certainly didn't represent the place I visited.

'This is an old map, from the fifties, and there was supposedly a secret military base here, not visible because the majority of it was concealed underground.'

'Do we know what it was used for?' I asked curiously.

'Not exactly sure but it was supposedly built in the early forties, originally as an ammunitions and vehicle store for the war effort. It was then later converted to some kind of military hospital, although there are suspicions that it was more of a centre for medical research, possibly used for biological and chemical warfare or, for the more hardened conspiracy theorists, extra-terrestrial genetic engineering. It was all shrouded in mystery so no one knows exactly what it was used for. It's really all based on rumour and hearsay.'

I found it intriguing but at the same time disconcerting. Even just seeing it on a map gave me goosebumps, but the prospect of actually physically going there again, knowing what I knew now, was quite terrifying. I had spent all these months desperate to find its location, but now I was beginning to wonder if actually locating it would be something I would come to regret.

Sam and I travelled back on the train together later that afternoon. I was expected at work the next day and I took it Sam was expected at the boatyard, although I got the distinct impression he wasn't too bothered about whether he turned up or not. We agreed with the rest of the group that those able to make it would meet up with us at my house on Friday evening in two weeks' time, and then we would travel to Devon straight from mine the next morning. Danny wanted to meet the immediate following weekend, but I was worried about sorting out work commitments and so asked to postpone it another week to give me some leeway. Danny was reluctant, although eventually agreed. He admitted that the extra week would allow them more time to do further research into the JAHL project, which still had so many unanswered questions.

We suggested meeting up with Sam somewhere in Devon as he was already so far down south in Cornwall, but he insisted he would come up to mine first, probably a few days beforehand. I played it cool, pretending I was indifferent to whether he met us there or came to mine first. Privately, I was pleased at the prospect of spending more time with him. Moreover, as it was his choice, I concluded he was eager to spend more time with me and for that I was rather chuffed.

'I can't believe we finally found the place. This is, like, exciting stuff,' said a cheerful Sam.

I raised my eyebrows. Exciting was not the word I would have used.

'No? Seriously? I thought this is what you wanted and you had been desperate about it?'

He was right. I had been absolutely desperate, spending huge amounts of time investigating to the point it had really taken over my life. Yet, on our discovery, I had not felt the elation that I thought I would. It felt more like trepidation.

'Well, no, of course I am glad we discovered where it is,' I said, as convincingly as I could. 'It's just that it is quite daunting. I mean, it's a government base. At least we think it is, and it's not exactly kosher. It's going to be dangerous. We could be walking into something very bad here, and we might not be walking back out.'

'It's still exciting, though.'

I found his response very naive and childish. He seemed to be treating it like a game.

'No. Actually, I don't find it exciting, Sam. It's extremely serious, potentially very dangerous, not to mention that I've just found out that I was involved in some kind of secret government experiment. For all I know, I could be part alien. Which, before you ask, I also don't find exciting.'

I crossed my arms, flung myself back into the chair and looked away in an act of defiance. Sam didn't speak and after a few moments I turned my eyes back towards him. He had his lips pursed, like he was trying to stifle a snigger. I glanced around the carriage, checking to see who might be in earshot and overheard my declaration of being an alien. To my relief, there were very few people on board; the nearest person to us was several aisles away and he had earphones in.

'Well, it's all right for you. You're not part of this government experiment thing. You weren't injected with some alien matter that's been flowing through your body for the last twenty-five or so years doing God knows what to me.' I flicked my eyes quickly about the carriage again, just to double-check no one had heard me, even in my lowered tone.

'I wouldn't worry too much about that.'

'No, I'm sure you wouldn't,' I replied sarcastically.

'Look, so they injected you with this stuff. It clearly didn't do anything. They abandoned the project because it failed. I mean, you're normal. You look normal. You act normal. You've got no antennae or superpowers, and I take it your blood isn't green. It's all quite disappointing.'

'Oh, for God's sake.' The conversation was bordering on ridiculous but he was right; I didn't feel anything abnormal and I had led a normal life, up until recent events, that is.

'Listen, seriously, if you think about it, people inject themselves with foreign bodies all the time. Cocaine, steroids, half the time they don't really know what is even in it. It can be mixed up with all sorts of crap. What about people who go through chemotherapy? They are well aware of how potent that is and the side effects that causes.'

'Well, I suppose. I don't know. I don't think it's quite the same.' I paused as the chap who had been sat a few aisles in front of us with the earphones on was now up from his seat and making his way past us, presumably on his way to the toilet or maybe seeking out the catering carriage. Our eyes briefly met as he inched past my seat, but he quickly averted them and soon disappeared through the doors into the next carriage.

I continued, 'Those people have chosen to have whatever they've had injected into them and are probably aware of what potentially it could do to them. I didn't have a choice. It was done behind my back, and I doubt they had any idea of any repercussions.'

'OK, so, yeh, I get the whole "you didn't know" thing. I mean, that is pretty bad. But I'm just saying, I know it's a bit scary wondering what they put in you, but it was, like, over twenty-five years ago and you seem normal to me, with nothing strange or weird about you.' He then gave me a warm smile and I felt reassured by his words.

Just then, the guy came back and reclaimed his seat a few rows down. I watched as he placed his earphones back in his ears and settled back down, listening to his iPod. I spent the rest of the train journey watching the scenery go by and thinking over everything I had found out about the last few days and what might be round the corner.

Eventually, we came to my stop. Sam had decided to go straight back to Cornwall, and therefore would stay on the train as it continued south. We'd swapped numbers, although Sam did not have a mobile or a home phone number and so gave me the number to the boatyard where he worked. He promised he would travel back up to my house in time for our next adventure, and I sincerely hoped he would stick to his promise. I felt a little sad at saying goodbye to him as we embraced and he gave me a peck on the cheek. I stepped off the train, looking back into the carriage and giving Sam a wave through the window. He waved back as I felt a lump come to my throat. I had grown accustomed to him being by my side, and leaving him made me feel abandoned and alone. I quickly turned away and left the platform, all the while fighting the urge to turn back around and get one last look of him before the train left. As I walked over the bridge, to cross the tracks over to the taxi rank, I heard the station master blow his whistle and I grabbed a last glimpse of the train pulling away. I started to wish that I had at least tried to persuade Sam to come back with me for a while and catch a later train, before reminding myself he would be back in a couple of weeks. However, two weeks seemed an age away, and I knew I would be spending the time just wishing it away.

CHAPTER NINETEEN

Returning to work the next day was hard. I was physically tired and mentally drained and I found it difficult to concentrate. Jess had given me a hard time of it as she squeezed every morsel of information possible out of me. She was convinced that I had gone to London with Sam for a romantic weekend away, and no amount of my protesting my innocence was going to change her mind. In the end, I decided it was easier for her to believe what she wanted. At least it saved me from having to try too hard to hide the truth from her. Of course, when I checked with Tom to make sure I wasn't on the rota for the weekend in two weeks' time, she immediately jumped to her own conclusions.

'Got something planned with Sam, have we?'

I flicked my eyes at Jess and then plucked up the courage to ask Tom for some extra holiday.

'Any chance I could maybe have the week off after as well? I'm happy to work the weekend shift straight after.' This was the first real moment that I had some good evidence and strong leads to follow up, and I wanted to have a decent amount of time dedicated towards it.

To my surprise, Tom was in a very affable mood and readily agreed to my request, while Jess's jaw had dropped wide open.

'So it's serious then? I don't blame you. He's such a hunk.'

'How do you know I'll be spending the time with Sam?'

'Well, are you?'

'Maybe, maybe not,' I teased.

'You are!'

Both Jess and I started giggling like lovestruck teenagers just as Harry came through the main hotel doors. I immediately stopped laughing, feeling strangely guilty, as if I had been caught doing something wrong.

Harry looked at us both suspiciously.

'Could you call the plumber? I think we have a problem with the boiler and it's a bit beyond my expertise.'

'Yeh, sure,' I said, followed by an awkward silence. We both then went to speak at the same time, and I could see Harry going slightly red with embarrassment as he talked over me.

'Sorry, you were saying?' he said.

'Oh no, it's OK. I was just pointing out about you being dragged into doing maintenance work again.'

'Yep. Nothing changes here. Although apparently I am told they are recruiting for someone, but I won't hold my breath. Well, anyway, I'd better get back on and do some gardening, seeing as I am behind on it. Again.'

I smiled and Harry started making his way back out the main entrance.

'Oh wait, Harry,' I shouted.

He had to step back in as he was already out the door as I shouted after him. He looked at me expectantly, waiting for me to speak.

'You didn't tell me what you were going to say.'

His eyes furrowed as he tried to recall what it was.

'Oh yes,' he said, his tone sounding slightly embarrassed again. 'I was just wondering if … if you were going to the party next week.'

'Party? What party?'

'The celebration party for ten years. You know, ten years since Tom has been running the hotel.'

'Oh right, yeh, I forgot that was coming up. When's that exactly?'

'Thursday, not this Thursday, next Thursday. Eighteenth, I think.'

I winced when he mentioned the date, knowing it was only the day before the guys would be coming to my house. Harry reacted to my expression with what appeared to be disappointment.

'Thursday the eighteenth,' I repeated back. 'Yeh, I should be free for that. Yep, I'll be there.'

Harry gave a satisfied smile and left.

I worked the next ten days straight, apart from one day off midway through. I barely thought about Roseville Resort, the JAHL project or any of the gang, although Sam did pop into my thoughts a few times. As the days counted down till our arranged meet-up, I began to feel nervous about our impending visit to Devon, but slightly excited at the prospect of seeing Sam again. I hadn't heard from any of them since I last saw them. I was confident that the gang would have been busy working on their research and would turn up on the day, but I wasn't so sure about Sam. I considered calling the boatyard to see if I could get hold of him, if only to remind him of the date. If Sam didn't show, I wasn't sure I would be able to go through with any of it. He was the one giving me the strength and confidence to keep going. In the end, I decided against calling and hoped he would come of his own accord. I needn't have worried, for he did indeed turn up, a day early, in fact, the night of the party.

Jess staggered over with a tray of Sambuca shots. By the time she reached us, she had slopped half of it into the tray and the glasses were sliding around, threatening to topple over the edge.

'Here we go, everyone, get it down yer,' she slurred.

We were all at least mildly inebriated, but Jess was definitely winning the 'most drunk' award.

I purposely picked the glass I thought had the least drink left in it as I was trying to avoid getting too bad a hangover the next day. I wasn't sure what time people had planned to come, but nowadays, hangovers seemed to linger for much longer, sometimes lasting the entire day if I had consumed enough of the hard stuff.

I could see Harry had seen what I was doing as he smiled while picking up a glass of his own.

Amelia turned her nose up at the tray and refused to take a glass.

'I don't know how you drink that stuff,' she sneered, and then took a sip from her flute of champagne.

'Oh, come on. We're celebrating,' Jess garbled in her drunken state. Amelia looked on with disgust at her behaviour.

'Tom. Come on, Tom.' Jess grabbed at Tom's arm and almost fell into him in the process. 'You'll have a drink with me. Come on, it's only a little teeny-weeny one.'

Tom wasn't looking too impressed, either, but he took one anyway.

'Right then, down the hatch in one,' and with that she flung her head back and gulped it in one go, with Tom quickly following suit.

Harry and I looked at each other, each waiting for the other one to make the first move. As soon as my hand started to lift, Harry immediately followed and we both downed our drinks together while maintaining eye contact the whole time. Harry smiled at my expression of revolt. I'd forgotten how much I disliked the taste of Sambuca, making this one of the rare occurrences when I actually agreed on something with Amelia.

'Who's for another drink?' asked Jess, sounding even less coherent than ever.

'Oh, Jessica, really? Haven't you had enough?' said Amelia, giving Jess a disapproving look.

'Yes, I think maybe you need to get some fresh air for a bit,' said Tom, taking her by the arm and gently trying to coax her away from the bar. Amelia grabbed Jessica's other arm and, more roughly than Tom, tried to pull her towards the exit.

Harry and I were left standing together, laughing as we watched the pair of them struggling to get Jessica away.

'Would you like another drink, Emma?' Harry kindly offered.

'Oh no, I think I need to slow down a bit myself.'

He gave a very flat-looking smile and I wondered if I had offended him.

'Perhaps a dance then?' He asked in a way that sounded like he expected me to say no. Lionel Richie's *Dancing on the Ceiling* was playing, and I concluded that was a song I could make a reasonable attempt to dance to.

'Yeh, OK.'

Harry's eyes lit up and he reached out his hand to grab mine. I was about to reciprocate when suddenly I could hear Jess wailing my name. Jess had looked to have sprung free from Tom and Amelia's grasp and was now staggering over to me.

'Emma!' she shouted. 'Oh, Emma! Guess who's here! I'll give you a clue. He's gorgeous and his name is Sam.' I was stunned into silence.

'Oops. Silly me. I said his name. That's a bit of a giveaway,' she sniggered, as she swayed from side to side, struggling to maintain her balance.

'Sam's here?' I couldn't be sure if she was being serious or playing a silly trick.

'Yeh, look,' and she pointed over towards the bar. I could see Sam, dressed in a deep blue smart shirt with black trousers, swigging from a bottle of beer as he watched us from the bar. He raised his beer in acknowledgement.

'Who's Sam?' asked Harry. Before I had chance to answer, Jess butted in.

'Her boyfriend.'

Startled by her reply, I quickly averted my attention back to Harry to downplay her answer, but it was too late. I could see the damage had been done.

'Oh right. Well, come on, Jess. Let's get you that fresh air,' and with Harry helping Jess, they both went off, leaving me standing on my own.

The dance floor was starting to fill up and I was gradually becoming cocooned. Before things got too boisterous, I slinked my way over to the bar to join Sam. He was looking particularly handsome in his outfit and as soon as he gave me his warm wide smile, my heart melted.

'Hi,' I said as I sidled alongside him.

'Hi.'

He took a sip from his beer, all the while gazing at me. I felt shy, as if we had only just met, and I couldn't think what to say.

'You look very nice in that dress.'

I could feel the heat on my face and was convinced I was blushing.

'You look quite good yourself,' I returned, regretting instantly my use of the word 'quite'. It made what was intended to be a compliment border on sounding like an insult.

'Did you just arrive straight here?' I asked, not convinced he would just turn up so smartly dressed.

'Nah. I went to your place first. When I realised you weren't in, I came here. Nice guy on reception, we chatted for a bit. I mentioned I was here to see you and I dropped Jess's name in. He told me you were all having a party, so I blagged my way in. He even let me change in the backroom and leave my suitcase there.'

That sounded about right. Sam, the master of persuasion, would make light work of Stefan, the gullible Polish porter who was temporarily filling in on reception duties.

'Come on, let's have a dance,' said Sam, grabbing me by the arm and whisking me away to the dance floor. I apparently had little choice in the matter and was horrified to see the dance floor was almost empty. Even worse, I didn't recognise the song that was playing, and it was at an awkward tempo where it was neither upbeat enough to be a dance track nor slow enough to smooch to. I found myself moving completely out of rhythm and incapable of coordinating my arms with my feet.

I felt like the whole world was watching me. Sam didn't seem to care about my lack of dance skills and grabbed my hand, giving me a twirl. As I spun round, I caught a glimpse of Harry watching from the sidelines and I felt instant guilt. As I completed the turn and was back facing Sam, he wrapped his arms round my waist and danced me around the room. I felt like a rag doll and was relieved when the song finally finished and my torture came to an end.

'Shall we go to the bar and get a drink? What would you like?'

'Bacardi and Coke,' I replied, as my feet ached and my pride was severely dented, 'and make it a double.'

CHAPTER TWENTY

The next day, I woke with an inevitable hangover, although not as bad as I had imagined and I would guess nothing in comparison to how Jess would be feeling. We had carried on drinking until the early hours of the morning. Jess had gone way overboard and had to be carried to one of the hotel rooms to sleep it off. Sam and I caught a taxi back to my home around 2am but stayed up for another couple of hours chatting, drinking and eating whatever snacks we could find from the cupboards.

It was now late morning and my eyes felt heavy from the lack of sleep. I instantly regretted staying up so late and I blamed Sam for being such a bad influence on me, although I had failed to put up much resistance.

I found Sam still fast asleep on the sofa, where he'd dozed off just before I'd finally gone off to bed. I decided to leave him be and take a shower. I wasn't sure what time the others would be arriving, but I wanted to be ready and presentable. They came earlier than I expected. I had only just stepped out of the shower and barely put on my change of clothes when I heard their vehicle pull up on the drive.

'Looks like they are here, Em,' shouted Sam from the lounge.

I was hastily rubbing my hair with a towel, enough to at least stop me dripping water everywhere. There wasn't going to be enough time to hair dry it and style it properly.

'I didn't think they would be here till later,' I said, feeling flustered.

Sam was still sitting on the sofa, hunched over like an old man. He looked bleary-eyed and very much the worse for wear.

'I'm going to take a shower,' he grumbled, clearly in need of more sleep.

'There's fresh towels in the cupboard in the bathroom. Help yourself.'

Sam trundled off and left me to welcome our visitors. I had just enough time before they rang the doorbell to dash up the stairs, give a quick comb-through of my hair and dump the towel in the corner of the bedroom.

'Hi. Come in.'

'Hi, Emma,' said Danny as he came in.

'Hi,' said Greg, closely following behind.

I smiled and held open the door, expecting the rest to follow, but no one else was there.

'Where's everyone else?' I asked, confused.

'It's just us,' replied Danny.

I closed the door and joined them in the lounge. Danny was sat in the armchair and Greg was stood with his back to the window.

'Teddy's got an assignment he needs to finish and Fiona couldn't get out of work. They've got some important exhibition on at the library and so it's all hands on deck,' explained Danny.

'And Patricia?'

I noticed Greg look awkwardly at Danny, and I could tell there was something up.

'She decided not to come. We've split up and she moved out last week. So she isn't part of the group anymore.'

I was taken aback as I didn't realise that Danny and Patricia were an item. They hadn't appeared like a couple to me, and I had assumed she was just another university friend. Although, thinking on it now, she had seemed like the odd one out of the group and did not hold the same level of interest in the JAHL project.

'Oh, sorry to hear that,' I said, trying to sound as sympathetic as I could and not let on I was unaware of their relationship.

Danny smiled weakly, although he didn't seem too upset. Maybe he was good at hiding his emotions, but I suspected they had been drifting apart for a while. I did feel quite disappointed that Patricia had not come as, out of all the group, she was probably the one I got on with the best.

Danny then quickly changed the subject. 'Did Sam make it?'

'Yes. He came down last night. He's in the shower. He shouldn't be long. Sorry, we've had a bit of a slow start. We went to a party last night and it turned into a bit of a late one.'

Greg flicked his eyes up in a manner that suggested he wasn't surprised, and Danny looked a bit irritated by my admission.

Coincidentally, Sam suddenly stepped into the room, his hair all fluffed up from the shower.

'Hi, guys.' His voice sounded hoarse and he was looking rather ragged.

'Good night, was it?'

I could detect a hint of sarcasm in Greg's voice and felt slightly ashamed.

'Yeh, it was a great night, thanks. Feeling it a bit this morning, though.'

'You don't say.'

Already, I could feel the tension in the air. Greg seemed to need little excuse to fall out with Sam, and I wondered what it was he disliked about him.

'So what's the plan?' asked Sam, seemingly unmoved by Greg's tone.

'Well,' began Danny, 'we thought we'd get an early start tomorrow to give us a good full day. We were thinking maybe leaving at five in the morning?'

Sam gave a sharp intake of breath at Danny's suggestion. 'Jeez, do we need to go that early?'

'Well. We want to get down there as soon as, don't we? Give us chance to find it and then investigate properly.'

I was in total agreement with Danny and so quickly added my support before things escalated and we wouldn't even be able to find agreement on timings.

'Yes, I think that's a good idea. Definitely want to start early. I just want to get down there as soon as possible.'

Danny looked relieved and Greg gave a wry smile. Sam shrugged his shoulders, mumbled something under his breath and disappeared out into the kitchen. Shortly after, I heard the sound of cupboards opening as Sam began to make his breakfast, or given how late in the day it now was, lunch would be a more appropriate term.

'Five it is then,' confirmed Greg, and that was the matter settled.

As Sam had slept on the sofa the night before, I assumed he would do so again tonight, so I let Greg and Danny have the spare room. Both had brought airbeds and sleeping bags, although there was a bed in the room. They tossed coins for the bed, with Danny winning, and so Greg was resigned to sleeping on the floor. I wasn't sure what Sam's reaction would be when he found out what the sleeping arrangements were, but he was probably capable of sleeping on a clothes line, so I was hoping he wouldn't be too upset.

'So, we thought we'd spend this afternoon going through the research we have been doing and everything we have found out so far,' stated Danny.

'Have you found out much more?' I asked, suddenly feeling quite inquisitive. I hadn't really expected to find out any new information until we had finally found Roseville Resort. Even then, I was feeling sceptical. I still wasn't convinced we would find it, and even if we did, would it really give us any more answers other than proof of its existence?

'Yes. We've managed to find out a bit more.'

My eyes widened and I felt a tingling sensation run through my body. I couldn't tell if it signified excitement or nerves. It was probably a combination of both.

'Sam,' I shouted out. 'Sam. Do you want to come and listen to this?'

Sam poked his head round the door. He had a mouthful of food so couldn't speak.

'They've found out some more stuff, they're going to go through it now.'

Sam nodded, disappeared for a moment and then returned with his cup of coffee and a plate heaped with several slices of toast. I noticed he didn't offer the rest of us any.

'Does anyone want anything to eat or drink?' I asked, as the smell of Sam's coffee and toast filled the room.

'No, thanks,' said Greg.

'No, I am good, thanks. We stopped on the way here and had something,' explained Danny.

'So what have you found?' I asked eagerly and, with that, Danny began to tell us about the research they had been doing and the discoveries they had made. It sounded like they had all spent a good many hours investigating and that their efforts had been worthwhile.

'We've been compiling profiles on the twenty-eight subjects that were selected as part of the experiment. We've been doing this for quite a while. I think the last time we saw you we'd covered about half of the names off the list, but now we've been through all of them and probably got about as much information as we can on everyone. Fiona has collated all this information and put it into this document.'

Danny opened up a red folder, labelled 'Subject Profiles'. Inside was a fairly thick set of hole-punched A4 paper sheets held together with a treasury tag. He opened the first page and ran his finger from top to bottom.

'This is a summary page, showing all twenty-eight people, their location and a very brief description of them.'

He then started slowly flicking through the pages. 'And then for each person we have a couple or so pages dedicated to them, giving any information we think is important. So it's got personal details about their background, various addresses, occupation, medical history, etc.'

He then flicked it back to the first summary page.

'What we found was quite startling. We'd already noticed a pattern forming from the very start, but with only small numbers we couldn't be sure if it was just coincidence. Now we have gone through them all, I think we can assume it is no coincidence.'

He then placed his finger just under the first name listed on the summary page.

'So this is Zoe Abbot,' his finger then sliding horizontally along to the next column of data.

'This is her date of birth,' his finger then sliding a bit further to the right and further still after he revealed each bit of extra information.

'Her last known address, the group she was listed under, taken from the original JAHL project document. So in her case, she was part of Group A, the same as you, and then this final one which gives just a short description of their current status.'

His hand had been covering the very right side of this 'Current Status' information, so it wasn't until he took his hand fully away that it was revealed.

I gulped when I read what it said. 'Deceased (01/07/03)'.

I saw the row immediately underneath also read 'Deceased' but with a slightly later date of '08/08/03'. I skipped the rest of the details, save to briefly read his name: Jeffrey Alcock.

Suddenly this 'Current Status' column was now jumping out from the page, demanding my attention. The names and their other details no longer seemed important.

Deceased (10/05/2001)

Deceased (27/01/1985)

Deceased (08/04/2003)

My mouth was going very dry and goosebumps were appearing on my arms as I began to feel cold.

'They're all dead,' I said in horror.

'Well, no, not quite,' replied Danny, with some strange sense of comfort.

My eyes continued scanning down the list. For one brief second, a wave of relief washed over me when I saw the next word did not begin with a D.

Prison (ABH)

The next wave to hit was nausea, and then, after seeing the next line was back to Deceased, I temporarily closed my eyes. But even in my mind's eye I could still see the dreaded words.

Out of the twenty-eight names on the list, thirteen were dead and seven were either in prison or some kind of mental institution. Only eight of us were alive and not locked up, and even then three of them had criminal convictions. I cringed at the statistics; they did not look good and certainly could not be thought of as pure coincidence. I averted my eyes from the document. I had seen enough.

'So the conclusion is, whatever they injected into us, all those years ago, eventually either kills us or sends us mad.'

I could see by the way Danny and Greg were looking at each other that was exactly what they thought but, nonetheless, Danny did his best to try and reassure me.

'Well, it does look like some of the group has quite probably had some adverse effects from it. But it's difficult to be sure. For example, this person here died when she was only ten. Her medical records show she was ill for some time. She suffered from a heart defect from birth and had a compromised immune system, eventually causing her death. We know the heart defect was apparent prior to anything she was injected with, so it is quite plausible that her death was not linked to the project and she would have died anyway.'

'I'm not sure that is particularly comforting, Danny. Let's say she hadn't been so unlucky to have had this heart defect. Looking at the maths, there is a high probability she would only have made it to the grand old age of twenty-something before she was six feet under or locked in a prison cell anyway.'

Danny's mouth opened as if he was about to say something but then decided better of it.

For a while, it stayed silent, apart from the occasional slurp or munching sound coming from Sam.

Eventually, Danny broke the silence.

'Do you want to continue going through this or would you rather stop?'

I gave a nonchalant shrug and rubbed my eyes firmly with the palm of my hands.

'OK, let me take a closer look at it,' and I reached out my hand intimating for the document to be handed over to me, of which Danny obliged.

I turned past the summary page and on to Zoe Abbot's detailed profile pages. She had exactly the same date of birth as me, living in Somerset with her husband and two children. Three days after she was born, she was handed over to the care of Saint María Convent, a nunnery based in Devon. Her childhood looked difficult, in and out of foster care, child homes and eventually adopted. She married young and had two children in her early twenties but looked to have settled, with her last known address registered in Somerset and her occupation listed as part-time cleaner. I imagined her to be a hardworking mother, probably struggling to make ends meet, and felt sympathy and pity for her. That was until I saw the newspaper clippings.

There was a rather grainy photo of a woman in handcuffs being led from a terraced house. The heading read, 'Mother arrested for the murder of her two young children'. I read the first part of the article which described how Zoe Abbot, the mother of an eighteen-month-old girl and a six-year-old boy, had apparently killed both her children within minutes of each other, one by strangulation and the other by suffocation. As if the gruesome explanation of the words I was reading wasn't harrowing enough, it was the picture of her in the next article that really choked me up. This picture was much clearer than the first and was a photo of them all as a normal happy family. Zoe and her husband stood together, arms around each other, looking lovingly at their two children stood just in front of them. It was from this picture I instantly recognised the family. Not even two months from the date of these articles I had been sat on a bench in Roseville Resort next to Zoe, talking to her while her husband John and her two children played by the pond's edge. Now, finally knowing her actual name, I learnt that on the 1st of July she committed suicide while being held in a secure mental institution awaiting trial for the murder of her own children.

Shaking my head in disbelief, I finally managed to raise my head and looked straight at Danny.

'This is terrible. I've only read this first one. Are they all this bad?'

'Well, no, they are not all as bad, but granted, yes, there are a good proportion of quite distressing stories that involve extreme behaviour, typically of a psychotic nature.'

Hesitantly, I continued to look through more of the document. As I turned each page and learnt more about each of the 'subjects', it increasingly became a struggle to read. On some occasions, I found myself skipping over parts completely when it became too distressing. There were multiple examples of extreme violence resulting in either a serious physical assault or murder, which I found too much to bear. Other examples were much less violent, although not necessarily any less harrowing to read. Jeffrey, for reasons unknown, suddenly went deluded while walking his dog. According to witnesses, after letting his dog free from the lead, he spread his arms like an eagle and dived off the edge of a coastal cliff. He inevitably died from multiple injuries sustained from over a 300ft fall. Anthony died from an overdose after a wild weekend bender, deemed by the coroner as death by misadventure. A verdict that was almost impossible to accept by his family and friends, who described him as extremely shy and introverted, shunning any kind of party lifestyle and completely teetotal. Kathleen, a well-respected artist, regarded as a pillar of her community, was now committed to an asylum, undergoing assessment and treatment for severe mental disorder. She had been displaying signs of very odd behaviour for several months, but the final straw came when she appeared as guest speaker at her local village fete. Apparently, she launched into a massive rant while proceeding to strip naked in front of everyone. It was not long after that the men in white coats came and took her away.

And so it went on, and although each one had their own individual story, the pattern was more or less the same. Each one had suffered from some form of loss of mental control.

'I need a drink,' I said as I threw the document onto the coffee table and watched it slide off the other end and onto the floor. Danny picked it up and held onto it.

'Shall I put the kettle on?' offered Sam.

'I was thinking of something much stronger than that,' I replied, opening up the drinks cabinet and retrieving a bottle of brandy. I could see I was raising a few eyebrows but I didn't care.

'Anyone else want one?' I asked, as I poured myself a large glass. Everyone declined and watched me as I glugged it down and then poured myself a second one.

'Perhaps a bit early, do you think?' asked Sam concernedly.

'I don't know. Is it?' I taunted.

'Well, it is a bit. We've got a big day tomorrow, don't forget, early start an' all.'

Sam's reply really riled me and I almost launched into a tirade before thankfully managing to stop myself. Instead, I ignored him, drank the last of my drink and whisked myself off to the kitchen to wash the glass up.

I washed the glass up repeatedly as if it was badly stained and used such vigour that it was a wonder it didn't shatter. Eventually, I managed to break myself out of the cycle and place it on the drainer. I stood at the sink and stared out of the window, watching a magpie strut across my back lawn as if he owned the place. Two pigeons making a ruckus in a silver birch tree then caught my eye, and I couldn't make out if they were fighting or mating.

'Everything all right?'

I jumped as Sam placed his hands on my shoulders and peered round me, trying to catch my gaze.

'Oh, I don't know, Sam. This is all getting too much for me. I just want to go back to my normal simple life. I have this thing burning in me, desperate to find out what this is all about, but every time I find out something, it's just all horrible and ... and ... well, just a nightmare. My life has turned into a complete nightmare.'

Sam hugged me and I willingly fell into his arms and lapped up the comfort.

'You know you can stop this anytime. You can stop looking any further and go back to your normal life.'

I lifted my head from his shoulder and looked him square in the eyes.

'How can I? It's too late. I know too much. I can't just go back. I can't just forget it. It will always be there, weighing down on my shoulders, haunting me.'

Sam didn't say anything, but I knew what he was thinking. He knew I would have to keep looking until I had exhausted all avenues and found out everything I could and that there was no chance of ever going back to my previous life.

Just then, Greg entered the room but quickly left when he saw Sam and me in each other's arms.

Feeling embarrassed, I immediately relinquished my grip and parted from Sam.

I rejoined Greg and Danny in the lounge, as if the last few minutes were just a glitch. Sam followed only moments later, and we continued to go over the research.

We spent the best part of the rest of the afternoon going through the details, trying to make sense of what it all meant and to plan our journey in the morning. We stopped only occasionally for some light relief and to refuel. While the JAHL project was starting to uncover some of its secrets, there were still so many unanswered questions. Two of which for me were the standout questions that bothered me the most and would keep me awake at night. How long did I actually have left of my life, and would I stay sane until the very end? The prospect of a premature death was extremely scary, but the thought of going mad, losing control and possibly committing some heinous crime was beyond bearable.

CHAPTER TWENTY-ONE

The weather was atrocious. A storm had moved in overnight and the rain lashed down so hard it was bouncing back up from the road. Danny had the wipers on at full speed, and even that was struggling to keep the water off the windscreen. Danny was forced to be careful as he struggled with visibility as well as coping with all the surface water that had created rivers in the roads. I had been reluctant to even embark on the trip when I saw how bad it was, but all the guys were insistent that we should go and I was outnumbered and overruled. Even after we had set off and the thunder and lightning clapped overhead, I persisted in suggesting we should postpone. Now I just sat quietly in the back. We had come too far to turn back now, and after a troubled night's sleep I had very little energy left to waste on talking to a brick wall.

Sam, who was sat in the back of the vehicle with me, had tried a couple of times to pacify my mood. I wasn't having any of it, now feeling like the outsider. He had clearly grown tired of me snapping back at him and so was now giving me the silent treatment. I kept my eyes fixated out of the window, purposely avoiding any eye contact with Sam, although I wasn't really taking in much of what I was seeing. I could feel my eyes growing heavy and it was a struggle to keep them open. Eventually, I succumbed, allowing my eyelids to drop firmly shut.

'Emma.'

Startled, I opened my eyes. Sam had been shaking my leg, trying to rouse me from my sleep.

'Huh? Are we here?' I wasn't sure how long I had fallen asleep for and I was feeling very disorientated.

Greg was straining his neck as he peered round at me from the front passenger seat.

'We should be close. We've just driven through those crossroads back there, you know, the white sign you remembered with the Bamdale and Tifford names. We're just getting some petrol.'

As my eyes started to refocus and I felt like I was returning to the land of the living, I began to recognise where we were. It was still early in the morning so most places in the village were still shut, but I instantly recognised the pub on the corner with its white picket fence. Further along the road, between the post office and an antiques store, I spotted the second pub, except this time it looked more attractive than I last remembered. I guessed it must have had a lick of paint since I was last here.

'I've been here before. Lisa and I stopped at this exact same petrol station.'

'Great,' said Danny enthusiastically. 'Can you remember how much further it was?'

'Not really. We had difficulty finding it, and we kept making wrong turns which added to the journey. I don't think it was probably that far, though.'

Greg had jumped out of the car and was refilling it while the rest of us got out to stretch our legs. The weather had begun to abate and there was now only a light drizzle. Even the sun was threatening to make an appearance from behind the clouds.

'Anyone want anything?' asked Danny.

'Yeh, can you get me a bottle of water?' I replied.

'Sure.'

Danny and Sam made their way into the station shop while Greg finished filling the tank.

I walked to the kerbside and looked up and down the street. It was very quiet and there was no one about besides us and an elderly gentleman in a tweed jacket across the way walking his dog. I watched them, mesmerised, until they eventually disappeared round the corner, past the pub with the white picket fence and out of sight. It seemed very eerie being back here, and I wasn't sure that I felt overly comfortable. Just then, the pub door opened and another gentleman stepped out carrying a watering can. He proceeded to water the hanging baskets that adorned the pub walls. I watched for a while, amused he was watering the plants after having so much rain, until I was distracted by the sound of Sam and Danny returning.

'Come on, Emma. Let's go,' hollered Danny.

I made my way back over. Greg was already sat back in the car. Sam was just jumping in the back with an armful of snacks and drinks, and Danny waited for me to get closer before hurling me a bottle of water. I caught it just in time before it smacked me in the face.

'Thanks,' I said sharply.

'Jelly baby?' asked Sam as I sat back in the car with him.

'Only if it's a black one.'

Sam smirked and then fished around looking for one. He handed me two blackcurrant-flavoured jelly babies.

I popped them both into my mouth together and gave him a strained smile.

He grinned and it was at that moment I knew we were back on good terms.

As Danny pulled away from the petrol station, we passed the pub where the man was still watering his flowers. As we drew alongside him, he turned his head towards our car and for a brief moment our eyes locked as he spotted me watching him from the car window. Instantly, I shrank back and lowered my gaze in the hope that he hadn't recognised me.

Sam watched me curiously as I cowered in my seat.

'Everything OK?'

I nodded as I unscrewed the lid on my bottle and took a swig. He watched me as I slowly screwed it back on again. His expression was one of suspicion.

'You sure?'

As we drove out of the village and turned onto a new road I felt much better, as if we had now reached some sufficient safe distance. I leant in and almost whispered to Sam, 'I think I recognised that man watering the plants outside the pub back there.'

'What?'

'He was at Roseville Resort. He worked there. He was at the main gate, and later I spoke to him at the main reception.'

'Are you sure?'

‘Fairly. I think it was him. It looked like him.’ In fact, the more I thought about it, picturing him in a smart burgundy outfit, the more convinced I became.

‘Stop the car,’ shouted Sam.

Greg turned to look back at us and gave Sam a very peculiar look.

‘Stop the car,’ repeated Sam, more demanding this time round.

‘Why? What’s up?’ said an unamused Greg.

‘Just stop the bloody car.’ Sam sounded very impatient, and yet again I was witnessing two people who really did not see eye to eye.

Danny did as he was told, pulling into a layby.

‘What’s your problem?’ Greg glared at Sam and he glared straight back.

‘There isn’t a problem,’ I said, quickly trying to diffuse the situation, knowing that Sam’s only real problem was with Greg.

‘Well, why have we stopped the car then?’

‘Because … Emma here recognises that guy back at the village we just stopped in as someone from Roseville Resort.’

‘Which guy?’

‘Some guy watering plants at the pub.’

‘Did you?’ asked Greg, now looking hard at me and sounding like he didn’t believe me.

‘Uh,’ I stuttered, now feeling less sure about myself. ‘Yeh, I think so.’

‘You think so?’

‘OK. Well, I am almost certain I recognised him as someone who worked there,’ I said, with much more conviction. This was enough to convince everyone in the car we should turn around and go back. Convince everyone, that is, except me.

By the time we arrived back outside the pub, the man had just finished watering the last hanging basket and was about to make his way back in.

Sam leapt out of the car and managed to get between him and the door.

‘All right, mate?’

The man didn’t answer and looked very wary.

‘You got a minute?’ asked Sam, a bit too intimidating for my liking.

Greg was now standing alongside Sam, while Danny and I hung back.

'I'm busy. Pub doesn't open till 11am. Excuse me.' He brushed past Sam and headed for the door.

'Did you work at Roseville Resort?'

Sam's question immediately made the man halt in his tracks. He paused for a moment as if carefully considering his answer.

'No. Never heard of it,' he said steelily. Then, before anyone could react, he disappeared into the pub, shutting the door firmly behind him, after which we heard the distinct sound of a bolt being slid across. Sam spent several minutes repeatedly banging on the door and shouting for him to open it so we could talk to him. Greg wandered round the back to see if he could gain entry, but he too came back defeated.

'He's holed himself up in there. Don't think we are going to get to talk to him,' said a deflated Greg.

'You definitely sure it was him?' said Danny, turning to me to check for proof.

'Now I've seen him up close, and also now heard his very distinctive voice, I am absolutely sure it was him.'

Danny surveyed the pub, as if he was trying to formulate a plan.

'We'll come back later, when the pub is open. Maybe we can get to speak to him then.'

Sam banged on the door one more time, but unsurprisingly there was still no answer. In the end, even he gave up, and we made our way back to the car and continued on our way.

'Oh, for God's sake, where is this place?'

Even Danny was beginning to lose his rag, and he had more patience than the rest of us put together.

'We've already been down this road twice,' said Danny, slamming his hand on the steering wheel in frustration. We'd been driving around for ages, stopping at numerous points along the way trying to find what was becoming ever elusive.

'Did you guys recognise anything?' Danny sounded desperate and fed up.

'Nope. Not a thing,' said Sam, in a tone not helping the cause and undoubtedly winding both him and Greg up.

'Sorry, no. Nothing looked familiar,' I added nervously.

Danny spun the car round in a wild manner that even alarmed the usually casually relaxed Sam.

'We aren't getting anywhere here, so we may as well go back to that pub. It'll be open by now. Maybe that guy can tell us something.'

'Well, only if he is willing to talk to us. He didn't look too pleased to see us before. I'm not sure he's going to suddenly want to talk to us now.'

Greg's negativity seemed to rattle Danny's cage, making him answer in an uncharacteristic stern reply.

'Well, you got a better suggestion? Do you want to drive around in circles for a few more hours?'

'OK, fine. Let's go back.'

Sam and I looked at each other, slightly shocked by the other two's responses. We both stayed silent and kept ourselves out of the argument.

The pub was indeed open. The parasols on the picnic-bench tables were all now fully open, flapping in the wind, and the advertising boards were placed out on the kerbside. The bolted door was now wide open and enticing us in. The man we had approached earlier was behind the bar, waiting for the first punters to arrive. He was obviously very disturbed at our return and looked on anxiously. Only Danny approached the bar; the rest of us sat at a table nearby and easily within earshot of the conversation.

'Hi there,' said Danny in a friendly tone.

The man said nothing and gave him a cold stare.

'Look, we don't want any trouble. We just want to talk to you for a few minutes. We are looking for Roseville Resort, and my friend here recognises you as someone working there.'

The man looked very disturbed at the mere mention of Roseville. I noticed he gave me a brief glance when Danny told him I recognised him even though Danny never singled me out as the one who had seen him.

Just then, a young lad walked through the door. He walked in with purpose and a bounce in his step.

'Hey, Frank. Sorry I'm a bit late.' He threw his jacket on the coat stand with great precision and joined Frank behind the bar.

'Can you serve this gentleman, please, Jack?'

'Sure thing. What can I get you, sir?'

Frank then came out from behind the bar and anxiously beckoned the rest of us to follow him.

He took us to another table, right in the corner, well away from the bar, and we all sat down.

He spoke in a very low and hushed tone and had an uneasy demeanour.

'Look, I can't talk about that place. You need to leave me alone and stop pestering me. I can't tell you anything.'

Danny arrived at the table with a tray of drinks and Frank almost jumped out of his seat, only narrowly avoiding knocking the entire tray clean out of his hands. Luckily, Danny was quick to react and managed to move the tray out of harm's way. Danny then sat alongside me. There wasn't much room, so I had to shuffle along to the point where mine and Sam's legs were touching. Sam cheekily winked at me as I sat uncomfortably wedged between the two of them.

'Listen, Frank,' began Danny, 'we really aren't here to cause you any trouble. We just want to know where Roseville is. Can you help at all? We've all been looking for this place for an age, we just can't find it. Anything you can give us, just anything, we would really appreciate, and then I promise we will leave you alone and you won't see us again.'

Frank looked like he was about to actually tell us something when in walked a group of young men and put an abrupt stop to him speaking. He watched them with suspicious eyes as they went to the bar and ordered their drinks from Jack. They were too far away for us to hear what they were saying, but to me they were just a group of ordinary mates ordering a round of drinks. Frank was watching them like a hawk, like he suspected them of being hitmen. However, once they had taken their seats at a table at the furthest distance away from us and partly obscured by a pillar, Frank seemed to settle and leant in towards us. He then spoke quietly but sternly.

'If I show you where it is, you will leave me alone and never hassle me again?'

Danny nodded vigorously. 'Of course. Definitely.'

‘Then meet me back here in a couple of hours. Don’t come to the front entrance, come round the back,’ he ordered, and then looked Danny square in the eyes with real intent and added, ‘and make sure no one is following you.’ With that, he stood up and left us all sat slightly dumbfounded as he took his place back behind the bar.

‘Well, he was an interesting chap,’ said Sam, trying to lighten the mood and reaching across to grab a drink. ‘Maybe now we will actually get to find this bloody place after all.’

For the first time, I too actually believed with Frank’s help we would finally find it. Although Frank’s stark warning did nothing to heighten my enthusiasm, only my nerves.

CHAPTER TWENTY-TWO

As agreed, we came back exactly two hours later. Greg went to the back door as instructed while the rest of us stayed in our vehicle. Danny tapped impatiently on the steering wheel as we waited until eventually Sam could stand it no longer.

'Will you quit the tapping? It's driving me nuts.'

'Sorry, mate,' apologised Danny, and ceased his compulsion.

'What do you think is taking them so long?' asked Danny, sounding jittery. Greg had been gone for a good ten minutes now, and I too was feeling a rise of panic. I wasn't too sure about Frank's bona fides.

'Do you think everything is all right? Shall I go and check?' I offered, far too boldly. In reality, I was feeling very cowardly and no way inclined to leave the vehicle.

'Nah, Greg's a big boy. He can look after himself. He'll be out in a minute.'

I gave a secret sigh of relief at Sam's calm and unconcerned response. He was forever my saviour.

Danny began tapping on the steering wheel again. Sam tutted but made no remark this time, instead taking out his baccy from his inside jacket pocket and rolling a fag.

'Here he is,' said Danny, distinctly relieved.

'Where's Frank?' I asked, puzzled.

Greg jumped in the front passenger seat.

Danny looked at him, equally puzzled. 'Everything all right?'

'Yeh, fine. He took a bit of convincing. He's far from keen. But he has agreed to take us there. But he will literally take us as close as he can and then he's going to scarper, and we must never, in no uncertain terms, ever contact him again.'

'OK, but where is he?'

'Oh. He's not coming with us. We have to follow him in his car.'

'Jeez, he's not seriously going to drive across that, is he?' Greg's question did nothing to deter Danny, and he did indeed follow.

No wonder we had had so much trouble finding it. The route Frank was now taking us looked challenging enough for a 4x4; it certainly wasn't something that either of our cars was designed for. The car jolted and lurched its way across the very rough terrain, sending us bouncing about in our seats. At one point, I was thrown so high my seat belt cut harshly into my shoulder as it held me down, and even then I was sure I felt a faint brush of my head against the roof of the car. I'd been on roller coasters less aggressive than this ride.

'He's stopping.'

Greg's words were a huge relief, and my anxiety lessened as our car gradually came to a stop.

Frank was true to his word. He stopped for only a brief moment, stepping out of his car and pointing out to us an area beyond, before getting back into his car and driving back in the direction we had come.

'Bye then,' said Sam sarcastically, waving to him as he drove past us. Frank gave us no acknowledgement.

We all got out, with Danny and Greg surveying the damage done to our vehicle.

'Well, this doesn't look anything like the place I remember,' said Sam, who was now looking out in the direction Frank had pointed out. I was inclined to agree; the place was a wilderness and I could see nothing that remotely resembled a holiday resort. Danny was now on his back, half underneath the car, with Greg crouching down beside him. Judging by the expression on Greg's face and the disagreeable tone of Danny's voice as he was relaying back his findings, I doubted very much we would be using the same method to leave. I wondered how many miles walking it would be to get back to civilisation.

I walked over to stand alongside Sam and cupped my hand over my eyes as I looked out into the distance.

'Can you see it?' he asked.

I squinted, looking harder as I scanned the area afar. At first, all I could really see were a few trees and unkempt hedging. But as I looked and focused harder still, I could see, just beyond the line of trees and hedgerow, a fence.

My heart skipped a beat. I immediately dropped my hand away from my brow and turned and looked at Sam.

'Yes. I do see it. I can see some fencing. It must be the perimeter fence.'

Sam smiled and gave a single assured nod. He then made his way back to the car. I gave one final look back out, swallowed hard and followed him.

Sam had retrieved a rucksack and was filling it with what was left of the provisions we had bought from the garage. Greg and Sam were now stood alongside the car in serious conversation about the state of our vehicle. It seemed like the car had now taken precedence and they had completely forgotten our main purpose.

'You lot coming or what?'

Sam, with the rucksack now on his shoulders, was already making his way over to the site.

'Wait,' I shouted after him. 'Shouldn't we just talk about this first before we go gallivanting off?'

Sam didn't even look back and was well into his stride. I knew there was no stopping him, and he wasn't going to wait for anyone.

'Oh, for God's sake,' I muttered. 'Are you guys going to come?' I urged. I was desperate for us to get going before Sam put too much distance between us.

Danny and Greg were watching Sam as he strode further and further from us. Greg was slowly shaking his head from side to side, with his hands on his hips in disbelief. Danny looked less aggrieved. Danny then switched his gaze to me and gave me an affirmative nod.

'Sure. We'll just grab a few things and then we will be there.'

'OK,' I said, feeling relieved, although not convinced Greg was quite so on board. I then hurried off in pursuit of Sam.

Sam walked at a very fast pace and was obviously much fitter and stronger than myself. I therefore struggled to keep abreast, although did not readily admit to it. No doubt the heavy breathing gave that away, with no need for any admission. Finally, we made it to the perimeter fence; myself arriving a few paces behind Sam, with strained calves. Sam was examining the fence up close, giving it a hard push and then stepping back to judge its height. The fence was made of solid metal with a corrugated effect, and barbed wire ran all along its top. It looked strong and imposing and something not to be crossed. If its appearance alone was not enough to deter you, then the stark warning messages emblazoned periodically along its structure were there, reinforcing the point.

The first sign I laid my eyes on read, in big bold red letters, 'Restricted Area. Keep Out, MOD Property. Trespassers will be Prosecuted'. Next, my eyes followed down to the sign just below it, which read, 'Danger. Hazardous Area'. This sign was in a less intense colour, black writing on a yellow background, although it did nothing to lessen the impact of its meaning. I found the words alone were enough of a threat to frighten me.

Just then, I heard the sound of muffled conversation and turned to see Greg and Danny had almost caught up with us. They both had huge army-style backpacks, and I nervously wondered what they were concealing inside them.

'How's it looking? Any way in?' enquired Danny.

Sam let out a slow, exasperated-sounding puff of air.

'Well, unless you have a really long ladder then I can't see a way over it, and unless you're carrying a grenade launcher or just happen to have a tank with you, I can't see us getting through it, either.'

Greg scoffed at Sam's sarcasm. Sam simply ignored him and started to walk further down along the fence, examining it as he went.

'Does this look familiar?' Danny asked me.

'No. Not at all. This fence wasn't here, definitely not all these warning signs. And there's no road leading to it. This whole area looks nothing like when I came here before. I guess we must have come to it from a different direction.'

Greg trotted off to Sam, who was now a good few metres away, further along the fence. I watched until he caught up with him and they started to engage in conversation. I continued watching them for several minutes, half expecting them to erupt at any moment and break out into a fight. They were too far away for me to hear what they were saying, so I could only gauge the mood by their expressions and actions. To my relief, it seemed amicable, and I felt relaxed enough to look away.

'Do you want a drink?'

Danny was sat on the ground drinking from a water bottle. My calves were still aching from the walk and so I sat down where I stood. I nodded, as my throat was beginning to feel dry.

'Yes, please.'

Danny screwed the top back on. I had a sudden flashback to earlier and this time readied myself before he threw it in my direction. This time, he threw it underarm with a looping trajectory and it was an easy catch.

'So are you and Sam an item then?'

I almost choked on the gulp of water I was just in the midst of sipping. After several coughs and splutters, I finally managed to answer.

'What? No. No, we're not together. We're not a couple.'

Danny looked at me with disbelieving eyes.

'We're just friends,' I insisted.

'OK. I just wondered.'

I could feel my face flushing and wasn't sure what to say next or even where to look. After composing myself, I instinctively looked for Sam. He and Greg were both gone. Feeling panicked, I quickly got up and looked again, straining to see as far as I could.

'Where are they?' I said accusingly to Danny, as if it was his fault for waylaying me.

'Don't worry. They'll be back. Let's just wait here for them.'

Eventually, after several minutes of standing there willing them to come back into view, I sat back down. Danny didn't look the least bit worried, and I began to wonder if my reactions were too overblown. I tried to reassert myself and appear more casual.

'So what happened between you and Patricia?'

I balked at asking such a forward question. I wasn't sure what came over me; it just suddenly popped out of my mouth without even really thinking. I suppose I was simply following Danny's lead, although it was very unlike me to ask someone such a personal question and I instantly wished I could retract it. Much to my relief, Danny didn't seem fazed.

'Ah, I don't know, we just sort of grew apart. Patricia was never really into all this extra-terrestrial stuff. She thought it all a bit far-fetched. At the beginning, I think she just found it amusing and saw it as my hobby. But then I probably spent a bit too much time with that and not enough with her, and I guess she got tired of it.'

I gave a sympathetic smile and made sure to bite my lip and prevent myself prying any further.

After a few moments of silence between us, I could hear Greg calling to us.

We both got up to go over and meet him. He was panting and had obviously been running.

'We think we've found a way in,' he told us breathlessly. He bent over, placing his hands on his knees as he tried to catch his breath.

'Where's Sam?' I asked in a worried tone.

'It's OK. I left him back there, just setting up a few things.'

I screwed my eyes up in puzzlement, wondering quite what that meant. I was inclined to think it wouldn't be to my liking.

CHAPTER TWENTY-THREE

'I really don't think I can do this,' I said, shaking with fear.

'Come on, Em. It's fine. It's not that far. You'll be fine.'

'Bloody hell, Sam. I could break my sodding neck.'

I was perched precariously halfway up a tree on a branch that I wasn't convinced was strong enough to take my weight. The tree was partly uprooted and was leaning at quite a severe angle out towards the fence we were trying to get over. It had taken me an age and a lot of courage to get up this high. Now I was up here, I realised that was the easy bit; the jump down looked terrifying. Sam and Danny had already made the death-defying leap. Sam had landed with not even a scratch and had acted like it was a breeze. Danny had had a more awkward landing and was limping from what was probably a sprained ankle.

'Come on, just jump.'

Sam was beginning to lose patience with me. I looked back down to Greg, who was still to make the climb. He too looked like he had had enough waiting for me. I began to realise that I may as well jump. The climb back down the way I had come looked just as harrowing. Readying myself into position, I closed my eyes, took a deep breath, told myself it would all be fine, opened my eyes and jumped. I landed only a fraction from where Sam was stood and knocked him clean off his feet from where I lost balance and rolled sideways into him. We ended up in a tangled mess with me on top. Sam was laughing his head off, and I could feel my blood starting to boil. I did not find it funny. I tried to get up off him but he wrestled with me on the ground, still laughing right in my ear, acting like it was some kind of game. I was full of rage and fought hard to get up, punching him several times in the side of the head.

I shouted at him to get off me and let me get up, intertwined with a barrage of expletives. I probably swore more times in that one instance than I had in my entire life.

Sam immediately relinquished his grip and allowed me to get up. He looked stunned and was no longer laughing. I went to give him a sharp kick in the side of his ribs while he still lay on the floor. He quickly moved his hands in the way in self-defence, but the only contact I made was with thin air. Danny had grabbed me from behind in a bear hug, lifted me off the ground and swung me out of harm's way. He then gently placed me back down but still held me in a tight embrace.

'Emma, calm down. Please calm down,' begged Danny.

My temper began to cool and I could feel the tension relinquishing from my body. I think Danny must have felt it too, as he let go of his grip and bent down to clutch his swollen ankle. His quick movements must have aggravated it, and he was clearly distressed from the pain it was giving him.

'What the hell has got into you?' Sam had got up and dusted himself off. He looked very aggrieved.

'I didn't find it funny, OK. You just kept laughing at me and wouldn't let me get up. I just jumped a bloody long way. You don't know if I was hurt or not.'

'Well, are you? You don't look hurt.'

I hadn't actually noticed what physical state I was in. I was too preoccupied with Sam laughing at me. I didn't feel in any real pain. Maybe a bit bruised, but only superficial. My arm was stinging a bit, though, and I noticed I had a scrape running all the way down the back of my forearm. It was bleeding but it didn't look too deep. I guessed I must have caught it on the hawthorns. All in all, I seemed to have got off fairly lightly.

There was a thud as Greg landed on our side of the fence. I turned just in time to see him perform some commando roll and then rise to his feet. He appeared unscathed.

'Everything all right here?' I had the feeling the question was directed more towards me than anyone else.

'Yes. Fine,' I replied.

'Sure? You looked like you were having a bit of a psycho moment.'

'No. All fine. Just Sam winding me up. I'm over it now.'

I wasn't sure Sam was over it. He hadn't said a word since the incident and in true Sam style was already traipsing across the field that we now found ourselves in, waiting for no one.

I was torn between catching up with Sam and trying to smooth things over or waiting for Danny, who was struggling to walk. Instead, I did neither and chose to maintain the middle ground, walking well ahead of the weakened Danny, who needed the support of Greg just to keep up, and staying well behind the striding Sam.

We walked for what felt like miles. Field after field, jumping hedgerows, a brook and clambering over more fences and gates, although none of the obstacles were of the magnitude we had earlier experienced. We were reminded at several points that we were trespassing and that our lives were in severe danger, but even that seemed less daunting now. It was difficult to imagine the danger when we were in such peaceful countryside.

Sam stayed well ahead of the rest of us but did stop from time to time to allow us to catch up, as he was far outpacing any of us. Eventually, he came to a complete stop and sat down amongst the wild flowers. The grass and poppies were so high I could only just see the top of his head. As I drew closer, I could see he was watching me.

'Hi,' I said nervously, like it was the first time we had met.

He nodded. 'Hi.'

It was hardly a riveting conversation, but at least we were on speaking terms. I sat down on the grass next to him and gave him a weak, apologetic smile.

'Sorry about before. I didn't mean to get quite so mad with you.'

'Well, you certainly seemed to mean it when you swung your foot wildly at me and almost broke my ribcage.'

'I'm really sorry. I don't know what came over me.'

The first statement was true and genuine, while the second was bordering on a lie. During the walk, I had thought over and over about my obvious overreaction and I was beginning to wonder if I was suffering from the same ill effects as many of my fellow test subjects. Paranoia was not something I would normally associate myself suffering with, and yet, in recent months, this feeling had featured heavily in my life. I also noticed that while, at one time, patience was a virtue I had in abundance, now I was easily irritated. In fact, rage was becoming an altogether familiar experience, and now I was displaying signs of uncontrollable violence. My only comfort was I felt remorseful and I recognised my unreasonable behaviour. That at least gave me some hope that I may be able to maintain some level of control and behave as a decent human being.

'I guess we should wait for the others before venturing in.'

I frowned in confusion. 'In? In where?'

'Roseville Resort. You know, that place we have been searching for to the ends of the earth?'

His sarcasm was lost on me as I felt the butterflies rising in my stomach and my head going very light and fluffy. I had been so preoccupied with how I was feeling and the potential damage I had caused to our relationship I had failed to notice we were sat right alongside a high steel mesh wire fence. The very same one I had first seen when Lisa and I had approached the complex all those months ago. I raised myself off the ground, needing to steady myself from the shock and realisation of where we were. Only a stone's throw away, I could see the security gate. Thankfully, this time, it was lacking any security guard, and yet curiously it still made me feel just as uneasy and under threat.

Danny and Greg took forever to reach us and I was becoming increasingly agitated as the time ticked by. I found myself pacing up and down alongside the fence as my blood pressure began to rise. I had to take some long and deep hard breaths in order to calm myself down and remind myself of the time and effort it had already taken to get this far. A few more minutes was really not going to be such a hardship.

Danny practically collapsed on the ground next to Sam, clearly in a lot of pain. He clutched at his ankle and gingerly tried to rub away the pain.

'You gonna be able to carry on, mate?' said Sam, looking very unconvinced.

'Yeh, I'll be fine. Just need a minute.'

Sam gave him a perplexed look, taking the last drag on his cigarette before discarding it.

'Is this it?' asked Greg, sounding disappointed as he peered through the wire mesh. 'It doesn't look much like a holiday complex.'

'In all honesty, it never looked like a holiday complex the day I first arrived. At least not from this entrance point. It looked much better once we got further inside.'

On this occasion, though, it wasn't to be. Even once we gained entry, by using cutting equipment we had brought along with us and quite a bit of brute force, it still in no way resembled a holiday resort. The beautifully landscaped gardens were long gone. The place looked severely neglected.

Where once elegant topiary stood, lovingly crafted into beautifully shaped ornamental structures, there was now nothing but a higgledy mess of unrecognisable shapes interwoven with ivy and bindweed, as if strangling the life out of them. The delicately laid-out borders, once awash with neatly cut roses surrounded by swathes of colourful flowers, were now overrun with weeds, and the roses looked practically dead. There was the faint hint of colour where some rose flowers had managed to bloom, but at this late stage of summer even they had given up the ghost and were now merely faded and shrivelled petals.

The main square fared no better. Although the buildings still stood, some had been badly damaged by the Japanese knotweed, which was running rampant. It was quite a shock to see it in this state and it was almost unrecognisable to me. The fountain in the centre, although relatively intact, looked forlorn, with its figurine statue appearing worn and tired, and the bucket it held aloft its head no longer spilled out any water.

'Jeez, this place has gone to the dogs,' said Sam, looking quite startled. He plonked himself down on the bench and lit a cigarette. For a moment, I was transported back to the night when I met Sam at the very same bench. But the moment passed and I was back in the present.

'So, where do we go from here?' Greg questioned Danny. Danny was now sat alongside Sam, trying to stretch his injured foot out while he used his good leg to prop it up.

'I don't know. This place looks big. It could take a while to search it all.'

'And what are we searching for exactly?' added Sam.

'I don't know really. Evidence. Something that might be linked to secret government operations. Maybe something related to the JAHL project.'

'Great. Sounds clear as mud and easy as pie. Do you wanna split up? Like you said, this place is huge. Maybe we can cover more ground if we separate.'

I got the impression that Sam's suggestion was about him preferring to work alone, away from us, rather than a logical calculation.

'No. No. Hang on, let me think.' Danny winced with the pain, and it was obviously affecting his ability to think and formulate a plan.

We waited patiently for his answer.

'We need to find the entrance to the underground. That's where all the real interesting stuff is going to be. This place was built for secret operations and it was all put underground. Anything above ground is just a ruse to hide what's underneath.'

Sam looked straight at me and had to squint from the sun, which was shining bright behind me.

'Do you want to lead the way or shall I?'

And with that, with me leading, all four of us made our way to lodge Number 126.

CHAPTER TWENTY-FOUR

The lodge stood starkly in front of us, looking largely unscathed. A few of the globe lights leading up to it had broken glass, and the gravel path was looking very spoilt by the weeds that had found a way to push their way through. In some places the dandelions were of quite an impressive height and gave a good display of pretty yellow. I was glad to see the Japanese knotweed had not spread to this part of the resort.

Sam kicked the door down to allow us entry. Inside was just the same as when I last left it. I was surprised to see it was all still fully furnished. Even the TV still hung on the wall.

Danny sat on the black leather sofa and lifted his foot up onto the coffee table. I could see his swollen ankle bulging, and I wondered how he managed to keep his shoe on.

'I'm just going to rest here a minute. See if you can find the way in.'

I nodded and led Sam and Greg to what was Lisa's bedroom. I tentatively opened the door. Nervous someone, even Lisa, might be behind it. To my relief, no one was there. I checked the bathroom just to be sure, before pointing out the mirror to the other two.

Greg looked astonished. 'Wow. That's the doorway? That is cleverly disguised.'

After admiring the craftsmanship, he removed the latches and revealed the secret compartment.

'I can't get this trapdoor open,' said Greg, after a few minutes of frustrated attempts to open it. 'We're going to need the gear.'

I left Sam and Greg to it and joined Danny in the lounge.

'How's it feeling?' I asked.

Danny shook his head. 'Very sore.'

'Do you think you can carry on? Maybe you should rest up here and let us search.'

Danny looked horrified at the suggestion.

'I'll be fine.'

Just then, Greg poked his head round the door.

'You two coming? We've got it open. You better hurry; Sam's already gone down through the trapdoor.'

'Oh, for God's sake. Can he not just wait two minutes for anything?' I said, annoyed. The question, of course, was rhetorical.

The descent was easy enough. A metal staircase, dimly lit by strategically placed lamps, took us down deep underground. I could feel the temperature dropping as we stepped lower and lower. Eventually, we stepped onto solid ground, and we began to make our way along the narrow cave-like corridor. The space was limited, making me feel very claustrophobic, and I had to duck several times to avoid low-hanging parts of the cave roof.

We had to walk in single file, with Sam leading, followed by myself, Greg and then Danny struggling along at the back.

Sam stopped abruptly and I almost walked straight into the back of his rucksack that he had on his back. He slipped the rucksack off his shoulders, fumbling around trying to retrieve something.

'Here. Take these.'

He handed me a torch, and then another. I passed both back to the guys behind and then took another one from Sam for myself.

We continued for a short part before the cave began to open out and the corridors got wider and the ceilings got higher. I noticed the ground had become wet underfoot and the walls were moist. Small stalactites and stalagmites were visible from the cave walls, and the place was beginning to feel more and more magical.

'Wow. Look at this,' said Sam in amazement.

As I took my next step forward, the cave opened right out into a huge cavern. It truly was amazing and very dramatic. All four of us stood looking in awe all around us. I shone my torch over to the right and saw an almighty stalagmite, standing several feet high. I walked over to it and arched my neck back to look up at its very highest point. It must have been twice as tall as me and as I strained to arch my neck even further and look even higher, I saw the mass of stalactites hanging just above it from the cave roof. For a moment,

I forgot the reason we were there. It was like I was a tourist, out for the day with my friends, exploring a local historical cave.

'Well, we have a choice, people. Any preference?'

Sam shone the torch at three specific points in order to highlight them to us, and they all looked worth investigating.

Danny purposely made his way over to one of them, seemingly ignoring the other two and strangely suddenly overcoming his impediment. I watched with interest as he studied the large wrought iron gate that blocked the way to a corridor leading off from the right of the cavern. I wondered what it was that drew him like a magnet to this one and made him so easily dismiss the others. Greg seemed more interested in the beauty of the stalagmites as he ran his hands delicately over them and studied them in detail. Sam simply watched Danny from afar, like a tiger lying in wait and preparing itself to pounce when Danny made his next move.

I joined Danny to see what it was that was so compelling. I could see a long corridor stretching out beyond the gates. It was unusually lit by a red glow. I could not see where the light source was coming from, but it must have been from a strong light at the far end that was emitting the light back up the corridor towards us. The light was enough to enable me to see there was a series of these gates all along the corridor, very similar to the constructs of controlling internal prisoner movement between sections of a prison. The gate that we stood in front of looked to be the biggest and thickest of them all. Danny was staring, as if wonderstruck, at one of the signs hanging from it.

It read, 'Unit 74 – IRVIN', in bold black letters.

Underneath hung a second sign, conveying words of a nature that was becoming altogether a familiar occurrence: 'Restricted Area. Authorised Personnel Only'.

The next sentence below was in much smaller letters, as if it was of less importance than the words that preceded it, and yet to me it was the most paramount piece of information.

'Warning. Extreme Danger to Life. Do not cross this point unless authorised to do so'.

Sam, who had most probably grown impatient from a lack of any decision to proceed, had now joined us and was rattling the gate.

The lock broke easily, presumably weakened by decay, and the gate only required a gentle push by Sam to swing open.

In a blind panic, I grabbed Sam harshly by the arm to prevent him from entering. He looked narked at my reaction.

'Have you not read the sign?'

'What?' Sam snapped.

'The one that spells out our possible deaths if we enter. Bloody hell, Sam, are you always this cavalier?'

Sam briefly scanned the signage and it apparently had little effect on making any change to his attitude. He strode straight through and on to the next set of gates. I refused to cross the threshold and instead stayed with Danny, who was still studying the sign. I found his level of interest and the length of time he had been staring at it rather unsettling.

'Does that sign mean anything to you, Danny?' I asked, trying to keep one eye still on Sam.

'Maybe.'

I noticed Sam was struggling to open the next set of gates and I relaxed a little.

'Maybe? Maybe what exactly?'

'Jeez, what was that?' shouted Sam.

Startled, I quickly turned my attention back to Sam. He had ducked to the floor with his hands over his head, as if protecting himself from something above.

'What? Are you all right?'

I was panicking again even though I could not see any danger.

Sam slowly raised himself upright, nervously looking about him as if he expected something to swoop down and attack him. Cautiously, he walked backwards, making his way back down the corridor towards us.

'What was it?' asked Danny.

'I don't know. Something moving around on the cave roof above me.' He sounded shaken, and I think this was the first time I had witnessed Sam's vulnerability.

'Was it a bat?' I asked. That seemed the most likely explanation.

'I guess so.'

Sam's answer did not sound convincing.

'What else could it be?' I was feeling quite scared.

Greg had now joined us. He had taken a small step past the gate and into the corridor, shining his torch all along the cave walls and roof. He moved the light along slowly, trying to root out what, if anything, was in there.

'Wait, go back,' said Danny suddenly, with an air of excitement in his voice.

I could feel the hairs on the back of my neck standing up as Greg slowly moved the torch back over the area he had just traced. Then I saw it. I was not sure what it was, but it was definitely not a bat.

The closest thing I could think of it resembling was a ray fish. Except it was clinging to a cave wall rather than a seabed.

'What the hell is that?' said Greg, taking a step backwards so he was now the right side of the gate.

He immediately swung the gate back closed so as to put a barrier between us and it. The sound of the gate swinging shut seemed to frighten it, and it slithered across the rock face before disappearing through a crevice. Its sudden and quick movement made me jump, literally. I stumbled backwards several steps and squealed like a mouse.

'I don't know what that was,' said Greg, 'but I don't think we should be going down that way.'

Danny looked intrigued and as if he would beg to differ.

'There is a doorway over the other side of the cavern. It's locked but I might be able to get it open with the crowbar. Maybe we should check that out.'

Sam needed little persuasion from Greg and headed straight over. We all followed, although Danny lingered momentarily longer, as if in two minds, before eventually joining us.

I was rather nervy as I stood waiting for us to commit yet another breaking and entering violation. I needlessly cowered several times, having convinced myself one of those things was crawling along the cave ceiling right above my head, but it was just my eyes creating their own fabrication.

The sign above the door simply read 'Control Room'. It was a very plain grey door with a matching grey frame blending it into the cave wall. There were no warnings of restricted access or threats to life, although this did not lessen the feeling of fear I held of what might be behind it once they finally managed to break the door down.

There was a large crack that reverberated around the cavern as Greg prised open the door. I noticed Sam uncharacteristically held back and let Greg enter first. Maybe his last encounter had affected him more than he had let on.

The room inside proved to be just as plain and grey. The walls were man-made, having been erected inside the cave itself to form a perfect square room. Very little now occupied the room, but I imagined at one time it housed expensive technical equipment and maybe operated as some kind of control hub. All that remained now were a few empty grey desks and odd bits of other office furniture dotted about. I ran my finger through the thick dust along one of the desks, noticing several stained coffee mug rings and various scratches and markings made through wear and tear. Sam was rifling through the drawers of filing cabinets, and Greg was searching through desk drawers and waste paper bins.

'There is nothing in any of these,' said Sam, slamming the last drawer shut.

'No, I can't find anything, either,' replied Greg.

'Well, I guess if they have abandoned this place then it was unlikely they were going to leave any evidence behind,' said a despondent Danny, who had sat himself on one of the office chairs while the search commenced.

'We may as well search this last bit of the cavern,' said Sam. 'There is another corridor leading off the far end. I had a quick peek earlier and it looks to be quite a long and wide corridor leading further into the cave. Might be something of interest down there.'

'You lot, go ahead. I'm going to wait here for you. My ankle is killing me and I'm going to have to rest it for a bit.'

'I don't think that's a good idea,' I said, horrified at the thought of leaving someone down here on their own.

'I'll be fine, don't worry about me. Go ahead.'

I looked at Sam and Greg for backup, but none was forthcoming.

'I don't think we should split up,' I protested.

Danny waved us on, directing us to go on through the door. Sam and Greg left the room while I hung back. I considered staying put and keeping him company, but curiosity had got the better of me. Besides, I always felt compelled to follow Sam.

'Are you sure?'

'Yeh yeh, I'll be fine. Go on.'

I quickened my step in order to catch up with the other two, who had already pressed on ahead.

'Guys, can we be quick about this? I don't want to leave Danny for too long on his own,' I pleaded, once I had caught up with them. It felt too much like a classic horror movie scene where the person left on their own would inevitably meet some terrible fate.

The cave continued to display its wonders as we travelled even further. This part of the cave was much more open, and it was difficult not to be distracted by all the spectacular rock formations. Eventually, it opened up into another cavern, except this chamber was much bigger than the previous one. In the very centre lay a rock pool and as I got closer to it I could see the water was absolutely crystal clear. I stood staring at it, mesmerised by its beauty, until I was interrupted by a tap on the shoulder.

'There are quite a few rooms off here, so I think it's better if we split up to search each one.'

Greg then pre-empted what I was about to say. 'I know it means we'll each be on our own for a bit, but we're all in the same vicinity and you said you wanted to get back to Danny as quick as possible, so this is going to help speed things up. OK?'

'OK,' I replied, not really feeling particularly OK about it at all.

I searched four of the rooms in total. I'm not sure exactly how many the others covered each, but it must have been at least equal to, if not greater than, my share. The area we were in looked likely to have been used as a hospital or maybe for medical research. As before, the rooms had been stripped of most equipment and articles, but there was enough remaining to give the general gist.

The first room I searched resembled an operating theatre with its operating table in the middle of the room anchored to the floor, a cracked porcelain basin attached to the side of the wall and many medical cupboards along the walls of the room. There was nothing of interest to be found here. The next two rooms I took for labs. They still had some scientific equipment left on the workbenches and in some of the cupboards. Several glass vials had smashed on the floor, and I was careful to avoid treading on any of the broken glass. I smiled when I spotted a Bunsen burner, invoking memories of my school chemistry lessons. Once again, neither of these rooms really contained anything of significance. The final room I searched appeared to be an office, or maybe a staffroom. There was a large black leather sofa, not dissimilar to the one in the lodge above ground, and an old dirty coffee maker on a table nearby.

After searching the white cupboards on the walls, where I found only mugs and crockery, I moved on to the dozen or so filing cabinets lining one of the walls. Most were empty. A couple still had their file dividers and I became overexcited when I found one of them actually had paperwork in. But as I flicked through the contents, I was soon overcome with disappointment when I found them to be only blank sheets and empty envelopes.

I ran my fingers through my hair and gave a long sigh in despair. I was about to move on to search the next room, when I spotted something poking out under the end filing cabinet. From this angle, all I could see was the very corner of a white piece of paper, but as I got closer and crouched down to retrieve it, I could see that there was a great deal more to be found. Tucked behind the cabinet were reams of paper that looked to have accidentally fallen down the back and had been long forgotten. I inched the filing cabinet far enough away from the wall to allow all the paper to fall to the floor and give me enough space to gather them up. I felt a sensation of sudden thrill when I realised that these papers were not blank and contained plenty of writing. I gave a quick scan of the pages; many of them looked to be highly scientific and beyond my comprehension. However, I saw enough to know they were worth hanging on to as I spotted more than once the word JAHL.

I came charging out of the room, desperate to find the others. Sam was sat on a rock in the middle of the chamber, and Greg was just coming out of another room.

'Nothing in there,' he said, sounding very fed up. 'That's the last room.'

'You got something?' asked Sam, looking quizzically at what I was holding.

'Yes. Yes, I think I have,' I replied, waving it around in excitement like I had a winning lottery ticket in my hand.

'Well, what is it?'

'I'm not sure, scientific papers about the JAHL project.'

'OK. Well, it's something.'

'We can look at this properly later. Can we get back to Danny first?' I was really worried we had left him for far too long on his own.

'Sure,' said Greg, and led the way back.

To my complete and utter relief, Danny was exactly where we had left him, still sat in the chair.

Without thinking, I ran up to him and gave him a hug. He did not return the affection. Embarrassed by his flinching, I quickly released my hold and backed away. I could see in the corner of my eye Sam grinning, making me feel even more uncomfortable.

'How's the ankle?' I asked, trying to deflect away the unwarranted attention.

Danny was nonplussed by my question, and instead threw me one of his own.

'Did you manage to find anything?'

'Oh yes,' suddenly remembering the papers I had wedged under my arm. 'I found these in one of the rooms down there.'

I handed them over to Danny, who began to cast his keen eyes over them. He remained silent for quite a while and I worried he was not impressed.

'OK, well, this looks like it could be useful. Let's make our way back to the surface and we can go over this in more detail later.'

Greg helped Danny up while Sam did his usual trick of shooting off as soon as he got wind we were ready to make a move. I held the door open to allow Danny and Greg through and then followed behind. Danny looked in real pain and struggled to walk unaided, so Greg acted as his crutch. As we made slow progress back through the cavern, I nervously looked about me, half expecting one of those creatures to fly down from the ceiling or crawl out from one of the rock faces. I felt a shiver down my spine as we began to pass the entrance to the Unit 74 corridor where we had encountered one before, and I really wished the guys would speed up a bit so we could get past it as soon as possible. If it wasn't for Danny and his invalidity, I would have chosen to run past and not dare look back.

Suddenly Danny came to a stop.

'Sorry, can we just stop for a minute.'

As he stood there wincing in pain, leaning heavily on Greg for support, I knew we had drawn right alongside the prison-style gates. I resisted turning my head to look directly at them, as if avoiding eye contact was the safe option, in the same way you should never gaze upon the face of Medusa. Danny, however, did not follow that protocol, and I watched him turn his head and give a long hard stare straight at them. The look on his face was disturbing, like he held some emotional attachment to them.

'OK, I'm ready, let's go,' he said, releasing his gaze before gingerly stepping forward.

I could resist no longer and was impelled to look.

The red glow that was emanating from deep within appeared much stronger than before, but that was not what shook me the most. I focused hard as I dared to believe what I was seeing. Each of the internal gates, as far as my eyes could see, was wide open. I felt the sudden rush of a need to get out of there as quickly as possible. I made a quick dash along the short distance Greg and Danny had put between us and alarmed them both as I came upon them.

'You all right?' Greg asked, with deep concern in his voice.

'Let's just get out of here, can we?' I begged, with my innermost thought focused on how on earth those gates had come to be opened. I just knew it had to be Danny, but I couldn't bear to think why. Even worse was the thought of why he had blatantly done it without our knowledge. This was reminiscent of Lisa's betrayal all over again. I was beginning to wonder if there was anyone I could actually trust. I hastened my speed, passed Danny and Greg and caught up with Sam.

'Hi.' Sam was surprised to see me and looked back behind me for the others.

'Hi. It's OK, they're coming. Just a bit slow with Danny's foot.'

Sam smiled, that reassuring smile that I had so greatly missed, and I felt my uneasiness lift.

CHAPTER TWENTY-FIVE

We travelled back to London that very same night. Miraculously, Danny and Greg had managed to get the car going although I doubt it was legally roadworthy. The idea of returning to London was instigated by Danny and as none of us opposed it, the decision was made. I was quite glad to leave the place as it was really starting to make my flesh crawl. The trip, for me, had served its main purpose and that was to discover its location and prove that it really existed. It helped to qualm my feelings of paranoia that I hadn't just dreamt the place up and, of course, it also affirmed its link to the JAHL project.

Sam and I stayed overnight at their flat. I got only very disturbed sleep. The sofa bed I was sleeping on was not particularly comfortable, and I suffered with nightmarish images of strange creatures crawling over the duvet cover.

The next day, I was feeling quite rundown. I mainly kept myself to myself while the others looked over the papers I had found and discussed what to do next. I began to wish Patricia was still around to sit with and chat to. I wondered what she was up to now and how she was getting on. I considered asking Fiona if she knew how she was but thought it was maybe not appropriate. In any case, she was, as always, head down in the books.

The buzzer sounded on the intercom. Danny looked up from his studying and frowned at the annoyance of being disturbed.

'Emma, can you see who that is?'

'Sure.'

My only duties now seemed to be making the tea and answering the door, making me feel rather insignificant. I wondered if that was how Patricia felt.

'Hello?' I enquired.

'Hi, got a parcel here for you that needs signing for.'

'Oh right, yes, sure. Come on up.'

I turned to Danny to let him know who his visitor was, but he was obviously disinterested as he was head down and lost in his work.

There was a knock on the flat door and I opened it to a rather large and rotund man. He handed me the parcel, which I fervently took from him, and I signed the paperwork with a scrawl that barely resembled my signature.

He grunted as he left, which I took for a goodbye, and closed the door behind him.

I realised that I hadn't even checked the name of whom the parcel was actually for and hastily read the name tag, fearing the parcel wasn't even meant for anyone here. I breathed a sigh of relief when I saw it was for Danny. I placed it down on a side table, deciding it was best not to disturb him, but as I did so, my eyes fixated on the addressee name. 'To Mr Danny Irvin'. Irvin, for some reason, was ringing bells in my head. Where did I know that name from? It didn't take long for it to come to me, and it made me feel queasy as the realisation hit me.

I stewed for many hours on the information I had accidently uncovered. I almost convinced myself it was pure coincidence, but the reality was that it was highly improbable. At one point, I got tantalisingly close to broaching the subject with Danny, but it was trumped by a more urgent topic that needed discussion on what our next move was.

The contents of the papers I had found were highly scientific and unintelligible to anyone in the group. Although I was surrounded by very bright university graduates, none were well versed in the subjects of biology or chemistry, and therefore a lot of the text was beyond their understanding. There was, however, one very useful piece of information it supplied, and that was the name of the person who headed the project: Anthony Haywood, Head of Program. The group had spent many hours attempting to locate him before eventually finding he was retired and residing in Texas, USA. He was the person we would attempt to visit and extract information from. Volunteers to actually travel to America were few and far between. It was interesting to see the energy and enthusiasm poured into the research task compared to the complete lack of it when required to act upon. I sensed that interest amongst the group was waning. I was never convinced of how interested Fiona and Teddy were, even from the beginning. They treated it more like a theoretical piece of coursework for university. Greg was worried about the prospect of losing his job, and given that he had been fired from his previous one, he couldn't afford a repeat. Although his discipline was Computer Technology, finding employment had proved difficult with a lack of reference, and so he now worked as a chef in a London restaurant. He had already missed a busy weekend shift for our trip to Roseville. Asking for even more time off was not an option. Even Danny, who had been by far the most eager and enthusiastic of the group and really the leader, seemed to be losing interest, and his previous high energy and drive had all but disappeared. His excuse was he had no valid passport as it had expired but, to be honest, his injury alone was probably enough to prevent him from being able to travel. That left only me and Sam, and I automatically ruled him straight out. The likelihood of him carrying a passport on his person seemed a ridiculous thought, and for one horrible moment I thought I would have to do this alone. But, to my astonishment, apparently that was the one thing he treasured and always kept with him. His explanation was someone as fancy-free as him never knew when he might want to take off somewhere. He had a point. After all, I knew he was well travelled, but it was still hard to believe. Either way, we both seemed to have the means and also had no work commitment issues to speak of. I was not due to return to work for another week, and Sam treated his job like some casual affair that he could drop in on as and when he felt like. So, by default, we were the ones to travel.

We travelled the next day from Heathrow, but not before I finally plucked up the courage to confront Danny.

'Did you see I left that parcel that came for you on the table over there?'

'Yes, I did, thanks. It's just a new hard drive for my computer. The other one went pop.'

'Actually, Danny, I did notice something with the name on the parcel.' I felt my throat drying up with nerves and swallowed to help lubricate it. 'Your surname is Irvin.'

'That's right, yes.'

'That's the same name we saw in the caverns on one of the signs.'

I watched for his reaction and I detected uneasiness.

'Is it?'

I raised my eyebrows at his attempt to dismiss the fact.

'I also noticed from those papers I found there is a science co-ordinator listed in the name of Gerald Irvin.'

He had no reply to that other than to drop eye contact and shift uneasily.

'That's quite a coincidence, don't you think?'

'Yeh, I suppose.'

I was beginning to get quite annoyed at his lack of responses. He was obviously trying to hide something. My annoyance fuelled my confidence and I began to question him more aggressively, determined to get the truth out of him.

'Danny. Your surname is Irvin. You are pursuing with quite some interest a project that happens to have a highly ranking scientist on it with the exact same surname. I also know you were so entirely engrossed with that corridor that was carrying the name of Irvin that you entered it while we weren't around.'

Danny looked quite astonished at my directness and looked particularly surprised when I made the last point.

'How did you know I entered Unit 74?'

'Because after watching you stare at it as if you were spellbound, I noticed the internal gates had been opened when we had most definitely left them shut.'

I waited for an answer as he shuffled nervously.

'Well?' I was growing impatient and was determined he wasn't going to wriggle his way out of this one.

'Gerald Irvin is my father,' he finally said. He looked relieved, as if a big weight had lifted from his shoulders. 'Look, I'm sorry I didn't say anything.'

'And why didn't you say anything? That's quite a major piece of information to leave out.'

'I don't know. I guess I was worried if you knew I had a personal link to Roseville then you wouldn't be so keen to help me find it.'

'Do they know?' referring to the rest of the group.

'No.'

'Did Patricia know?'

'No.'

I began to realise now that I had been used. The keen interest that Danny had in locating Roseville was not being driven by a desire to help me. It was purely for his own gain. I was the pawn in all of this.

'Where is your father now?'

'I don't know. He went missing a long time ago and he is presumed dead.'

'I'm sorry.'

'He was last seen entering the Unit 74 corridor, but he never came back out.'

At least now I understood why he was so mesmerised by that corridor and why he had entered it.

'Emma, you ready? We are going to miss our flight at this rate.'

Sam had appeared with bags in tow. I looked at my watch. He was right. If we didn't leave now, we would likely miss our plane.

'We'll talk more about this when I get back,' I said sternly to Danny, before grabbing my bags and heading out the door with Sam.

'What was all that about?' asked Sam.

'Another revelation about this weird and wonderful world I seem to have found myself in.'

Sam looked intrigued.

'I'll tell you about it later. Let's catch this plane.'

CHAPTER TWENTY-SIX

The trip to America was quite an experience for me. This was the first time I had ever flown or even been abroad. I did not find flying particularly enjoyable and was glad when we were firmly on American soil. According to Sam, I looked petrified on both landing and take-off, although I am sure he was exaggerating.

We caught a bus from the airport to take us to the town where Anthony Haywood resided. It was during this journey that Sam and I discussed the earlier conversation I had with Danny.

'Blimey. That's a turn-up for the books. I hadn't even thought he might actually have a link to the JAHL project. What a sneaky guy. He should have told us.'

'Yes, he should have. I have to admit my estimation of him has gone right down.'

I'd always quite liked Danny. Yes, he was extreme sometimes, but I always thought his obsession was driven by curiosity and a keenness to learn about a subject he just happened to be passionate about. I thought government conspiracies was his chosen hobby and not something that he was so personally attached to, although, in hindsight, his drive and sheer obsession on the subject were so great that maybe I should have suspected. The revelation, however, had a detrimental effect on how I now felt about him, and I was glad it was Sam accompanying me now and not Danny.

'You know what else I find weird? Apparently, no one else knew about it, either. You'd think Greg at least would have known.'

'Not necessarily. Why would you think that?'

'Because he was the one that found out about the JAHL project. Remember? Some government colleague of his blurted it out when he was drunk.'

Sam thought about it for a moment.

'Yeh, you're right. Oh, I don't know. I've never trusted Greg anyway. Wouldn't be surprised if he knows about it as well.'

'Well, Danny said he doesn't.'

'Well, Danny has already lied to us once, so we can't really trust anything he says.'

'True. But why would he lie about that? I've already found the connection out. So what does it matter if he knew or any of the others knew as well?'

'Protecting his mates. I don't know.'

Sam looked as if he was growing bored of the conversation and so I dropped it and stayed silent for the remainder of the trip.

'Hello. Can I help you?' asked the greying gentleman who answered the door.

'Hi. Are you Anthony Haywood?' I asked hopefully.

'I am. Who are you?'

'Oh. Um … I'm Emma and this is Sam. We have come over from England to see you.'

He frowned and kept his hand firmly on the inside door handle. I was expecting him to slam it shut on us at any moment, and so I smiled as sweetly as I could in the hope it would encourage him to continue talking to us.

'See me about what?' He was firm but still with an air of curiosity in his tone.

'The JAHL project.'

His expression did not change and he continued looking at me, briefly switching his eyes over to Sam before returning his focus to me.

'What did you say your name was?'

I was taken aback by his question and took a moment to reply.

'Oh, umm, Emma.'

'Emma what?'

'Maynard.'

'Well, in that case, you'd better come in.'

His home was comfortable and well kept. He offered us a seat on a deep red luxurious-looking sofa. I settled my feet on the deep shaggy rug that lay just before us and fixed my gaze on the open fireplace, mesmerised by the dancing flames that were roaring so brightly.

He sat in a well-worn but sturdy armchair closer to the fire and waited for me to speak.

'Thank you for letting us come into your lovely home and talk to you.'

I waited for his reply, but he remained silent and expressionless. I couldn't tell if he was willing to talk to us or unhappy with our presence. As he had invited us in, I assumed he would at least have some discussion with us.

'As I said at the door, we've come over from England and wanted to find out more about the JAHL project.'

He still said nothing, although his eyes appeared soft and I felt no animosity.

'I know you originally headed up the project and so I was hoping you could fill in some blanks for me. I was one of the test subjects, you see.'

I hesitated to continue while I monitored his reaction at my announcement.

'I know you were, Emma.'

'Oh, OK.' Relieved that he had finally spoken.

'Yes, you are right. I did head up the project from its inception in 1975 until 1978, the point at which it was closed down. I remember you as a young child. I knew your father, Theodore Maynard.'

His confession to knowing my father startled me. I swallowed hard before speaking.

'How did you know my father?'

He raised his eyebrows, clearly expecting me to already know that.

'He worked with me. He was on the project.'

The revelation knocked me for six. I could see Sam watching me out of the corner of my eye.

'I guess you didn't know that.'

I slowly shook my head and closed my eyes in dismay, before finally finding my voice again.

'Did you know that my father died? A long time ago now.'

'Yes, I had heard. I was very sorry to hear that. He was a good man. The last time I saw him, it was in the mid-eighties. I came to your house to say goodbye before leaving for America. You must have been about nine or ten years old. I remember seeing you playing in the garden on a swing and you waved to me.'

I couldn't recollect that memory and I felt slightly bad for it. Anthony spoke to me warmly, as if he knew me personally and we had a connection. Yet to me this was like the first time I had ever met him.

'I'm confused. My father was part of the JAHL project, I was part of the JAHL project, and yet he didn't adopt me until ... when would it have been?'

I pondered for a moment, trying to establish the dates in my head. I couldn't work out how it all fitted together. It did not make sense to me.

'It must have been 1983. You said the JAHL project was abandoned well before that and I was in care for years. Does that mean he specifically sought me out? Why would he want to adopt me so long after the project had ended?'

This was not going how I expected. I had come here to seek answers on details on the JAHL project, not about my family and how I came to be adopted. I'd chosen to block all those types of questions out long ago and had come to accept it as it was.

'The main ethos of the project may have been abandoned, but the monitoring of the test subjects continued.'

'So I was watched for all those years?'

'To a degree. You were kept in a reasonably controlled environment that allowed us to keep a minimal eye on you. This was a risky experiment, groundbreaking. We could never be one hundred per cent sure what the effect would be.'

'So, I've just been a lab rat for my entire life with scientists or whoever watching me?'

Even Sam was now shifting uncomfortably in his seat, and it took a lot more effort to unnerve him than anyone I knew.

'Maybe it would be easier if I started at the beginning and just told you how it all unfolded and how you came to be adopted. It might put it in context for you to better understand.'

I couldn't see how any further explanation would make it any easier for me, and I didn't believe I could ever come to really understand how this all came to be.

'OK,' I replied dubiously.

'In 1975, the JAHL project was formed and a team of highly skilled scientists and like-minded people were put together to conduct an experiment. An experiment that was a first, that would push boundaries beyond anything we had tried before and that was deemed highly risky and, of course, highly controversial. Your father, who was highly regarded and an expert in his field, was one of those in the team, a team that was led by me. I am not going to tell you the details of the experiment. It is highly classified and it is not in anyone's best interests to divulge this information, but I suspect that you already know enough to know what was involved.'

That, of course, was not true. I didn't know much at all about what was involved, but I decided at this point not to interrupt him.

He paused for breath. The fire suddenly popped and crackled, as if to interrupt him with its own commentary. He was only momentarily distracted, before he turned his attention back to me and continued.

'A site was located to facilitate the experiment. An already well-established government base that was already well equipped and had the necessarily facilities available.'

'Roseville Resort,' interrupted Sam.

Anthony frowned at him, possibly in annoyance.

'The place in Devon, disguised as a holiday resort. Got lots of underground rooms and stuff.'

Anthony's frown subsided, and he instead arched his eyebrows with an expression of surprise.

'Well, yes, it is in Devon, and most of it is concealed underground. I've never heard of it referred to as Roseville or a holiday resort.'

'Well, it is now,' stated Sam, as if he was an authority on the subject.

'Well, maybe. But certainly not back in the seventies. Back then, it was off-limits to the public. Only government staff with the right clearance were allowed on site. All staff, along with their immediate families, lived on site in lodge-style homes above ground. Only the actual employees had authorisation to enter the underground facilities. Family members were heavily vetted and were not permitted to enter the underground facility. In fact, they were kept completely in the dark about the actual nature of work that was going on literally right beneath their feet.'

'Jeez, sounds like a concentration camp. Were they prisoners?' asked Sam.

'No. Not at all. They were free to come and go as they pleased, but as the majority of amenities were provided directly within the complex, there was often little reason to venture out. There was an in-house school, a few shops, leisure facilities, etc., and this in turn provided jobs for many of the non-government family members. Although they were not restricted to obtaining employment or using other amenities outside of the facility, the preference was they remained in-house.'

I flinched at his attempts to normalise it, as if they led ordinary lives just like anyone else, when to me it all sounded very underhand and far from normal. In fact, I would go as far as to say verging on a cult regime.

'Once the team was in place, we arranged for the …' Unusually, for someone who appeared so articulate, Anthony stumbled over his next words. '… the, shall we say, unusual beings to be transported to our base, where they were placed in a secure unit deep underground.'

'Was this unit called Unit 74 – IRVIN?'

Anthony looked surprised by my comment.

'Yes,' he confirmed with an astonished tone, 'although at the time it was only referred to as Unit 74, a nod to the year the beings were first utilised. Irvin was added at a much later date in recognition of the loss of the main scientist who was in charge of looking after the unit.'

I glanced over at Sam and our eyes met. He stayed silent but I could still tell, just by the look in his eyes, that he wanted me to ask the burning question that was already on my lips.

'What were these beings that were kept in Unit 74?'

Anthony appeared discomfited by the question and did not immediately respond.

'I am not sure I can really answer that.'

'Were they from this planet?'

Anthony, clearly stunned by my remark, took a deep intake of breath before replying.

'I wasn't involved with this part of the project, nor was it my concern or even responsibility. So I do not know the origins of the beings, but I do know that they were not natural. My assumption was that they had mutated due to genetic experimentation. The thought of them originating from somewhere other than our planet had never crossed my mind. That is all I can tell you. I cannot discuss anything more about them.'

It was a bold statement and I wanted to push him more, but I knew he was adamant. Even if he was covering it up and did know more, I didn't think I would have any chance of getting him to reveal anything further about them. Instead, I decided to press him about Danny's father.

'What happened to Irvin?'

Anthony gave a deep sigh, lowered his head and stared pensively into the rug.

'Gerald was involved in a very serious and unfortunate incident. It was just after the JAHL project had ceased. I was no longer there and neither was your father, but some of the team stayed on to continue with other projects. Unit 74 had been growing in capacity over time and was being used to house many different creatures that had been transported from other various government installations. I remember Irvin raising concerns, even during the JAHL project, that capacity was being overstretched and that it was dangerous to keep multiple species in such close proximity, but the higher powers chose to ignore the warnings.

'Eventually, the inevitable happened. A situation occurred whereby supposedly something escaped from its container, and then it all escalated when it managed to free other species. A team, which included Gerald, had to go in and try and contain the situation. Eventually, it was brought under control, but in the midst of the chaos they did not realise that Gerald had gone missing. An extensive search of the caverns was made, but he was never found. He is presumed dead.'

Anthony looked solemn; his eyes were now staring at the fire. Suddenly, snapping out of his trance, he got up to add more logs to it.

'Unit 74, which then became Unit 74 – IRVIN, lasted only a few more months after that. Apparently, similar incidents were occurring all too frequently, and it was becoming too dangerous. It was decommissioned, everything was moved out to other sites and so the demise of the whole government facility soon followed.'

'When you say everything was moved out, I'm not quite so sure,' Sam quipped.

'What?' snapped Anthony. It was becoming increasingly obvious that Sam was really starting to grate on him, and I worried he would soon be thrown out.

'I'm just saying that I personally am not convinced they actually cleared it completely out. Maybe left a few behind?'

'Why would you think that?' The tone of Anthony's voice gave the impression he thought Sam an idiot.

'Well, because I saw something in there. I don't know what it was, but it didn't look like anything from this planet.'

'You've been in Unit 74?'

'Uh, yeh, did we not mention that?'

'No, you didn't,' he said firmly, and looking very intense. 'What did you see exactly?'

Sam let out a sigh. 'I can't tell you exactly; it moved really quickly across the walls and over the ceiling. I didn't stick around for very long.'

Anthony looked long and hard at Sam, studying him as he tried to deduce Sam's revelation.

Eventually, he reverted to focusing his attention back on me.

'And did you enter Unit 74?'

'No.'

Sam gave me an accusing look, suggesting I was lying.

'I didn't actually enter the unit,' I said defensively, 'but I did stand at the entrance and had a look in.'

'And did you see anything?'

I thought for a moment, trying to remember what I had seen. With the passing of time, the images did not seem as vivid as they once were.

'Maybe.'

Sam looked astonished at my reply.

'What do you mean, maybe? You screamed and ran a mile after seeing it.'

'Well, yeh, I think I did see something. But I'm not sure.'

Sam looked disappointed with me, and Anthony was still trying to suss us out.

'Look, can we just forget about Unit 74 for a minute and get back to the JAHL project and how I came to be adopted?'

I was becoming frustrated that we were digressing from the real point of me being here.

Anthony looked like he was contemplating a further question, and I was sure he was eager to find out more about what we had discovered at the unit, but he managed to relent.

'Over the course of the next few weeks, the subjects that we were going to experiment on were brought in.'

I hated the way he referred to me and my fellow compatriots. Dehumanising us before the experiment had even begun.

'They ranged from newly born to a few months old. I think you were one of the older ones, about three months old maybe.'

The fire cracked and spat out a cinder of wood onto the hearth, making me jump.

'Once initial medical tests had been run on you all to determine your overall health and genetic makeup, the experiment began. The group was divided up into three groups and each group was administered with varying degrees of doses of DNA extracted from the Unit 74 beings. The first group was given substantial doses, the second group was given slightly less and the final group was given minimal amounts.'

I cast my mind back to the document Danny had shown me that first night we met them in London and remembered reading the list of names divided out under the three groups A, B and C. Mine was under Group A, and I wondered which group that fell under. I presumed the higher dosage one. I was acutely aware that, apart from myself, everyone else in Group A was long dead, and it would make sense that the ones receiving the higher doses would be the first to succumb. Anthony had briefly paused speaking as he watched me deep in thought, until he saw my eyes had refocused and I was once again listening properly.

'For the first few months, there appeared to be no ill effects, and all the subjects integrated well into our little community. However, as time went on, it became quite noticeable that the children's behaviour was fast deteriorating. In the early days, it was passed off as the natural development of children. The effects of growth spurts, the attempt to try and push the boundaries, the terrible-twos phenomenon, whatever excuse we could come up with to keep us in denial from the unbearable truth. But things got more and more out of control, and it could no longer be attributed to natural child development.

'What kind of things?' I asked nervously, remembering again the document I had read from Danny about the terrible crimes that had been committed by many of them in their adulthood.

'Extreme tantrums, often volatile and sometimes violent behaviour. Shocking behaviour to see in any single child, but horrendous to experience amongst the entire group. I distinctly remember one child had somehow managed to obtain a knife from the cafeteria and threatened to use it. She hadn't even reached three years old, and yet here she was brandishing a knife.' I gulped and prayed that I was not that three-year-old.

'She was, of course, easily overpowered, but it was a harrowing experience and one that firmly called into question the continuation of the experiment. Naturally, as head of the project, the heat soon turned on me. Unrest developed amongst many of the staff, and some of the braver ones were beginning to find their voice. Understandably, the overriding opinion was that the experiment should be halted immediately and the children should no longer be part of the community and instead be locked up for our and their safety.'

'My God, that is absolutely awful. You locked them up, like prisoners, when you were the ones that caused them to be like this? You're the ones that should be locked up.' Sam wasn't holding back; he was giving off more heat than the fire.

'You make me sick,' he barked, as he abruptly got up and stormed across the room, before finally slamming the front door behind him.

Anthony made no move, although I was sure I detected remorse in his expression. I hoped he felt remorse.

'Was I locked up?' I was barely able to whisper the question.

'No. None of you were locked up. I refused to follow that course of action, against much opposition.'

I breathed a sigh of relief and relaxed a little.

'A few difficult weeks passed but gradually our scientists began to find that the non-native matter was becoming harder to trace within the children and, with it, their bad and aggressive behaviour began to wane. After a few more weeks, we could find no trace in any of the children, and the opinion was that the matter must have broken down, unable to survive within a human person and thereby completely eradicated. The project continued for a few more months, but with no evidence of its existence, along with the children returning to normal behaviour, the project was deemed a failure and was soon wound down.'

'And what happened to all the children? I assume they were put into care homes, like me?'

'There was much debate about what should happen to them all. Some were adamant that they should be allowed to return to normal society, while others were strongly opposed. They were fearful of what damage the children may have incurred and what they might be capable of.'

Anthony sighed heavily as he recalled the events, clearly uncomfortable with what had occurred.

'Eventually, we came to a consensus. We would still maintain some control and be able to monitor the children, but we would not keep them completely segregated from normal life. At least not at the beginning. It would be a gradual release into society before eventually releasing them completely from the programme.'

The fire was dying down and in danger of going out. I noticed the temperature in the room had decreased, and I was beginning to feel a chill in the air.

'So the JAHL project came to an abrupt end, and so too did my role. Operation Watchdog was launched, headed up by someone else on the outside but still including many of the original staff, who were simply transferred across to this new project. The hope was all the children could be adopted or fostered by anyone who was attached to the JAHL project. Some did volunteer and thereby some of the children were immediately placed into family homes and integrated into society quite quickly. But there were not enough volunteers, so an arrangement was made with some children's homes to take these "special" children in and not to allow them to be adopted as that was to be arranged strictly by the government only.'

'Were the children's homes not suspicious about this? Did they not ask questions?' I asked, confounded.

'Well, like I said, I was removed from the project at this point, so I don't know the exact details. I am sure specific ones were picked that were more likely to conform, shall we say, and not ask too many questions. I do know they were paid handsomely for their troubles.'

'To keep their mouths shut, you mean.'

I hung my head as if in shame. At least now I knew why I was so often looked over when prospective adoptive parents turned up and it took so long before I was eventually taken in.

'So that's what happened to me,' I said, slowly raising my head to meet Anthony's gaze. 'I was not allowed to be adopted until someone the government had approved came forward. That took years. I was stuck there for several years, deprived of any love or proper family life.'

'The government did not have many options to pick from; it was a very secret affair. Few fitted the criteria to be allowed in on the secret. Eventually, Theo decided to adopt you. I think they had wanted another child for a while but were struggling to conceive, and now age was against them. Obviously, this was a dilemma for them given your father's involvement with the project. He was all too aware of certain special children in need of adoption, ones that his employers had desperately asked for volunteers to adopt.'

'Was he paid to take me in? Like the children's homes were?'

Anthony looked at me softly and looked hesitant to reply.

'I am sure there were incentives to encourage people to adopt, yes.'

I stared at the fireplace. The fire had now completely gone out. I was feeling weary and cold.

'What happened to you?'

Anthony looked surprised at my question. I guess everything so far had really been about me and that he was not important to the story.

'I remained with the government, but I was transferred to a different project.'

'And what do you know about the new JAHL project now? Part two.'

'Nothing.'

'Nothing?' I found that unlikely.

'I was not aware that the project was in existence. As far as I knew, Operation Watchdog remained for a few years after, until that too was disbanded. Once every subject had been integrated back into society after showing no signs of harbouring any of the non-native matter during those years of monitoring, it was assumed they did not pose any sort of threat.'

'Well, in that case, it pains me to say that Operation Watchdog can also be deemed a completely failed project. They were wrong.'

Anthony looked aghast at my statement.

His expression was enough to make me believe he did not know anything about the resurrection of JAHL. Anthony had seemed like a warm and gentle character, but the truth was he was not just part of a very secretive and controversial project, one that pushed the boundaries of what is morally right, he was the man in charge. I could not help but feel anger towards him. He was, after all, responsible for what had happened to me. It was his fault and I could not forgive him.

I stood up to leave – there was nothing more to find out here – but not without first leaving a parting shot.

I looked him sternly in the eyes. 'We do pose a threat.'

CHAPTER TWENTY-SEVEN

The next day, we immediately flew back to London. I felt the journey here to be a big disappointment and largely a waste of time. I was not really sure what I truly expected; maybe I was searching for solace or some kind of salvation. Whatever it was, I found neither, only more hurt and unrest, although admittedly a few more pieces of the puzzle had been found.

Sam had tried to persuade me that we should stay a few more days, explore the place and enjoy ourselves. I made clear my indignation to his act of folly, and for once he listened and the idea was quickly quashed.

By the time we reached the London flat, it was very late into the evening and we were both exhausted. Our flight had been delayed by several hours and the London traffic had been murder. I was too embarrassed to ring the buzzer at such a late time, but Sam had no such qualms. As it turned out, everyone was still up, playing Monopoly and evidently fairly inebriated. To see Greg drunk was mildly amusing and not particularly surprising, but to see Fiona in such an intoxicated state was quite shocking, and Teddy was barely able to form a word.

'Emma!' Teddy bellowed, as he realised my presence. He came running towards me, arms flung open wide in preparation to embrace me. He made it only a few short steps before he tripped over Greg's outstretched legs and fell head first into the coffee table, knocking the Monopoly board flying. Fiona almost split her sides laughing so hard, and Greg was more annoyed at the game being spoilt.

'Bloody hell, Teddy, what you playing at? I was winning that game.'

I watched the scene before me in disbelief, not quite believing these were the same people I had left behind only a couple of days before. Fiona was still laughing uncontrollably, with her hair flailing all across her face. I couldn't remember ever seeing Fiona with her hair down, never mind it looking so wild. Teddy was sat on the floor, rubbing his head and looking very pale. I was worried he may be on the verge of being sick.

'Well, look at you crazy kids. And there was me thinking Monopoly was a boring game.' Sam's quip lightened Greg's mood and even he was now smiling. Greg headed to the fridge and grabbed himself and Sam a beer.

'You want one, Emma?'

'No.'

'Suit yourself.'

'Where's Danny?' I asked curiously.

'Dunno,' he answered, shrugging his shoulders and taking a sip of his beer.

'You don't know?' I said in frustration. I still had unfinished business with him.

'He's gone, packed his stuff just after you left for America.'

'Gone where? When's he coming back?'

'No idea. Not sure he is coming back.'

'Oh, for God's sake. This just gets better, doesn't it?'

Teddy could no longer hold it in and spewed all over the floor, setting Fiona off in hysterics again.

I could take no more and headed straight for the spare room, leaving the carnage behind me.

Naturally, I was the first to rise in the morning, everyone else inevitably still feeling the after-effects of the night before. I carried on regardless, making myself some breakfast and riding out the time till they returned to the land of the living. Sam was the next to surface, and it came as quite a comfort and relief to see him. He was wearing only his boxer shorts, and I found watching him ruffle his hands through his hair with his muscular torso exposed rather seductive.

'Morning,' he said, chirpier than I was expecting, although perhaps he had not had such ill effects from the night before as he had joined them much later in the day. The others would have been far more advanced in the amounts of consumed alcohol.

'Morning,' I replied, trying not to stare too hard at his finely tuned body.

He joined me at the breakfast table and stole a piece of toast from my plate.

'Oi.'

He gave me a cheeky grin and my heart melted.

'So what is the plan today?' he muttered in between munches.

I gave a deep sigh. 'I really don't know. I am not sure what else there is to do.'

I was feeling vulnerable and hoped Sam would give me some words of comfort, or perhaps a hug. Instead, he looked unconcerned and grabbed another slice from my plate.

'I'm going to have to go back to work the day after tomorrow, so I guess I need to make my way back home today really,' I said, with not much enthusiasm.

'Yeh, me too. I'll probably come back with you and stay at yours for the night if that's OK? Then I'll head off in the morning.'

'Yeh, of course, that's fine.' My enthusiasm suddenly returning.

'Cool. I'm going to have a shower. See you later.' And with no word of warning, he planted a kiss on my forehead before striding off, leaving me with a warm tingle inside.

'God, my head hurts.'

Greg had now appeared, not looking as fresh as Sam but at least fully clothed. I put the kettle on and retrieved some paracetamol from my handbag for him.

'Thanks. Any sign of Teddy and Fiona yet?'

'No. Well, apart from one brief sighting of Fiona rushing to and from the bathroom earlier this morning.'

Greg chuckled but that quickly turned to a grimace, before he delicately held his head, clearly in some pain.

'Sam and I are travelling back to Bath today.'

'Oh right.'

'Well, I need to get back to work. I only had the week off.'

'Yeh, yeh, sure.'

'You said last night that Danny has gone?'

'Yeh, we are not sure what is going on. He left in a bit of a hurry.'

'Is he coming back?'

'I don't know, I don't think he will be. He has packed up all his stuff. He hasn't got any belongings in his room.'

'Do you know why?'

'No. Well, I think it is something to do with this JAHL project. But I don't really understand the reasoning.'

'Yes, I think it is to do with the JAHL project. Danny has a closer connection to that project than I first realised.'

Greg looked at me in bafflement, and I genuinely believed he had no idea what I was talking about.

'He was one of the test subjects? His name wasn't listed.'

'No. He wasn't directly part of the experiment. His dad was a scientist on the project.'

'He never said anything to me about that. Are you sure?'

'Yes. He told me himself.'

Greg looked stunned.

'I think he has gone to look for him.'

'What, gone where? I thought his dad had died. A long time ago.'

'Unit 74, the underground tunnel we came across at Roseville.'

'What?'

I wasn't sure Greg's hangover was helping him with his mental capabilities and ability to really grasp the situation, so I spent a while explaining it all to him and eventually he cottoned on.

Sam and I took a late-afternoon train back. I never got to see Fiona and Teddy before leaving as they were still in a comatose state. At least I got to say my farewells to Greg and clear up some of the misunderstandings around Danny. Apparently, Danny had been spoon-feeding Greg with odd titbits of information to casually mention to Greg's ex-colleague in the hope of making him spill the beans. So although it felt like Charlie had been the one to bring forward the JAHL project revelation, he was in fact being steered towards it by these feeds of information. Sam, of course, who was not a fan of Greg, was not convinced. So any excuse to dislike him a little more was always pounced on.

The train journey was a pleasant one. The weather was good and sometimes the sun was so bright I had to shield my eyes from its rays penetrating through the glass windows. Sam and I chatted away quite happily about all sorts of things but never once referring to anything related to JAHL, and that was a very refreshing change. I couldn't remember the last time I felt this relaxed, and maybe the weight was starting to feel like it was lifting from my shoulders.

'So you're going to stay at mine tonight?' I asked as the train pulled up to the station.

'Yeh, if that's all right with you?'

'Sure,' I squeaked. Embarrassed by my high-pitched response, I quickly cleared my throat and repeated it again in a much lower and less excitable tone.

'What's your plan after tonight? I suppose you need to get back and work and ... sorry, I mean get back to work?' I was getting all tongue-tied and losing all credibility. I knew there was a good chance that this would be the last time I would see him, and the thought of this was making me wobble.

'Yep,' he replied emphatically as he flagged us down a taxi.

I felt downhearted by his answer, although it was no surprise.

CHAPTER TWENTY-EIGHT

I slept very little that night. Sam and I had spent a lovely evening together. A nice meal, a bottle of wine, plenty of merriment and wonderful companionship. There had been moments of obvious flirtation taking place, and it had been a real tussle on my emotions as I tried to figure out if it was nothing more than a bit of fun or if there was something more meaningful behind it. In the end, I avoided any complication by ending the night feigning tiredness and planting a simple kiss on his cheek, before retiring to my bedroom. Sam stayed up for another hour, watching TV, before I heard him trudge up the stairs and delicately close the spare bedroom door.

Now, here I was, all on my own in my quaint little cottage, breakfast untouched and with only the sound of the birds for company. Sam had left early to catch his train and I had only a few brief minutes to speak to him before he left. It was not enough to muster enough confidence to say I wanted to see him again. It wasn't even long enough to say a proper goodbye. All night, while I had been restless, I had thought over and over what it was I wanted to say, and I didn't even get the chance. I kicked the bin over in frustration and stomped around muttering derogatory comments about myself, before working my way up to a final act of grabbing the nearest object, which happened to be my favourite mug, and hurling it against the wall. As it smashed into smithereens, I stepped backwards in horror at my aggressive actions and fell into the sofa sobbing.

Once the sobbing had subsided and reduced to merely a snivel, I got myself off to the bathroom. Looking in the mirror that hung over the sink revealed just how dreadful I looked. It wouldn't be long till I had to leave for work, and I couldn't go looking like this. I splashed cold water several times over my face to try and lessen the puffiness and redness around my eyes. It seemed to be making little difference and I was getting more and more frustrated as time went by. As the frustration in me rose, I began to give myself a serious talking-to.

'Come on, Emma, pull yourself together.'

I grabbed a towel off the rail and vigorously rubbed it over my face. I am not sure what I thought that would achieve. If anything, it made it even redder. I repeated the action thrice more, each time with more pressure and vigour. Each time talking more and more sternly to myself. I was working myself up into a frenzy and by the time I had finished my ritual, the towel had been flung across the other side of the room and my knuckles hurt where I had punched the mirror. By this point, I had not a care in the world what I looked like and stormed off to work regardless.

When I arrived, thankfully, there was nobody in sight at reception. This gave me the opportunity to nip to the ladies' toilets, freshen myself up, apply a little make-up and at least look presentable.

I took a deep breath and inwardly told myself to just stay calm and keep it together.

By the time I made my way back to reception, Jess had returned to her post.

'Emma!' she squealed. 'You're back.'

I tried to summon the biggest smile I could manage and hoped it would be enough to convince Jess I was all fine and dandy.

'I am,' I replied, as I took my station behind reception with Jess. I fumbled around with some paperwork that was lying around, hoping there was something I could turn my attention to and avoid too much conversation.

'Morning, Sam,' said Jess in a cheery tone.

The mere mention of the name Sam made my legs buckle beneath me, but when I heard his voice answer, I dropped all the paperwork I was holding and about to file, all over the floor.

I stood dumbfounded as he chatted away to Jess from across the reception desk.

Jess could see my reaction and looked nervously on as I crouched down to pick up the papers. As I was down on the floor, almost in hiding and avoiding the situation, Sam hoisted himself across the reception desk so he was lying on his belly and was able to look down on me on the other side.

'Hey, Emma.'

'Hey,' I said casually, but underneath I was still in shock and not quite believing what was going on.

As I tried to rise back to my feet, I misjudged the position of the reception top and hit my head on it on the way up.

'Oh, Emma, you all right?' asked a concerned Jess. Sam merely chuckled.

'Yeh, fine,' I hastily replied, giving it a quick rub. In reality, I gave it quite a clonk and it was hurting, but I was too embarrassed to admit it.

'Bet you're surprised to see me?' quipped Sam. I raised my eyebrows at his understatement.

'Just a bit,' I said.

'Does she not know?' Jess asked, eyes wide open in amazement.

Sam chuckled again. I was feeling a bit annoyed at Sam finding it so amusing and that Jess was seemingly more in the loop than I was.

'Know what?' I directed the question at Sam, but when he gave no answer I turned my gaze towards Jess.

At first, she also stayed silent, looking over at Sam in anticipation of him spilling the beans.

When that was not forthcoming, she finally spoke.

'Sam has taken on the handyman role we have been recruiting for.'

'Have you?' I almost choked the words out.

'Yeh,' he replied, sounding very pleased with himself. 'Thought I'd give it a go.'

'Right, yeh, OK.' That was all I could manage to say. I was still trying to digest the information.

'Cool, right?' Sam asked, with a big grin.

Jess had started to pick up the papers I had strewn all over the floor and file them away. I think she was finding the situation all a little uncomfortable and so was trying to busy herself.

'Yeh. Yeh, that is cool.' There was an awkward pause in the conversation, and I became distracted by Jess clearing up while I was still trying to process what was being said. I was feeling very excited that Sam was still going to be around in my life but also confused and a bit annoyed that I had found out like this.

'You didn't think to mention it till right now?'

'I thought it would be a nice surprise,' he said mischievously.

I wasn't a fan of surprises. If he'd told me before, he would have saved me a whole lot of heartache and sleep deprivation.

'Well, I better get on with some work as at this rate I'll be sacked before the end of the day!'

He gave a cheeky wink, thrust his hands into his boiler suit trousers and casually strode off down the corridor.

'Sorry, Emma, I didn't realise he hadn't told you.'

'Ah, it's all right,' I said, trying to sound like I was shrugging it off as unimportant in an attempt to hide my embarrassment. 'That's Sam all over. It's how he is. Carefree and just makes it up as he goes along.'

As my eyes fixated on the corridor that he had just walked down but from where he had long disappeared from view, I realised he was the complete opposite to me. I wondered what it was that attracted me so much to him when he obviously lived by entirely different principles to me.

'So how was your time off? Get up to anything good?'

I felt the energy drain from my body at the mere question. True to form, Jess was on the hunt for information and would probably hound me all day until my head throbbed. I decided to get it over and done with there and then. So, for the next hour or so, in between a few work tasks as the hotel was fairly quiet, I gave an account of my week off. The account was relatively truthful; I just chose to leave out certain bits. As far as Jess was concerned, myself and Sam met up with a group of London friends and we went on a short trip to Devon. Jess asked a few awkward questions which I think I successfully managed to either dodge or bend the truth a little. The reality was, Jess was more interested in the development of any relationship between Sam and myself. She of course ended up bitterly disappointed. Come to think of it, she wasn't the only one. The whole trip had been disappointing; I was not sure anything good had come from it. It was really starting to hit home for me now that I had to put this thing to bed. It happened in the past; there was nothing to be done. It was over now and I had to try and forget about it and move forward with my life.

But it wasn't over.

How could it be over when I knew full well that I was finding it difficult to control my emotions? Sometimes, I could feel the rage bubbling within me, and I was finding it harder to keep it contained below the surface. So far, my bouts of anger had not escalated to a point that had caused anything bad to happen, but I felt sure it was only a matter of time before this would change.

CHAPTER TWENTY-NINE

The next few weeks were like a breath of fresh air. Dare I say it, but life seemed to be almost normal again, and I had begun to remember how to enjoy myself. Sam joining the team had made a big impact on my life. Going to work each day was a much more pleasurable experience with Sam around, and my social life had dramatically improved, with several memorable nights out on the town. Sam had become my true companion and the bond between us was as strong as ever, but the relationship had remained purely platonic, with only some mild flirtation. There had been a couple of stronger advances on Sam's part, but I had not felt ready to allow the relationship to develop into anything more than good friends and so I always gently rejected them. However, I was now beginning to come round to the idea and I had decided that tonight, should the opportunity present itself, I would feel comfortable allowing things to progress further.

The day had been a busy one; the hotel was gearing up for a Halloween evening party in the main function room. The event had proved a popular one, with tickets all sold out to within less than a week of being advertised. Tom was true to form, running around the place like a headless chicken, barking orders at anyone who came within his vicinity. This was the first time the hotel had run such an event at this time of year, and Tom was anxious for it to be a success. Thankfully, I had managed to keep out of most of the activities required in order to prepare it, remaining firmly fixed to reception duties. Alas, I failed to avoid it completely and was roped in to decorate the reception area with some of the giant helium balloon Halloween figures.

'Do you think we should put the ghost alongside Frankenstein or the witch?' asked Jess, who was enjoying this all far too much.

I puffed out some air across my lips as I pretended to deliberate which would be the ideal pairing. In truth, I couldn't care less.

'Frankenstein,' I said with conviction.

Jess thought about it for a moment. 'Yes, I think you're right, then we can put the pumpkin with the witch.'

I left Jess to tackle the cumbersome balloon decorations while I handled the much easier task of hanging pretend cobwebs along the length of the reception desk. I checked my watch and was relieved to see I had only minutes left before my shift ended and I could escape and concentrate on getting myself ready for the party, before eventually joining in the event itself. Although it was a public event, many of the staff who were not working that evening had complimentary tickets to also attend. Jess, of course, was immediately on board, snapping up a ticket the minute the event was announced. I took a little more persuasion but once I had found out Sam was thinking of going, I was more easily convinced.

'I am going to head off now, Jess.'

'Yeh, OK, see you later!'

'See you in a few hours,' I replied with a quick wave as I left through the front hotel door.

I skipped down the stone steps feeling quite excited about the prospect of the night ahead.

As I pulled up on my drive I could see Betty in the front garden bent over deadheading some flowers. *Just typical*, I thought to myself, knowing it was unlikely I would be able to get inside without her detaining me. I tried to be as stealthy as I could by avoiding all eye contact and moving quickly and quietly. Shutting the car door proved the trickiest, with the door failing to catch properly on the first attempt at closing it. I winced as it made a clunk sound on the second attempt, and I couldn't resist taking a quick sneaky peek over at Betty. She was already at our dividing fence boundary, peering right at me.

'Oh good, you're home,' she snapped.

My heart sank, as I knew I would now be losing vital minutes on an already tight schedule.

'Hi, Betty,' I said cheerfully, as if I was delighted to see her.

'Could you do me a favour, poppet?' she asked.

Poppet? Well, this was new, calling me by a pet name.

'Could you collect a prescription for me? Only I am not feeling up to going out and getting it myself.'

'Sure, I can pick it up tomorrow for you,' and then as I thought about it, I realised I may not be on top form so added, 'in the afternoon.'

'Tomorrow afternoon? Can't you go now?'

This woman was unbearable and probably the rudest person I knew.

'Well, it's not convenient for me right now, Betty. Can it not wait till just tomorrow?'

'No, it's fine, just let a poor woman suffer in pain and then I'll probably be bloody dead by tomorrow,' she huffed, turning her back on me and trudging back towards her house.

I gave a low growl and a tut before the guilt got to me.

'OK, Betty, I'll get it now.'

'Great,' she said, with a sudden chirpy tone, 'I'll fetch the prescription.'

The minutes ticked by and I was getting increasingly frustrated, wondering how much longer she was going to be. After several agitated looks at my watch, I decided to follow her in and find out what on earth she was doing. I found her in the kitchen rifling through a pile of papers on her sideboard.

'Have you found it, Betty? I need to get on really.'

She muttered something I couldn't fathom as she gave up on the pile and moved to a kitchen drawer.

'I know it is here somewhere,' she said, sounding confused.

'Aha,' she said triumphantly, waving the paperwork in the air at me before passing it over.

I took it, feeling very much relieved, but still that did not let me off the hook.

Before I even had chance to think about leaving, the kettle was filled and a tea tray with a plate of biscuits was being laid on the table. My heart sinking at the thought of more precious minutes slipping away, I couldn't bring myself to say anything. Instead, I accepted defeat, sat at the table, grabbed a bourbon biscuit and waited patiently for tea to be served.

'I can't stay too long, Betty. I'm supposed to be out tonight.' I felt like I needed to set that straight in case she had other plans. 'After I've got your prescription, of course,' I quickly added wryly.

'Oh, anywhere nice?'

'It's a Halloween party at the hotel that I work at.'

'Oh, not fancy dress rubbish, is it?'

'Well, yes, it is actually.'

She turned her nose up disapprovingly as she took one of the shortcake biscuits.

'And what are you going as?'

'A witch. The Wicked Witch of the West, to be specific.'

'How original!'

I was put out by the sarcastic response. I was not a fan of fancy dress, either, already finding it difficult to know what to wear without the added pressure of a theme.

'So, is your friend going?'

I screwed my eyes up in puzzlement, not sure which friend she was referring to.

'The one you had a falling-out with a while back?'

Oh, she meant Lisa. I hadn't thought about Lisa much during these last few months.

'No. She won't be there.'

'You not made up yet then?'

'No. I haven't spoken to her for a long while.'

'That's a shame.'

I took a gulp of the last drop of my tea and gasped when I saw the time and realised I still hadn't even got the prescription yet.

'Right, I've really got to dash, Betty.'

'Well, don't forget—'

'Yes, I know, I'm getting it now. I'll be back as soon as.'

She looked a little astonished at the directness in my tone but to my relief didn't bite, and let me get on my way.

Fate was, of course, against me. Endless traffic, traffic lights that seemed stuck on red and no parking available anywhere near to the pharmacy. Even once I managed to get into the place, there was a queue a mile long, and when my turn finally came there was some confusion with the prescription and it took an age to sort out. If I thought the trip there was bad, the journey back was even worse. A car accident on one of the main roads had caused all sorts of mayhem, and I got stuck in a tailback that robbed me of time I was already running short of. By the time I arrived home, I had barely ten minutes to get ready before the taxi would be arriving. I considered calling to try and delay it but we were picking up other people on the way, and as I was first in the queue I would be delaying everyone else. Instead, I ran to Betty's door, banged as loudly as I could on it and left the prescription on her doorstep. I didn't hang around to see if she came to pick it up.

Panic-stricken, I did the best I could in the circumstances to get myself ready for the party. It of course fell woefully short of what people would be expecting. I threw on a run-of-the-mill black dress, gave a quick spray of deodorant and a misting of perfume followed by a quick brush and disentanglement of my hair. I didn't even have time to touch up my make-up before the taxi was beeping his horn to make me aware of his presence. This had so not gone to plan. I had envisaged making a real effort with my hairstyle, producing long curled locks draped over my shoulders, using much more bold and exuberant make-up than I would normally. I had even bought bright green neon nail varnish for the occasion, a colour I would never dare to normally wear and probably now never would. I felt like crying but then the taxi gave another blast of the horn and so I had to dash out to it before it gave up on me and drove off. Sitting in the back of the taxi, I managed to grab a few glimpses in his rear-view mirror and was dismayed to see how plain I looked. I had remembered to grab the witch's hat on my way out, but that was really the only thing that made me resemble the character I was supposed to be going as. As well as the lacklustre attempt at my general appearance, I had also completely forgotten the black and green cape and the broomstick I had specifically bought for the occasion. The night was already beginning to feel like a disaster, and I hadn't even got there yet. I closed my eyes and prayed things would be fine once I got to the party, imagining myself there with Sam.

'Hey, Emma!'

I abruptly opened my eyes to see the taxi had pulled up outside Jess's house. She had opened the back door nearest to where I was sitting and was coaxing me to shift along and allow her to get in.

She was struggling with the size of her costume to even get in the car. She was dressed as a pumpkin and although the costume was clearly homemade and a little tacky, it was still a much better attempt than mine.

She got a fit of the giggles and I suspected she already had a few alcoholic drinks inside her.

I tried to help her in but she was like an unruly child. I could see the taxi driver was getting impatient and giving her some disapproving looks. Jess was oblivious and was still giggling but did eventually manage to squeeze herself in.

'I'm in,' she squealed, 'we are good to go!'

Once she was settled, she then turned her attention to me and immediately dropped her grin and began to frown.

'Oh,' she exclaimed disappointedly, 'I thought you were going to dress up and come as a witch?'

Although not unwarranted, the comment still stung my feelings, and I was beginning to wonder if I should have skipped the evening altogether.

It turned out I wished I had. It was, without a shadow of a doubt, the worst evening of my entire life.

CHAPTER THIRTY

We arrived to find the party already in full swing, with the place heaving. Immediately, I felt incredibly self-conscious when I saw the great lengths people had gone to with their costumes and was convinced everyone was staring at me with disapproving eyes. I kept telling myself I was probably just being over paranoid, but once Amelia had caught sight of me there was no question of what her thoughts were.

She was stood with a group of female friends, none of which I recognised, near the bar, and they were clearly having a good gossip and laugh at my expense. Amelia was dressed up to the nines, having chosen to come as a very convincing Morticia and making me feel incredibly inferior.

'Let's get a drink,' said Jess, tugging at my arm and dragging me along, closer to the enemy.

Jess managed to grab the last available space at the bar and I was left hovering on the fringes, leaving me little option but to open dialogue with them.

'Hi, Amelia,' I whimpered, acting as if I was too lowly a person to speak to her.

I could feel her friends' eyes burning stares. I longed for Amelia to at least have the decency to reply and acknowledge my existence so as to end the agonising awkwardness I was feeling.

'Hello, darling, lovely to see you. Glad you could come.'

I gave a feeble smile, revolted at her calling me darling and her blatant lie about how glad she was to see me.

I nervously cast my eyes round the group, smiling politely. Some managed to conjure a smile back, while others just glowered.

'Sorry, how rude of me, let me introduce you to my friends.'

I barely took any note of their names, and I certainly didn't bother conversing with any of them.

I gave a desperate glance over to Jess, hoping she would come to my rescue, but to my horror she had disappeared. I frantically looked around and finally caught sight of her further along, chatting to Tom and Sam. Once Amelia had finished the niceties, I gave them my best wishes and scurried away in the direction of my saviours.

'Hey,' said Sam in a warm and welcoming tone as I joined their circle.

'Hi,' I returned, already feeling much more relaxed.

I could see Jess was holding two bottles of lager, one in each hand.

'One of those for me?'

'Oh God, yeh, sorry,' and she handed me one with an apologetic look. 'You looked deep in conversation with Amelia so I left you to it.'

'Thanks for that,' I said sarcastically, and took a swig from the bottle while I put the encounter with Amelia and her cronies to the back of my mind.

We all happily chatted for a while in our secure circle of four. The rounds of drinks kept coming and the conversation easily flowed. Inevitably, as the night wore on, the volume of the music went up and the level of drunkenness increased. Conversations were harder to follow and people were loosening up, mingling more and wanting to dance.

Our circle of four had expanded and now resembled less of a circle and more of a wobbly oblong. To my distaste, Amelia and her group had joined us and were evidently swooning all over Sam. Where once I had stood right alongside him, I was now several feet away where they had pushed their way in and split us apart.

'So anyway, Emma, what is it you are supposed to have come as?'

I stood there trying not to react to Amelia's unkind comment, which had been a blatant attempt to embarrass me. Sam had one of his hands in his pockets and Amelia had her arm hooked round it.

'Wicked Witch of the West.'

'Oh,' she said, looking down her nose at me, 'I wouldn't have guessed.'

I grimaced a smile and thought how much I wanted to slap her.

'Well, no, thinking on it, that is a character I am sure you could pull off much better than me,' I quipped.

Sam spat out the drink he was swigging with laughter, and Jess tried but failed to stifle a giggle. One of her friends actually gave an audible gasp and, to my delight, Amelia looked horrified by my comment. I felt a moment of triumph, although I was sure I would be made to pay.

Amelia turned her back on me as she turned her attention to Sam. She whispered something in his ear, and he reacted by smirking and then taking another swig from his bottle. Although I could not hear what she said, I was sure it was something unpleasant or humiliating about me.

'Emma, come on, let's dance!' Jess yelled in my ear, pulling me hard by the arm; so hard it felt like she would yank it off. I reluctantly followed and as we danced to Whitney Houston's *I Wanna Dance with Somebody*, I was thinking how much I wanted that somebody to be Sam.

I lasted for another three more songs, all the while trying to avoid laying my eyes on Amelia in the distance, who I could see was all up close and personal to Sam and looked to be making a play for him.

'I'm just taking a break from all this dancing for a bit,' I shouted to Jess. She gave me a look of puppy dog eyes as I backed away from the dance floor, trying to entice me back, but she soon got swooped up in a wave of other dancers and I was able to complete the full retreat.

I lingered on the sidelines on my own, feeling very conspicuous and vulnerable as I watched people on the dance floor. I mused at the different dance styles, some only shuffling left to right, not always to the beat, and others who had no inhibitions and flailed around at will.

I jumped as someone snuck up behind me and wrapped their arms around my waist.

'I thought you were going to be on the dance floor all night,' Sam said gently into my ear, sending a tingle all over my body.

'Why? Jealous?' I mischievously replied.

'Yes,' he said firmly.

'Well, in that case, perhaps we should have a dance together.'

'Perhaps we should.'

My heart raced at his answer. I couldn't tell if we were just having playful banter or if he was being serious. For a moment, we stood in silence smiling at each other, until Sam finally spoke.

'Are we going to dance then?'

I felt my eyes widen in astonishment as I realised he was actually being serious.

'Sure,' I said with glee.

He grabbed my hand and led me to the dance floor. The first couple of songs were typical disco dance tunes, and I did my best to strut my stuff and not look too awkward, but then on the next tune the tempo of the song changed. The slower beat took me by surprise and I completely lost my rhythm until eventually I just stood there as I watched others coupling up and swaying together.

I assumed that this signalled the end of my dance session with Sam, and I prepared to leave the dance floor. As I took my first steps, Sam made a grab for me, pulling me towards him and placing his hands around my waist. I reciprocated, wrapping my arms around his body and clasping my hands together behind his back. He gently led me round the dance floor, and I was in seventh heaven as we swayed and spun around the dance floor together in each other's arms.

When I spied Amelia watching on, I snuggled in closer and flirtatiously whispered in his ear how much I was enjoying our dance together. He gazed into my eyes and at that moment I was sure he was about to kiss me. But as he leant in, I could see over his shoulder Harry watching us. Harry's forlorn expression sent a pang of guilt through me that made me retract from Sam, and the moment was lost. I immediately regretted the action, not understanding why I felt this guilt. I did not hold any romantic feelings towards Harry and, as far as I was aware, I had never given any hint of the possibility of a romantic relationship developing between us. All the same, I did care deeply for him, and to see his face looking on like that felt troubling.

Sam and I finished the dance, but I distinctly felt like he wasn't holding me as tightly and that a slight gap had developed between us. As soon as the song finished, Sam let go of me and made his way off the dance floor. He did look back towards me and give me a smile, but I noticed he did not reach out to hold my hand. I smiled back weakly, knowing the damage had been done, and watched him walk away, over towards Amelia.

'What's up with you? You've got a face like a wet weekend.'

I was sat at a table on my own in the furthest corner of the room, drowning my sorrows.

Jess sat opposite me and helped herself to my bottle of wine. She only managed to fill half her glass up as I had already drunk the rest of the bottle.

'Is it Sam?'

'Yeh, course it's bloody Sam,' I blurted, slumped over the table, drunk, staring at the empty bottle and wondering if I could be bothered to go and fetch another.

'I thought you two were hitting it off? I saw you smooching with him earlier. Looked like things were progressing well.'

'So did I, till I blew it.'

'Why? What did you say?'

I huffed and puffed, with Jess looking on, confused, and went to drink my last dregs. Half of it sloshed over my face, and I was about to wipe it off with the back of my hand when Jess handed me a tissue.

'Thanks,' I slurred.

'So what happened? Did you have an argument or something?'

'No, we didn't argue, we didn't anything. We danced, he went to kiss me and I backed away. End of.'

Jess started laughing.

'It's not funny. I actually thought something might spark tonight,' I said, feeling upset.

'Is that all? You need to pull yourself together. What's the matter with you? I thought you had had a big barney or something. Honestly, you are acting like a teenager on their first romantic encounter. You need to get a grip.'

She downed the last of her wine and promptly got up out of her chair.

'Come on, get out of your chair. Stop moping and try letting your hair down a bit.'

She glared at me like a mother scolding her child. When I made no motion to move, she seized hold of my arm and tried hauling me out of my seat. She did not have enough strength in her to get me up, but she did manage to tip my chair. On the first tug she only managed to tip it for a second before it tipped back, which was shocking enough for me, but her second tug was much stronger. This time, it tipped right over, bringing me along with it, and I fell onto the floor with the chair half on top of me as Jess toppled backwards and ended up flat on her back.

We simultaneously broke into laughter, and I am not sure if I was aching more from laughing so much or the force of the fall. We laughed even harder as people walked past us, looking at us like we were a couple of loons. After several failed attempts, we managed to get ourselves up. The incident had put me in a much better mood and given me a new lease of life. Jess was right. I was being pathetic. I needed to pull myself together and get this night back on track.

'Shall we rejoin the party and see if we can find Sam?' asked Jess tentatively.

'Hell yes!' I exclaimed.

I was feeling a little wobbly on my feet, so I made my way to the bar to get some water down me and try and sober up a bit. I scanned the room for Sam on the way but couldn't see him anywhere. It was only a casual look, though, and of course the alcohol had impaired my vision somewhat. I would look properly later. For now, water was my prime concern. The bar attendant looked relieved at my request for a pint of water. I was not convinced he would have been willing to serve me anything else, at least not of the alcoholic variety. I forced myself to drink the full pint, thinking I was in desperate need of some hydration. It at least took the dryness away from my lips and ceased the need to keep licking them. I placed the pint glass down on the bar and spun round to survey the room. I could see Jess on the dance floor, clearly abandoning me in my hour of need and leaving me to fly this mission solo. A general sweep of the room came up negative for any sighting of Sam. I decided a more detailed search was needed, so I proceeded to work my way round the function room looking for him. I couldn't find him anywhere and I was fairly sure he wasn't there. Tom confirmed this for me when I saw him at the main door as I made my way out to look elsewhere.

'Yes, I did see him a few minutes ago. I think he was heading off in the direction of reception.'

'Great,' I squealed, and planted a kiss on his cheek. He recoiled, bemused at my show of affection.

I trotted off to reception where I found Stefan, the Polish hotel porter, minding the desk.

'Hi, Stefan.'

'Hello, Emma. Having a good night?'

'Yes, thanks. Have you seen Sam?'

'Yes, just been speaking to him. He has just gone through those doors. If you are quick, you should catch up with him.'

'Brilliant.' I wanted to kiss him also but thought better of it. 'See you later, Stefan.'

'Bye,' he answered, and gave me a big smile.

I trotted on towards the corridor doors and could feel the excitement building at the prospect of seeing Sam on the other side.

I swung the doors open and sure enough Sam was there. There was no euphoria moment. There was only a heart-wrenching feeling of despair. However, this initial feeling was soon overtaken by an immense feeling of rage and I completely snapped. To see Sam in such a compromising position with another woman was bad enough, but when that woman was Amelia it was too much to bear.

I immediately went for her, straight for the throat. She looked petrified as I squeezed as hard as I could. Sam was yelling, swearing and frantically trying to pull me off her. I momentarily released my grip on Amelia and turned my attention to Sam. We locked eyes and he too looked petrified. With little thought or too much effort, I managed to simply toss him aside, slamming him into the wall and leaving him dazed on the floor. Stefan and Tom were both running frantically down the corridor towards me, yelling my name. They looked horrified at what they had witnessed and pleaded for me to stop. I ignored them and turned my attention back to the bitch, ready to continue with my attempts to throttle the life out of her. She was still choking and gasping for air following my previous attempt. She looked so pitiful, but I still grabbed her round the throat with one hand, picking her up off the ground and slamming her against the wall behind her. The other hand I used to fend off Stefan, who was attempting a rescue.

From then on, the situation got very complicated and muddled. I am not sure how much time had passed or how many people had joined the furore, but there was a lot of shouting and screaming and wailing and pulling and punching, until eventually it all came to an abrupt end when a dart was fired into my neck. I felt the effects almost immediately. The dart had been fired somewhere from my right side and was now lodged in the side of my neck. I instinctively pulled it out and backed away from Amelia. She was slumped against the corridor wall, her face covered in blood, choking and spluttering in between bouts of sobbing. The pain of the dart penetrating my skin was minimal, but whatever concoction it was carrying was now entering my bloodstream and causing me to lose strength and feel woozy. It reminded me of my spa session at Roseville Resort all those months ago. I took several more steps back and leant my back up against the opposite wall to the one Amelia was propped up against. I took a sweeping glance around me. My vision was starting to go blurry, but I could still make out some of the faces. Sam looked bewildered and exhausted, hunched over with his hands wrapped round his knees, huffing and puffing and trying to regain his strength. Jess had her hands over her mouth, crying and looking very distraught. Tom was on his knees and looked like he was about to collapse at any point, and Stefan was sat on the floor with his head in his hands. Two men dressed in commando uniform were coming towards me. I had no strength in me to fend them off, and so I simply allowed them to handcuff me and lead me away.

I could only just walk. My legs felt like lead and I was practically dragging them along the floor, having to rely heavily on the man either side of me for support. The fresh air hit me quite suddenly as we stepped outside, and I was beginning to feel nauseous. I knew it would not be long before I would pass out completely. My legs had now completely given way, and I was being dragged along the final part of the driveway to an awaiting van. Just before they bundled me in, they paused while they opened the van doors, and it gave me enough time to look at some of the people stood around watching my demise. It was difficult for me to focus and I had lost much of my peripheral vision, but as I turned my head there was one person who stood out in the crowd. She stood firm as she watched on, and it was the first time I had laid eyes on her in such a long time.

'Lisa? Is that you?'

She did not answer. She did not move. She only watched on. I was then bundled into the back of the van and shortly after I must have lost consciousness, as that was my last memory of that fateful night.

CHAPTER THIRTY-ONE

I gently opened my eyes. I was lying on the top covers of a single bed on my left side with my back to the wall and looking out onto the room. I was surprised to see it was a fairly comfortable albeit simple room and nothing like the jail cell I was expecting to awake in. I sat myself up and had a better look around. I noticed there was a water jug on the bedside table and as my throat felt very dry I helped myself. As soon as I had quenched my thirst, I got up and went over to the door to the room. I peeped through the porthole window. There was just a single corridor with no one in it. I tried the handle but it would not turn. I was locked in.

I sat back on the bed, poured myself another glass of water and started to think back to what I had done. There was no two ways about it. I had committed a violent attack, assaulting several people, and I was bound to be in serious trouble. It was possible that I could even be accused of attempted murder given the severity of the attack on Amelia. If it wasn't for the dart, which had stopped me in my tracks, I am sure I would have strangled her to death. Whatever I stood to be accused of, I was fully expecting a lengthy jail term to follow.

What I found most disturbing was I was not sure I was that bothered. In fact, I was not even sure if part of me was actually disappointed that I hadn't got to finish her off.

Just then, I heard some voices, and I could hear the footsteps getting louder as they approached my door. I could see someone looking at me through the porthole window as they unlocked it. Two men in black commando uniform entered the room. They had weapons but they were not drawn, instead just holstered to their sides. I wondered where it was they had brought me because it certainly didn't resemble a police station.

'Right then, Miss Maynard. If you could step this way, please.'

I remained sat on the bed, trying to work out if I should follow them. The commando gave me a long cold stare.

'Miss Maynard, you need to come with me,' he said firmly.

I stood up but did not step forward.

'Where am I?' I asked.

I noticed the other guy had his hand resting on his holstered gun, presumably ready to draw it.

'I am not at liberty to say. Now come with me.'

He went to forcibly move me but I moved first, making my way as instructed to the door and out into the corridor. They led me to another room further up the corridor. They gestured me into it and told me to sit down at the table that was in the middle of the room. They then left me on my own, and I heard them lock the door behind them.

I looked round at my surroundings. It was quite sparse with only the one table and a few chairs around it. There were no windows. Even the door was solid, so the only light source was artificial, coming from the strip lights on the ceiling. I noticed there were security cameras in each of the corners of the room and assumed I was being watched. I sat down on one of the chairs at the table and waited.

A few minutes later, the door opened and a familiar face greeted me.

'Hi, Emma.'

'Hi, Lisa.'

Lisa closed the door. I noticed she did not lock it, but I did catch sight of a black commando milling around outside. I guessed he was standing guard. She came over and sat opposite me, and for a few moments we said nothing and just stared into each other's eyes. It felt like we were competing in a staring contest. I blinked first.

'Where are we?' I asked.

Lisa did not answer, but I was not really expecting one.

'It doesn't feel like we are in a police station.'

'No, we aren't at a police station.'

I waited for a better explanation but none came.

'Emma, do you remember what happened?'

I joined in the game of no replies.

'Emma. Do you remember what happened at the hotel?'

'Yes.'

'What happened?'

'Well, you know what happened. You were there.'

'But I want you to tell me what happened.'

'Well, I want you to tell me where the hell I am and why you are here questioning me. Why am I not in a cell in a police station and being charged?'

Lisa sighed and leant back in the chair, as if she was feeling somewhat defeated.

'You are in a secure government building in London and I am employed here.'

'Employed to do what?'

'Well, right now, this minute, trying to sort your mess out. Emma, believe it or not, I am trying to help you.'

I screwed my eyes up. I was not convinced.

'So, tell me, what exactly do you remember?'

I now sat back in my chair and was now the one feeling defeat. My life had turned into one exhausting nightmare. I could not understand how it had all come to this, and I couldn't see a way out.

'I remember being at the Halloween party and seeing Sam with Amelia. I completely lost it and attacked her. I remember trying to strangle her, people trying to stop me, but they couldn't, until one of your people shot me with a dart that knocked me out.'

Lisa nodded her head but said nothing.

'I am affected by this JAHL experiment, aren't I? Like the other people on the list who have all gone mad and done terrible things. I felt extreme rage. I wanted to kill her. I would have killed her had you not stopped me.' I paused for a moment as I thought more acutely about the incident. Lisa sat quietly and allowed me the time to process more information.

'But what I also remember is no one was able to stop me. Grown men, far bigger in stature than me, could not stop me. I easily fended them off. What am I now? What has this experiment done to me?'

Lisa looked very much ill at ease, and I felt my shoulders and head drop as I awaited my fate.

Lisa leant forward, placing her elbows on the table and clasping her hands together in front of her face. Her face looked serious, and I waited nervously for her to speak.

'Emma, I know things have been very difficult for you lately. I know you have embarked on some kind of voyage of discovery about yourself. That you have discovered the existence of a government project that you think you have been a part of. But ... you have been misled.'

I felt the tension return to my shoulders. I could not believe that after all this she was still trying to convince me it was not true. I immediately stood up and slammed my hand down on the table. Lisa jumped and only a moment later the door swung open and two commandos entered with their guns drawn, pointing directly at me.

Lisa beckoned them to lower their weapons. She then turned to me. 'Perhaps you should sit back down.' I did so and as soon as I was back in my seat, the commandos left and we resumed our conversation.

'I don't know what is going on here, Lisa. These past five or six months have been so completely unbelievable. I don't know how everything has fallen apart. I was just an ordinary person in an ordinary world leading a relatively normal life. Now, it's all been turned upside down. Nothing is normal about my life, and the world I live in also seems unreal. Government experiments, secret facilities; it's like a science fiction movie. It's just unbelievable. If someone had told me this story, I wouldn't have believed them. But it is real because I am living through it. So don't sit there and belittle me, telling me I have been misled.

'It happened. I know it happened because I have spent the last six months desperately trying to discover the awful truth. And now,' I took a breath and tried to compose myself as my voice began to waver, 'and now, it's there for all to see. The terrible consequences that your employer has caused.'

I closed my eyes, worn completely down and wanting to just give up, for it all to end. When I reopened them, Lisa was watching me with an expression of pity. She genuinely looked very sorry for me and for a moment I felt friendship and not that a government official was interrogating me.

'Please, Lisa, can't you just admit that I am nothing more than a failed experiment? I know my life is over.' I was begging her now.

I didn't see the point of all the secrecy anymore. Surely, I would be locked up away from society, eradicated.

Lisa cleared her throat and swallowed hard. It felt like a confession was forthcoming.

'Emma, you are not part of any government experiment ...'

'Oh, come on ...' I was exasperated. Even after all this, she still insisted on continuing with this charade. 'Don't tell me. It's all been a dream. Yep, I've just made it all up.'

Lisa looked perplexed by my snide remark.

'Let me finish,' she said very resolutely, 'I said *you* were not part of any government experiment. I did not say that the experiment itself did not exist.'

The statement struck hard. I was confused, astounded.

'So you admit JAHL does exist?'

'Yes.'

'But ...' I swallowed hard, as I felt like I was choking up, 'I was not part of it?'

She hesitated. 'Yes.'

I slumped back in my chair. To finally hear Lisa confirm it was real was a revelation, but it was not giving me the overwhelming feeling of relief I thought I would feel. In fact, I wondered if it would have been better for her to keep the original pretence of covering it up. It would have given me some small fraction of hope that there was some better explanation. Something that would allow me to revert back to my life before all this.

'What?' I started to feel dizzy; it did not make sense.

'What do you mean, I wasn't part of it? Of course I was. I saw the document. The list with my name on it. Emma Stanton. Right there under Group A of the listed subjects.'

Lisa looked on like I was some crazy, confused soul.

'I've still got the document to prove it. It's at home. If you let me get it, I can show you,' I said desperately.

'That won't make any difference.'

'Yes, it will. Of course it will,' I shouted. What was this woman going on about? There in black and white and yet still trying to convince me I was not involved.

'I know about the lists and I know Emma Stanton is on one of those lists.'

'Well, what's the problem then? I am listed. It's me. Same name. Same date of birth.'

'The problem is, you are not Emma Stanton.'

Oh my goodness. My head was seriously spinning now. I spluttered, laughed nervously, not sure how to respond.

'What?' I shook my head, as if trying to shake some sense into it. 'What? What do you mean?'

She said nothing.

'I am Emma Maynard now because I took my adopted father's name. But I was born Emma Stanton. I am Emma Stanton.'

Still, she said nothing, but I could tell she was not wavering from her statement.

'What do you mean?' I pleaded.

Finally, Lisa spoke.

'Emma Stanton was three months old when she was orphaned. Her father is unknown, and it is assumed she was the result of a one-night stand or casual relationship. He may have abandoned them or not even have known of the pregnancy. Either way, her mother was single, but she was a very troubled person and committed suicide. It coincided with the precise time that the JAHL project was beginning. Hence, she was a perfect fit as a subject to be included in the project.'

'Yes, and that is exactly what happened to my parents,' I exclaimed.

Undeterred, Lisa continued.

'The JAHL project was abandoned—'

'Yes, yes, I know all this,' I interrupted. 'We were all put into care homes, monitored and gradually fostered or adopted back out into society.'

I was getting frustrated and tired now of hearing the same story being relayed to me. It was all information I had found out way before.

'Yes, that is exactly what happened. Except what we didn't know, until recently at least, is that Emma Stanton died while she was in the care home.'

Lisa paused while she waited for my reaction. I was too shocked to respond. I could feel my hands going very cold and start to gently tremor.

'We also believed you were the Emma Stanton listed, and so all protocols of the JAHL project were followed for you, just like everyone else on the lists. However, it has transpired that the care home chose to cover up the death by replacing the deceased with a different child. That child was you.'

Tears started to form in the corners of my eyes.

'But how could they do that? How could they even get away with that?'

Lisa shrugged. 'I know, it all sounds awful. I'm sorry but it happened such a long time ago and the people in charge of the care home have since died, so it is difficult to know completely what happened. We have spoken to other surviving employees and others who were also cared for there and tried to piece it all together. But it is difficult to know what is true and what is faded memory or just rumour and speculation, so we will probably never really know.'

'I need some water.'

'Sure.' Lisa briefly left the room and returned with a plastic cup filled to the very top with water. She placed it on the table and some of the water sloshed over the sides, leaving a small puddle. Lisa sat back down and presumably she was waiting for me to take some drink, but instead I just stared at the spillage.

'How did she die?'

'We are not sure. Some sort of accident. We think some sort of a fall and her striking her head. The death was never reported and they have hidden the body. We think they covered it up partly around the dubious circumstances of the death and also to allow them to continue receiving the extra government funding.'

'What you mean is they got hush money.'

I shook my head in disbelief.

'And so how did they swap me for her?'

'Once again, a bit hazy. Sounds like they did a favour for a friend. Took in an unwanted child that happened to be about the same age.'

'And no one noticed!'

'No. Clearly not. I guess there weren't really any relations or anyone else that was interested in them.'

'What about the government? I thought they were monitoring and keeping tabs on us!'

Lisa shifted her eye contact away from me and appeared to be looking at the same puddle of water I had become fascinated with. Actually, it was less of a puddle now and more of a stream, trying to make its way to the edge of the table.

'So who am I?' I whispered.

Lisa finally looked at me but with a very troubled look in her eyes.

'We don't know.'

Then suddenly it hit me. A sudden sickening thought. If I was not part of the JAHL project, how could I explain my unthinkable aggressive actions?

'But, Lisa, are you absolutely sure? I was not anything to do with the JAHL project?'

Lisa took an age to answer and I couldn't help but think she looked shifty, but that was probably wishful thinking.

'Yes, we are sure.'

Her answer was firm and resolute, and just as I had been thinking things couldn't get any worse, they just had. The lifeline that I had just been given, that should have lifted the enormous worry I had carried all this time thinking something foreign was inside me doing untold damage, was worthless.

'Let's take a break,' said Lisa. 'Maybe you want something to eat?'

'No. I don't want anything.' There was no way I could stomach anything right now.

'OK, let me just grab some snacks from the machine outside. Just in case. I won't be long.'

Lisa left the room and was actually gone for a lot longer than I would have anticipated it would take just to simply grab a few snacks. I was glad to be left alone, and I was disappointed when she did finally return. Lisa threw an assortment of chocolate bars on the table and a couple of cans of fizz. She waited to let me select my choice first, but I only stared, emotionless, at them. Lisa returned to her seat, popping open a can and grabbing one of the chocolate bars. I watched her as she took a glug from the can and unwrapped her treat.

'What happened to me at Roseville?' I suddenly blurted.

Lisa now had her mouth full and so continued to chomp rather than answer.

'Lisa, why did you take me to Roseville?' I insisted.

Lisa had finished her mouthful and was now running her tongue along her teeth, removing the last remnants. I got the distinct impression she was stalling.

'Well? I know it exists and I know you took me there.' Lisa seemed unmoved and took a while to answer.

'We needed to run some tests on you along with others that had been experimented on.'

'What kind of tests?'

'After the original failed JAHL project, apart from the monitoring operations, everything else was stopped because we thought none of it had worked. We thought it had all left the blood system, possibly destroyed by the body's own immune system. Whatever, it was over. Except, many years later, the monitoring operations team started to find irregularities.'

I raised a brow, 'irregularities' for people who were going insane or killing themselves seemed a strange word to use, but I said nothing.

'So this is where the second stage of JAHL came in. We needed to get everyone back and check what was going on. Was there something still actually present in them and causing these irregularities? Now, you have to remember, nobody actually knew they had been injected with this stuff all those years ago. This wasn't like we could just ask people to pop in for a quick blood test at a conventional hospital. So that is where Roseville came in. The original facility still existed, so we had the means and the capabilities to carry out the tests we needed to. We just had to find a way of getting people there without blowing the secret.'

'So you disguised it as some sort of holiday resort and duped people into thinking they were there for a free relaxing break.'

'More or less.'

'And you're fine with that? Lying to people. Lying to me.'

'Look, Emma. I am so sorry. I can't tell you how sorry I am, but I genuinely believed it was the right thing to do and it was in your best interests. As far as I knew, you seemed OK to me. I didn't believe that you had been affected in any way, and hopefully they would still find no trace of it in you. Sure enough, the tests apparently showed you had none of the stuff present, and of course that was because you were not actually Emma Stanton, the person who had been injected with it.'

'But, Lisa, being dragged off to Roseville, performing these tests on me, dumping me back in my home days later and then denying it ever took place! Don't you understand the phenomenal repercussions that it had on me?'

'I know, you were not supposed to remember anything about it. Supposedly, we had the ability to wipe all memories of the trip, and the intention was for you to carry on where you had left off. Once I had discovered who you really were, your memories were purged and we returned you back home. As far as I was concerned, the plan was you wouldn't remember any of it and we would fob you off with a story about being in an accident, falling into a coma for a bit and suffering amnesia, and then you would just go on and continue with normal life.

'As it turned out, we had overestimated this ability, and you were able to recall much more of the trip than we ever anticipated, which made things very complicated for us.'

'Complicated? What an inconvenience for you that must have been,' I said, astounded. 'I thought I was going insane. I spent months trying to figure out what happened to me. It dominated my life.' Lisa looked anxiously at the door, probably expecting the commando security guards to re-enter now my voice had grown louder.

'I know, Emma. It was a terrible mistake that you were ever even involved with all this.'

'So what is going to happen to me now?'

'Well, you have committed quite a serious offence, but I can help you, Emma. I can help you put this all behind you.'

I hung my head in shame, realising that I could not blame Roseville or the JAHL project for my acts of violence. It was all my fault and mine alone. I was solely responsible, and I knew I had little choice but to accept Lisa's offer.

CHAPTER THIRTY-TWO

I spent the next few days here at the facility. At first feeling agitated and like a captive, but gradually relaxing and accepting my being here. Lisa spent a good few hours a day with me, where most of the time we just chatted like the old times. Thankfully, she had dropped the formal approach where she sounded like she had rehearsed from a script and was now actually speaking to me like a genuine friend. For the first couple of days, I had tried to get her to tell me more about Roseville, but she refused to answer any of my questions and always did her best to change the subject. After a while, I just simply gave up asking. Not only was it a fruitless effort but I actually became less interested. In fact, I did my very best to forget about it and try and move on by solely concentrating on my rehabilitation.

I had a few physical and psychological assessments to check I was ready to be reintegrated, but apart from that it was almost like I was just having a simple break away from the rest of society in my own little comfort bubble. Now the time had come for me to be released, and I was feeling apprehensive and unsure as to whether I was ready to leave.

'I am going to take you back to your house today. Are you ready?'

'I'm not sure.'

'Yeh, course you are. Let's go.'

Lisa had already had a good chat with me about what my next steps should be. She had persuaded me that I should sell up and move away to start a new life. For a while, I could not understand how this option was even open to me. I had assumed I would be dragged through the court system and eventually wind up imprisoned. Lisa was adamant it had all been sorted and I could continue with normal life as long as I left behind my old one. She explained it was not wise to continue where I had left off, and even I could not see how that would be even possible. I had all but destroyed my old life and there was no going back.

We arrived at the house on a cold frosty morning. I immediately noticed the 'For Sale' sign and felt a tinge of sadness. This had been my home for a good few years, and it served only as a stark reminder of what I had and was now about to lose. Lisa parked up on the drive and proceeded to get out. I just sat frozen in the passenger seat, unwilling to move. Lisa peered at me through the window, but I only gave her a glance before staring back at my house with nostalgia. I could feel my eyes welling up and knots forming in my stomach as memories of Sam and his big cheeky grin formed in my mind.

Lisa tapped on the window. Drawing my attention back to her.

'Are you coming then?'

I nodded as I wiped away a tear, and I could see the sympathy in her eyes.

As I walked up the path to my front door, I looked over at Betty's lounge window, expecting to see the curtains twitching and her ineffectively hiding behind them.

But they weren't. In fact, I actually stopped walking and stood for a moment, confused. Something looked different. Then I realised … the pot with the lion carvings that stood near her front door was gone. How on earth had she moved that? I for one knew how heavy that darn thing was, having dragged it myself not so long ago.

'You all right?' asked Lisa.

'There's a pot missing.'

Lisa gave me a concerned look, probably wondering if I was going slightly mad.

I pointed to the slab where it once stood. 'There was a pot there before,' I stated emphatically.

'OK. And it's a problem it's not there now?' Lisa spoke quite slowly and with a worried tone.

'Well, it is a bit weird.'

'Is it?'

'Betty's quite particular about things. She wouldn't have been able to move it anyway. And where has she moved it to?' My eyes shot around her front garden in search of it.

'Well, maybe someone moved it for her.'

'I doubt it.'

'Shall we just go in and start sorting your stuff out?' She spoke as if I was a five-year-old she was trying to coax back into the house while trying to avoid upsetting me.

But it wasn't just the pot. I had also noticed the curtains were drawn right back as far as you could get them, revealing as much of the window as possible. That was not how Betty would normally have drawn them. She only drew them so far back, still half draped across the window, and I was always convinced that was strategic, to allow her cover for spying.

'Emma! Are we doing this or what?' Lisa sounded like she was grasping at the last straw. I decided I had better go in before the camel's back broke.

As I stepped into my home, I immediately noticed a musty smell.

'Shall we start packing a suitcase?' asked an eager Lisa. She was already at the foot of the stairs, and I could sense she wanted to do this as quickly as possible.

'Yes, OK. I'm just going to open some windows and let some air in and then I'll be up. There is a large suitcase under the bed. If you grab that and I'll be up in a sec.'

Lisa nodded and proceeded up the staircase.

I went to the lounge and opened the front windows, but as I did so I saw a white transit van reversing up onto Betty's drive. The male driver jumped out and opened the back of the van up while a female stepped out of the passenger side. To my surprise, she had a key to the front door and was able to let herself in, with the male following her in shortly after. I felt compelled to investigate the situation. Although Betty had proved to be an extremely awkward and frustrating neighbour, she had at times shown me a glimpse of her ability to feel compassion. I believed that she did possess some human decency; it was just buried deep down inside and she used it sparingly.

'I'm just going to check on next door,' I shouted to Lisa up the stairs.

'What?' Lisa shouted back down, despairingly.

I knew she would be annoyed, so I quickly left through the front door before she had chance to stop me. As I started my way down the path, the man came out with a cardboard box full to the brim in his hands and placed it in the van. As he made a return trip back to the house, he noticed me staring at him from across the fence. He smiled but said nothing and disappeared back into the house.

Next, the woman came out, also carrying a box. She gave me a quick glance as she approached the back of the van but did not in any way acknowledge me.

'Hi,' I chirped, determined to catch her attention.

She carefully placed the box in the back of the van and at first I thought she was going to ignore me. But, eventually, although seemingly reluctantly, she finally acknowledged me.

'Hi.'

Now I had her attention, I decided not to beat around the bush.

'Where is Betty?'

'She is no longer here,' she answered awkwardly.

'Well, where has she gone?' I demanded.

Understandably, she was not pleased with my interfering, and I realised I was doing quite a good impersonation of Betty herself.

'Sorry, I don't mean to be nosy, but Betty and I are good neighbours and I'm just concerned for her, that's all.'

I may have slightly overstated the good neighbours bit, but we weren't bad neighbours, so it didn't feel like a lie. The change in my tone seemed to soften the blow and she became more amenable.

'She has not been well and we have had to move her into a home.'

'Oh God.'

I took a deep breath as I tried to take it on board. I knew physically she was waning, but to me she was like a stalwart. I couldn't imagine her needing to rely on others to care for her. I certainly couldn't imagine her moving willingly out of her home.

'Is she coming back?'

'No. We are clearing the place and getting it ready to rent out. It will help fund the care home costs.'

'Are you related to her then?'

'Yes, I am her niece.'

'Ah right. I didn't realise she even had a niece.'

She gave a weak smile, as if there was probably some story to tell. When it came to Betty, that came as no surprise.

'We have not seen her for quite some years.'

I nodded. A person like Betty would have instantly probed deeper, but I refused to pry any further.

'I can give you the details of the care home if you'd like to visit her sometime. I would warn you, though, she is quite poorly. The stroke has had quite an impact on her both physically and mentally.'

'She's had a stroke!' I said, shocked. I don't know why but I'd just assumed she had got a bit too frail to live independently anymore, perhaps having suffered a fall. I hadn't even considered it was something so serious.

'Yes. The doctor had been trying to contact her for several days because she had failed to turn up to a follow-up appointment. Apparently, she had been experiencing some heart trouble and was on some new medication for it. They sent someone out and ended up forcing entry as there was concern for her welfare. They found her collapsed on the kitchen floor. We are not sure how long she had been lying there. The poor woman was covered in flour because apparently she had been in the middle of baking an apple pie or something.'

'Baking an apple pie? Are you sure?'

The woman looked at me very oddly, and I realised how strange my alarmist reaction to such a small detail would have sounded to her.

'Anyway, she was still alive but not in a good way. She spent a few days in hospital, and although she has made a partial recovery there is simply no way she could come back here to live independently.'

Just then, the man came back out.

'What do you want me to do with these?'

The man was waving a white paper bag around.

'Oh, I'm not sure. I might have to contact the doctor. I don't even know if she is supposed to be taking these anymore.'

I squinted to try and see exactly what it was and then realised it was a prescription bag from the pharmacy. The man shrugged and took them back in the house.

'They found those on the front doorstep on the day they came round and found her collapsed. I don't know what they were doing there. She was supposed to be taking them every day for her heart, but they were unopened and she hadn't taken any. I don't know if she forgot them, didn't know if they were there or purposely left them there and refused to take them. But, whatever the reason, it certainly didn't help.'

I swallowed hard. The sudden realisation that the prescription the man had waved about was the very one I had picked up on her behalf and dumped on her front doorstep, was unbearable.

The woman looked on as if waiting for me to answer, but I was speechless, paralysed with guilt.

'Well, I best get on,' she said, breaking the silence.

'Yeh, sure,' I responded, eventually managing to return to life.

I plodded back into the house and slumped myself on the sofa. So now it turned out that I had almost killed two people, as if one wasn't quite enough.

Lisa flew into the room and looked at me despairingly.

'What are you doing? We need to pack your stuff up and get going.'

'Betty almost died, and it was my fault.'

'What?'

I stared back at her in disbelief.

'It was my fault. If I hadn't been so desperate to get to that damn party, she would have had her tablets.'

'Emma. No idea what you are going on about. Who are you talking about?'

'Betty,' I said, with a disapproving tone.

'Who the hell is Betty?'

'My next-door neighbour.'

'Oh.' Lisa sounded relieved, as if Betty was just an inconsequence.

'How is Betty dying your fault?'

'She hasn't died.'

'Oh, well, good.'

'Good? She very nearly died and is seriously ill and has had to go into care. How is that good?'

Lisa huffed. She did look like she had just about had enough of me.

'Isn't this the batty old woman you used to always complain about?'

I contemplated for a moment. Yes, she was batty. She was interfering. She was rude. But she was also genuine, honest and, above all, you knew exactly where you stood with her. There were no charades and no false pretences. That was more than I could say about most of the other people in my life, especially the one who was glaring at me right now. In fact, I had been hoping all along that returning here today would have given me the chance to go round and have a good conflab with her. Strangely enough, she was the one that I felt most comfortable talking to and the person I felt would give me the best advice. But that was not going to happen. Instead, I had to rely on Lisa to help me out and get my life back on track. A person who had only befriended me because she was instructed to, although she had assured me that our friendship was genuine and only the introduction to it was false. I wanted to believe her. I wanted to believe everything she was now doing for me was out of the goodness of her heart and not because it was her job. However, Betty seemed more of a friend to me than Lisa, and Betty was the one I wished was here right now. How ironic when I had spent most of my life as her neighbour trying to dodge her attention and stay out of her way.

My thoughts were then interrupted by the sound of the doorbell ringing.

I got up off the sofa, pushing past Lisa to open the door. It was Betty's niece.

'Hi,' she said tentatively, as if she was worried about disturbing me.

'Hi,' I replied.

'I've got the details here of the home Betty is in.' She offered me a scrap piece of paper with scrawled writing of an address. I willingly accepted it from her.

'Thanks.'

'I've contacted them and added you to the visitor list in case you wanted to visit her.'

'Yes, I will, definitely,' I answered sincerely.

'Good, because I think she would like that. I know you got on quite well.'

Even I couldn't hide my surprise at that comment.

'Oh, she mentioned you from time to time and spoke quite fondly of you.'

'Did she? I thought you hadn't seen her for years?'

'No, we haven't, but we kept in contact occasionally by letter and the odd phone call. Christmas and birthdays mainly.'

'Oh right. Yeh, of course. Well, thanks for this.'

She smiled to me before wandering back up the path. As I watched her close the gate, I did think I could see some physical resemblance to Betty. I wondered if when Betty was her age she smiled as sweetly.

I closed the door behind me and felt a wave of remorse. Lisa was hovering in the lounge doorway.

'Best get packing, I suppose,' I said to her. Lisa's eyes lit up at that response and I made my way upstairs. Soon, my old life would be left a long way behind me and I would be embarking on a new one. Maybe this time it would be better. Maybe.

CHAPTER THIRTY-THREE

I rested my head against the train window, letting the gentle vibrations reverberate against my skull as I looked on at the scenery passing before me. I was tired. It had been a long journey down from Scotland but thankfully I was on the last leg. It had been a little over six months since I was last in Bath, and I had been getting excited about my returning visit. But the closer my train got to its final stop, the more nervous I was getting. Although six months was a reasonably long period to be away, it had felt more like a lifetime. Apart from Lisa, I had not had any contact with anyone else from here since I left all those months ago.

I lifted my head away from the window, stretching and slowly rolling my neck about, as it was getting stiff and beginning to ache. In fact, my whole body was beginning to ache. I had been sat on this train for nearly ten hours, and it was obviously starting to take its toll. It was a relief when the train finally rolled into my station and I could uncoil and actually get up. I only had a short walk to my hotel. I hadn't booked anything elaborate, just a simple single room in a budget hotel and only for a few days. Lisa had tried her best to persuade me not to come, thinking it would do nothing for me and only set me back. I had assured her I was mentally strong enough now and would be able to cope with any emotional reunions. I also reminded her I was not a prisoner. I promised it would be a short visit and that I was firmly fixed on my life now being in Scotland, and I would return there straight after this visit.

Now I was here, I questioned what on earth I was thinking. My departure after my Halloween incident had been swift, with very little time for goodbyes and only a vague explanation about where I was going. What reaction would I really expect from others when I suddenly reappeared? I think I had dreamt of delight and open welcoming arms. That seemed quite stupid now. I decided to put off the dilemma by checking into my hotel and finding somewhere to eat before having an early night. After all, it had been a long day and it was getting late into the afternoon now. It would be better to start my visits tomorrow, after I had replenished and had a good night's sleep.

The nerves had not dissipated by morning, and I was strongly regretting my decision to come. So much for thinking I would feel better once I had slept on it. I decided the first person to visit would be Betty. She seemed the most likely to be more reciprocal towards me. I had called ahead to the care home to announce my visit, if only to check that she was still there and alive even. I was relieved to find she was and that it sounded as if her condition had improved since she was first admitted. On the way, I nipped into a local shop that was selling flowers. There was only limited choice, but the one bunch of mixed colours of tulips seemed the best option. As I walked down the road clutching them, they reminded me of my home and the red tulips that would no doubt be in full bloom. I could feel the sadness sweeping across me, but before it had chance to engulf me I had arrived at the care home which thankfully quashed my thoughts. I rang the bell and, after a few minutes waiting on the doorstep, someone eventually answered the door.

'Good morning. Can I help you?'

'Hi. I'm Emma Maynard. I'm here to visit Betty. I called earlier this morning.'

'Oh yes. Come on in.'

I followed her down the corridor, right to the end, into a very large communal room filled with many elderly residents. Some were partaking in activities, such as the two men at a table in the corner playing dominoes. Others were just sat quietly sipping tea or gazing out the large windows into the garden beyond. One man was fast asleep in a chair, snoring very loudly, while a couple of women knitting were tutting and frowning at him.

'She's over there.' The lady pointed to a woman sat in a large comfy armchair positioned very close to one of the windows, giving an ideal view of the garden. Betty had her back to me and so did not see me approach.

'Hi, Betty.'

'Oh, my goodness!' she exclaimed, clutching her hand to her chest, as if calming her heart. She studied me for a few moments, and I feared she did not recognise me.

'It's Emma. I used to live next door to you.'

'Yes, I know who you are,' she snapped. 'I am not senile.'

Her sharp comment only made me smile with relief that she was of sound mind.

'I've brought you some flowers.'

'Kelly,' Betty yelled across the room, 'could you put these in a vase in my room for me?'

Kelly did as she was told, but she did not look overly enthralled and I felt guilty for bringing them.

I pulled up a nearby seat and took a pew.

'So how are you? I was so sorry to hear you had fallen so ill. I hope you don't mind me visiting. Your niece passed on the details. I haven't been able to visit until now but, well …' I trailed off. Betty was listening to me with what felt like contempt.

'I'm perfectly fine. I don't know why I am still here. I should be back home by now. If it wasn't for family thinking they can meddle in my affairs, I would be.'

I could feel the hostility as she practically spat the words at me. Suddenly I felt like I was coming into the middle of something I really needed to stay well out of.

Kelly had returned and brought us a pot of tea and a plate of biscuits.

'I thought you might like these while you have your little chat.' Kelly gave me a wink and I gave a grateful smile before she then tottered off to the needs of one of the other residents.

I poured the tea. A welcome distraction.

'They better be taking damn well good care of my place while they have shoved me in here. No doubt the place will be a tip, and I will have a job and a half on my plate when I get back. God knows what state the garden is in. A jungle, I expect. Have they been mowing the lawn?'

'Umm ... I don't know. It was six months ago when I was last there. I don't live there anymore. I sold up and moved to Scotland.'

'Scotland? Why an earth would you want to live there? Far too cold and there's nothing there.'

I wanted to ask her how familiar she actually was with the country. I doubt she had even visited it once.

'Well, admittedly, the climate is colder. But I am getting used to it. It was difficult to adjust in the early days, but I am starting to grow quite fond of the place.'

'Pfff … You don't intend to stay there for long, do you? Who's looking after your place while you are away?'

I was already starting to tire of this visit; I wasn't sure how much longer I could last it out.

'No, I am not moving back. I sold the house. I don't own it anymore. Somebody else lives there now.'

'Who? Oh, I hope they aren't noisy. They haven't got kids, have they? I don't want them running about the garden shouting and screaming, kicking footballs into my garden. I hope they haven't hit my greenhouse!'

I was starting to doubt now if she was actually of sound mind.

'Sorry, I don't know who bought it. So you are definitely going back then?'

'Oh yes. I am not staying here.'

I watched her struggle as she took her cup to sip her tea. I noticed she held a tissue permanently in her hand that she would use periodically to dab away dribble at the corner of her mouth. She seemed fairly coherent, but I could see she had physical problems.

'So did that fella of yours move up with you?'

Her question took me aback a bit.

'Fella?'

'Yeh, that one you had round at your house all the time.'

'Oh. You mean Sam. No. I went alone.'

'So he stayed here?'

'Yes. I guess so. I haven't spoken to him.'

'But that's why you came back, to see him.'

She said it as a statement, not a question.

'Left on bad terms, did you? Hoping to patch things up, no doubt. You know what they say. Absence makes the heart grow fonder.'

I didn't quite know how to respond. Worryingly, she was probably quite close to the truth. I hadn't come down here to try and reconnect to my old life and catch up with everyone because I was missing them. I had gone to Scotland to break away and start a new life. I had almost accomplished it, with no desire to reconnect to anything from my past. Except, that is, for one thing. One thing that I could not stop thinking about and I yearned for. I just hadn't been able to admit it to myself.

I thought I'd best change the subject before my emotions started to run too high.

'The garden looks nice,' I said, referring to the view that was presented right in front of us. One of the windows was slightly open, letting in a fresh warm breeze and the sound of the birds that were dancing between an olive tree and some other small tree, unrecognisable to me. They looked like they were working up courage to feed from the bird feeders placed nearby.

'Yes, it's OK, I suppose, but I keep telling Harry he's pruning the roses all wrong, and he's practically killed off that rhododendron over there.' She was pointing frantically at a plant that admittedly did not look the healthiest.

I smiled, surmising that Harry was probably just as keen as Betty that she returned home as soon as possible.

'And I don't know what it is he is planting over there. It just looks like grass and weeds to me,' she said, continuing with her rant.

I felt sorry for Harry. Whoever Harry was. Although I couldn't help but picture him as our very own Harry from Sapphire Hotel. For a moment, I even wondered if he might have left there and come here instead, but it was unlikely, just a funny coincidence.

'Anyway, I am sure you have got better things to do than just sitting here listening to an old woman like me. Probably better off spending time with that fella of yours.'

I took the final sip from my teacup and placed it down on the table.

'Yes, I probably ought to go and get on.'

I felt slightly choked by her words and also somewhat heartless. Had I really come here just to see how Betty was, or was I hoping to get some reassurance that it was OK to visit the person I really wanted to see?

'It was nice seeing you, Betty, and I am glad you are recovering well. I hope you get your wish to go home soon.'

I got up from the chair and gave her a peck on the cheek. She was startled by my action and never said a word as I left.

As I passed the main desk on my way out, I saw Kelly.

'Did it go OK?' she asked apprehensively.

'Yeh, fine.'

'Oh good. I know she can be quite awkward. She doesn't really get many visitors, nor does she get on with any of the other residents. It's nice to see her actually getting on with someone and having a proper conversation.'

'Is she going to be here much longer? I know she is keen to get back home.'

'Oh, she won't be going home. She is a permanent resident. In fact, I think her family has sold her house.'

'Right.'

I could feel the anger starting to mount on hearing that. I thought I ought to leave quickly before it became insurmountable.

'Thanks for the tea. Bye.'

'OK, bye. Hopefully, see you again soon. I am sure Betty would enjoy another visit.'

I smiled weakly and waved goodbye. It was highly unlikely I would return.

As I stepped into the fresh air, I did a few breathing exercises that I had learnt over the last months to help control my temper. I wanted to be in the right frame of mind if I was going to see Sam.

CHAPTER THIRTY-FOUR

The hotel was a bit further away than I had realised. I decided to catch a bus rather than walk it. Luck was on my side as the bus pulled up just as I got to the bus stop. It was only a short ten-minute journey by bus, and I could feel my excitement building. There was another five-minute walk or so at the other end and then finally I arrived. I had forgotten what a magnificent building it was. This was the first time I had walked down the entire length of the drive to get to the main building. I had only ever driven down it before, and I hadn't appreciated quite how long it was. I marvelled at the lovingly kept lawns and the tulips in full bloom. It made me think of Harry, and I wondered if he was still here and in charge of the gardens. I looked around for him as I made my way to the main front of house, but disappointingly I could see no sign of him. The closer I got to the stone steps leading up to the main door, the faster my heartbeat. The door swung open as someone was about to come out, and I waited in trepidation to see who it was.

'Afternoon,' said the elderly man dressed in a fine country tweed suit.

'Afternoon,' I replied. I was sure he was a hotel resident, maybe out for a leisurely stroll.

He held the door open for me and I smiled sweetly as I passed through.

'Thank you very much,' I said in a formal tone, as if he was royalty.

Now I was inside, my heart was at full pelt and in danger of jumping out of my chest. Jess was behind reception and gave me a beaming smile.

'Emma!' she shouted in astonishment, lifting the reception hatch with such vigour I thought it would come off its hinge. She immediately embraced me and squeezed me very tightly, uncomfortably tightly.

'You're back! It's so good to see you.' Thankfully, she loosened her grip and stepped back out of my personal space.

'Hi, Jess. It's good to see you too. How are you?'

'I'm fine. How are you? I didn't know if you were ever coming back. Everyone was very coy about it.'

'I'm good, thanks.'

'Look, I've almost finished my shift. Do you want to grab some lunch and catch up? I'm not due back till later this afternoon.'

In true Jess style, she caught me off guard and I responded without thinking it through.

'Yes, sure. Sounds good.'

I could have kicked myself.

'Great, Stefan should be here in a minute to take over reception. Once he gets here, we can go. We can pop into town if you like. There's a nice café I go to sometimes. Food's good, especially the cakes,' she said, grinning.

So Stefan still worked here at least. I wanted to ask her if Sam was still here, but I couldn't summon the courage just yet.

'We can go in my car if you like?'

'OK, yep.'

Jess went back round behind reception to tidy up a few things while I waited and sat in one of the guest reception chairs.

In the distance, I could hear voices coming from down the corridor. The double doors obscured who it was until finally they swung open and two people stepped through. I immediately recognised Stefan, but it took a little longer for the penny to drop for the second person.

'Oh damn, I've forgotten my purse,' said Amelia frustratingly as she had her head down, rummaging through her handbag. The distraction meant she had not actually seen me and judging by Stefan's expression that was probably some relief to him. He had been looking open-mouthed between me and Amelia, as if he was watching a tennis match, until finally settling on me.

I stared back at him for as long as I could, but my eyes were eventually drawn back to Amelia. She was now waddling back down the corridor the way she had come. Even after she had gone through the swinging doors and out of sight, I was still looking after her.

Eventually, I managed to break my gaze. Stefan was still staring at me in amazement, and Jess, who was still the other side of reception, was now also staring at me. I felt like I was a freak.

Suddenly Jess snapped into gear.

'Right, let's go. Stefan, reception is yours.' She lifted the hatch but this time made sure it stayed aloft, marched through, grabbed me by the arm and waltzed me out. It felt like a definite attempt to avoid a situation.

'How many months pregnant is she?'

At first, I thought Jess had pretended not to hear because she took so long to answer.

'Six,' she winced.

'She's very big.'

'It's twins.'

By now, we had reached the car. Jess was at the driver's door and I was at the front passenger's, waiting for her to unlock it, but before she did, I had time for one more question.

'I take it, it is Sam's?'

She nodded. I heard the click of the centralised locking mechanism as she turned the key. We both got in and said nothing more until we were sat at a table in the café, by which time I had completely lost my appetite.

'So what happened to you? You just sort of disappeared. Tom said you had gone away for a while up north somewhere?'

I had a cheese jacket potato in front of me that was still steaming. I had attempted to eat one mouthful, but it was so hot it burnt my tongue. I had been eager to spit it straight back out, but I had better etiquette than that. Instead, I juggled it around in my mouth for a while, hoping that it would lessen the impact if it was in minimal contact with my tongue, before I eventually managed to swallow it.

'Yes, I went up to Scotland.'

'Oh? Do you have relatives up there?'

Jess was stuffing her face with a jam and cream doughnut, and I wondered how someone in such fine figure could get away with eating something that was so calorie laden.

'No.'

'So you were on your own?'

I cut another piece of potato off, but as I brought the fork to my mouth, I could still see steam rising from it so thought better of it and let it drop back down on the plate.

'Yes. Well, I had some help. My friend Lisa, she organised somewhere for me to stay.'

'Did it help? I mean, are you all right now?'

I was perplexed by her question. I couldn't remember anyone actually asking me if I was all right for such a long time.

'At first, we thought maybe you were in prison or something. You know, for the attack. But then when Tom said you had moved away, we thought maybe you had suffered some kind of breakdown and needed to get away for a while to recover.'

Jess was making me feel very uncomfortable with her reference to the attack. I had learnt to keep that awful memory at bay and not let it consume or overwhelm me, but now Jess was in danger of making it resurface.

I placed my cutlery back on the plate together, to intimate I was finished with my meal. I wasn't even hungry, and all it was doing was burning my mouth. I decided to speak frankly to Jess.

'Look, Jess. It was an awful time. I could very well have been suffering from some mental episode, I don't really know. I had been going through some really difficult stuff, and I think it must have affected me somehow. I just lost it. I had to go away. Sort my head out. Get control of my life again.'

'And have you?'

'Yes. I think so.'

'So how did going to Scotland help? What's so special up there?'

I chuckled and Jess chuckled back.

'Well, for a start, it took me well away from what had happened. Then gradually I was able to come to terms with what I had done and begin the process of moving on from it and rebuilding my life. I have been taking various courses to help.'

'Courses? What … like anger management-type stuff?'

'Yeh, I guess. Meditation, self-healing, that kind of thing, and I took classes locally in yoga and tai chi.'

‘Really? Wow, are you some kind of martial arts expert now then? I mean, you looked like you were already able to handle yourself pretty well before.’

I smiled wryly. She still couldn’t help herself referring to the incident. I was not so uncomfortable talking about it now. In some ways, it was quite refreshing someone was willing to talk about it with me. Up until now, everyone had tried to bury it, as if it had not even happened.

‘No, I wouldn’t say I am an expert, but I am not bad.’

In actual fact, I had trained in these disciplines for hour upon hour each day, as if it was my sole purpose in life and up to a point that I had become quite proficient. Even my teacher seemed amazed by my progress, and I was easily equal to his skills, if not surpassing them.

‘It’s not so much about teaching me how to fight in combat. It is more about learning to stay in control and finding peace within myself.’

Jess grinned. I wasn’t sure if she thought I was just talking mumbo jumbo or if she actually believed in what I was saying. She took the last mouthful of her cake and then brushed off some of the sugar coating that had fallen off onto her jumper.

‘So are you back for good now?’

I hesitated in my answer. The intention was always to return to Scotland, but the longer I was down here, the more I was beginning to wonder.

‘No. I don’t think so. Anyway, I’ve sold my house and I’m just in the process of buying the one I am in at the moment.’

‘Oh! So you have moved permanently?’

‘Yes.’

‘Oh, Emma. I thought you’d come back. I thought you would be back at work and everything.’

She appeared genuinely upset and I felt touched, if not a little surprised.

‘I don’t think there would be any way I could come back after what I did. Do you?’

She thought about it for a moment, and I could tell by the expression on her face that she didn’t really think I could return.

'So, anyway, enough about me. What's been happening here? I see Stefan is still about.'

I purposely omitted Amelia's name.

'Yes, he's still here.'

'And Harry?'

'Yes, and Harry. Still managing the gardens. I don't see him that much as he generally stays outside or hides in his shed.'

'How is Tom?'

'Oh, you know. Tom is Tom. Stressed most of the time. He worries about having nothing to worry about. He is away at the moment on a break. I expect when he comes back he will be doubly stressed because he hasn't been here to keep an eye on things. I think he is back next week. Will you still be here then?'

'No. I am probably going back the day after tomorrow.'

'That's a shame. It would have been nice for him to see you.'

I doubted that very much.

'And what about Sam? Are he and Amelia still together as a couple?' I almost choked on the words. It seemed inconceivable that they were not only a couple but were about to start a family together.

Jess looked very uneasy and as if she wasn't sure what to say.

'No. Not exactly.'

Jess wouldn't even give me eye contact as she said it.

'So they split up?' I asked, hardly able to contain my glee. Suddenly I had a glimmer of a reason for not returning to Scotland.

Jess looked incredibly sheepish as I waited impatiently for her answer.

For the second time that day, I found myself clutching a bunch of flowers to take for my next visit.

I wasn't even sure if Sam liked flowers, but I wanted to take something, and this seemed appropriate.

'Hi, Sam. It's been a long time.'

My voice wavered and the tears started to flow. I wondered if my visit would have brought him happiness or resentment. I hoped for happiness, but I would never know.

I placed the flowers at the foot of his gravestone. I was sobbing so hard I was not even able to read the words on his stone.

Jess had broken it to me that Sam had died in a motorbike accident only two days after the Halloween party. Apparently, he stood no chance and it was instant. He had failed to give way at a crossroads and got completely taken out by the car he should have given way to. Sam of course was judged to have been excessively speeding, and I could just picture him now, showing off. It wasn't even his bike and he didn't have a licence.

'Oh, Sam. How could you be so stupid?'

I had been so angry with him for going off with Amelia. Although the anger had simmered over the last few months, it had only turned to sadness and dismay. I had wrestled with my emotions on the basis of how we parted. The last time I saw him, I had fought him. Hurt him. It was forever etched in my memory; the disdain in his eyes and the disbelief at my actions. I believe at that moment he hated me, and to know that was his last feeling towards me cut me to the quick.

'I am so sorry, Sam. I am so sorry for what I did. I cannot believe you are gone and that I can never even begin to make it up to you.'

Lisa had begged me not to come to Bath. Over and over, she had told me nothing good would come of it. Now I wondered if she knew Sam had died and she was trying to protect me. Could it have been that the hope of thinking he was alive and that one day I might get to see him again was providing me with the energy and motivation to keep going? Now I knew he was gone, that light of hope was extinguished, and perhaps I was only destined to fail.

I took one long last look at his grave through my tear-stained eyes. I would forever regret that I did not show him my true feelings earlier and would always wonder what could have been.

'Goodbye, Sam,' blowing him a kiss as I left. I did not look back. I did not know what the future would hold, but I knew that there was nothing left here for me. I vowed never to return.

CHAPTER THIRTY-FIVE

There were some days when I had no idea why I still did this job. In the early days, it was thrilling and so exhilarating. I had loved all the secrecy, the risk-taking and daringness. It made me feel special and important while feeding my addiction for adventure and living on the edge. That was the early days, though. Now it had become tiring, cumbersome and often a moral dilemma.

I had about five minutes before my meeting with the boss, and I had no idea how I was going to play this. Worse still was that the little whippersnapper was coming as well, and even if I decided to keep quiet, I doubted he would keep his mouth shut. That was the trouble with these youngsters. They thought once they had made it past the initial probation period that they had not just proved themselves worthy but were somehow God's gift and knew it all. Andrew was worse. He actually thought he knew better, and I had a hard job keeping him in his place.

I could see Andrew was getting twitchy, shuffling and reshuffling papers. Reorganising items on his desk while glancing back and forth at the clock. I always left for meetings at the last possible minute, which did not suit Andrew's obsession with time and the need for him to turn up early.

'OK, Andrew, let's go.'

He jumped up immediately to leave and looked mighty relieved.

'Now remember,' I said, as we walked side by side down the corridor, 'let me do the talking.'

I gave him a long hard stare as a warning shot, but he quickly dropped his eyes to avoid eye contact and I knew I was asking for the impossible.

I took a deep breath and opened the door to the boss's office. I was not looking forward to this, and I was contemplating that maybe I should just resign. That was if I didn't get fired first.

‘Lisa. Come in, come in. Take a seat.’

I smiled, closed the door and sat directly opposite him at his desk.

Andrew looked lost and was frantically trying to work out where he should sit.

Stanley hadn’t so much as looked at him, never mind spoken to him. I wasn’t even sure if he had noticed him. I had to contain my smugness and joy at seeing Andrew being reduced to insignificance. The only other chair in the room was placed right in the far corner, and I could see Andrew was not going to accept that as his seat. He predictably picked it up and moved it alongside mine. Andrew momentarily gained Stanley’s attention, but it was soon returned to me.

‘Now then, Lisa. What’s the update on Stanton?’

That was Stanley, straight to the point. No niceties or small talk.

It always amazed me that they still insisted on referring to her as Stanton. She hadn’t been a Stanton since the age of seven, when she was adopted, and anyway, I had discovered that she hadn’t even been Emma Stanton in the first place. Still, to them, it was only a file name to identify her by, nothing human or personable about it.

‘Yes, sir, it all seems to be going just fine. I think we’ve got over the worst of it and she seems quite settled.’

‘What’s this I hear she returned to Bath?’ I could sense the displeasure in his voice. I knew that was not going to go down well with him. I’d tried to stop her going but she had grown quite stubborn over the last few months, and I was beginning to think I had softened.

‘A small hiccup, sir, but it hasn’t been a problem. She’s back now. We don’t think she has any intention to return in the future.’

‘Hmm …’ he murmured. He didn’t sound very convinced.

‘And she has been attending all the sessions?’

‘Yes. That’s all going very well. The instructors are very pleased with her progress.’

‘Hmm …’

‘She seems very dedicated,’ I added, trying to persuade him it really was all OK.

‘And has she been displaying any extra abilities?’

I coughed to clear my throat. I had hoped he wasn’t going to go down that avenue, and I wasn’t fully sure how best to respond.

He looked at me impatiently as I delayed my answer.

'Nothing confirmed yet, sir. We are still looking into it.'

He screwed his eyes up at me, and I felt I needed to maintain eye contact to help convince him I wasn't hiding anything.

'Well, actually, sir, there have been some reports of enhanced abilities.'

Oh great. I forgot he was still sat there next to me. Up until now he had been as quiet as a mouse. Biding his time, no doubt, before he could find the appropriate moment to pipe up and make sure he got himself heard.

Stanley still had his eyes fixated on me, and I swear he hadn't blinked once in all that time.

'As I said, sir, nothing confirmed. We are going to need a bit more time, I think, to fully establish the facts.' If I thought I could get away with it, I would have given Andrew a quick short kick, but I was already treading on thin ice and the last thing I needed was an HR reprimand.

'What kind of things?'

Stanley was still directing his questions to me but I knew if I did not provide satisfactory answers, he would turn his attention to Andrew.

'Well, there's obviously the enhanced strength.'

'We knew that already.'

'Exactly.'

'Which we believe has increased significantly in the last six months,' uttered Andrew.

Stanley looked at Andrew. I couldn't tell if it was an inquisitive stare or if he was just irked by him. He certainly irked me. I really needed to find an excuse to fire this guy.

Andrew seized the chance of having finally succeeded at gaining some attention. Referring to the papers he had brought with him, he began to spill the beans.

'For example, on 17th March, she was in receipt of a washing machine. The driver, which of course was actually one of our undercover guys, reported he couldn't get the tail lift on the lorry to work in order to lower the appliance down to ground level. Apparently, Miss Stanton was able to just pick it up and lower it manually herself. Furthermore …' He had now turned the page. I scoffed at how he was incapable of being succinct. Andrew seemed to think the more you said, the more intelligent you sounded. To me, it was all waffle.

'She didn't even wait for the driver to get the trolley sack to take it down the path to the house. She just picked it up and carried it in.'

Andrew looked back up from his notes and stared back at Stanley as if he was waiting for a reply of admiration. Stanley said nothing and just continued to stare in bemusement at him.

'It weighed over ninety kilograms.' He sounded desperate, confused as to why he was not showing him the slightest reaction.

'That's over fourteen stone.'

Yeh, that's right, Andrew. Why not insult Stanley by assuming his age dictates his inability to have any perception of weight in kilograms? Idiot.

I don't think Stanley appreciated the patronising tones of Andrew because he ignored him and switched his attention back to me.

'Is that it? Isn't there anything else? I was told there was a high probability Stanton was going to be something pretty special. All I'm hearing is she happens to be able to carry her own bloody washing machine into her house.'

I looked at Andrew in disgust, placing the blame entirely on his shoulders. We could have been in and out of there in fifteen minutes tops if only he could just learn the skill of not talking. Of course, the real solution would be if he didn't have to tag along with me to these things in the first place. However, company protocol dictated that these young whippersnappers that were placed under my supervision had to follow me around like long-lost sheep in order to give them the best exposure and experience for their career progression. Well, I was not sure Andrew was doing much for his career progression right now. He certainly wasn't doing mine any favours.

Giving Andrew another long hard stare was a mistake. I think Andrew took that as a signal to continue with the waffle and get us into a bigger hole.

'There is more, sir.' He was frantically rushing through the pages, trying to dig up more dirt.

'Yes, here.' He cleared his throat, ready for the big announcement.

'Multiple instances. 5th Dec, 19th Dec, umm …' more rustling of pages ' … again, 4th Jan,' he droned, and looked up to see if Stanley was listening.

'I'm not interested in the dates,' he barked.

Andrew looked rattled and I thought he might break. In fairness, he managed to pull himself together, although I didn't want him to say anything. I was, after all, trying my best to protect Emma because I knew what it meant if they realised she was something special.

'We think she has developed a type of sixth sense.'

Now, that perked up Stanley, and I could see the glint in his eyes. Andrew must have noticed it too because he regained his confidence and was talking with much more authority in his voice.

'She seems to know when she is being watched. Like she has eyes in the back of her head. Whenever we send some guys up there to watch her, they are finding it difficult to remain covert. Apparently, as time goes on, it is getting increasingly difficult. They are having to watch her from further and further afield, and yet still she seems to pick up on their presence. She can even be in the house and then suddenly comes out to look for them and stares right in their direction.'

'You didn't think to mention this?' he said accusingly at me.

I was usually quite good at thinking on my feet and giving a quick response. It had got me out of no end of scrapes, particularly with Stanley. Today was not one of those days. I was flailing. I couldn't think of anything to say. Andrew was outwitting me. I was going to have to write that letter of resignation sooner than I thought. Right after this meeting.

'What's more, we think this sixth sense goes even beyond this.'

Stanley looked away from me and cocked his head at Andrew, clearly intrigued. How the tables had turned, and Andrew seemed to be on quite a roll.

'Her tai chi instructor said from her first lessons she appeared to be an average student. But she has advanced to what he states are incredible levels. He says, and I quote, "It is as if she can predict my moves before I have executed them."'

Stanley remained in the same head-cocked position, but he was now frowning.

'She is displaying the ability of foresight, sir.'

Stanley leant back in his chair and looked pensive. Andrew mimicked him by also sitting back, and waited. I noted how Andrew looked quite pleased with himself, and I was surprised he was able to stay quiet. I was mortified. I was hoping to keep this information away from them, but it was getting increasingly difficult and not just because of motormouth over there. There were just too many incidents and they were getting more elaborate. I don't even know why I thought I could keep it hushed up. Maybe I was getting far too overconfident and a bit too big for my boots.

'Is there anything else I should know?'

I suddenly sparked into life. I could see Andrew was about to spout more, but I got in first.

'No, sir. The incidents Andrew refer to have been sporadic and possibly a bit presumptuous. There is nothing really concrete yet, which is why I hadn't mentioned it. I wanted to continue with some more monitoring to gather more substantiating evidence before reporting it as fact.'

I sneaked in another quick hard stare at Andrew, but he didn't notice as he was fixated on Stanley.

My answer appeared to satisfy Stanley, which was surprising given I had not been very forthcoming.

'OK then. I want surveillance on Stanton substantially increased. I want more thorough investigation on this sixth sense you keep going on about and the foresight.'

'Yes, sir, of course.'

'If that means getting her back into one of our facilities, then do it.'

'Oh, I don't think there is any need for that,' I quickly replied.

Stanley glared at me. That was the wrong answer.

'I mean, we should try not to at first at least,' I rapidly backtracked.

Still didn't look like it was the right answer in Stanley's eyes, but it was a better one.

'I want a report in exactly one week on what you have found.'

I nodded while absentmindedly wondering if they would make me work my notice period out or would let me leave straight away.

'Right. You better update me on what's happening with Unit 74.'

I took another deep breath. At least this would be a shorter conversation as we really didn't have much information on what was happening there.

'So the seismic activity that was detected in the area has been explained away as small earthquake tremors. That seems to have calmed the situation down a bit and hopefully satisfied the locals.'

'And do we actually think it was an earthquake or is there really some chance we have left some down there?'

'We can't find any evidence that there is any presence of them in the caves. We are certainly not picking up anything on any radar or sensor equipment, and a team did go up and do a visual search and found nothing.'

'Hmm.' Another groan from Stanley, suggesting he was not convinced, which was perfectly justified. The caves were so extensive and in some places extremely deep that I doubted we could really be sure we had thoroughly covered everything.

'Well, they did find some damage,' Andrew blurted.

Oh, good grief. Someone, help me, please, and take me away from this nightmare. What was wrong with this guy? I felt sure we were just tying up the loose ends and bringing this meeting to a close. But not now, opening up a whole can of worms.

I needed to sting this one in the tail quickly.

'It's true, sir. There was some minimal damage on the surface, just outside the caves.' I put strong emphasis on the word 'minimal' and made sure I looked hard at Andrew as I said it. He saw me this time but didn't flinch. I think this guy was making a ploy for my job. He was welcome to it, but he wouldn't be able to cut it, and I doubted he would last five minutes.

'Some kids had got into the resort and just been messing around.'

'Kids? Are we sure? How did they get in?'

'Yeh, it was picked up on CCTV. Something about one of the fences damaged or something. It's all been sorted now.'

'I don't think there were any reports of kids.' Andrew was rifling frantically through his papers, trying to find the evidence. He wouldn't find it because I lied. But no one had been able to give me an explanation of what had caused that damage, and I was just making a best guess. We'd had trouble in the past with people trying to get in and had to keep beefing up the security. It was the most likely answer, and any possibility of *them* still being down there was just so miniscule it seemed silly to even entertain it.

'So, if there is nothing else, sir. Shall we call it a day and I'll get straight on to the Stanton case?'

I jumped out of my seat and edged towards the door. Andrew was still sitting there, looking very bewildered.

'You're sure that Unit 74 is all secure and there is nothing to worry about?'

'Absolutely, sir. It's all good.' I said it with such conviction even I was impressed. The question was, however, was it enough to impress Stanley?

'OK, Lisa. I'll see you in a week.'

Phew. Dodged another bullet. I was getting good at this. I was gone like a shot. Leaving Andrew for dust. I wasn't bothered about Andrew saying anything more to Stanley. I bet he tried once I was out of the picture, but he wouldn't have got anywhere. Once Stanley had terminated a meeting, that was it. It was final and he was already on the next thing. In any case, Stanley was very much about status and hierarchy, and Andrew was far too low down the ladder from him to warrant any meaningful attention.

I skipped down the corridor and was already thinking about what I could get up to that night. It was Friday and I always went out on a Friday. I remembered when Emma and I used to go out sometimes. She usually tried to make an excuse not to come, but I could nearly always convince her. I missed those nights. She could be a bit strait-laced but she was a good friend, and sometimes she would let her hair down and could be quite fun. There were many times when I forgot that the real reason we got to know each other was because of my involvement with the JAHL project. It seemed unbelievable at times that ours was an artificial friendship. Of course, to me it wasn't an artificial relationship. She was a genuine friend. It made me shudder to think of some of the things I had done and the lies I had told. At the time, I believed it was my duty and an absolute necessity. Now, I think I was young and easily led by other more confident people. But I had grown stronger and wiser since those days and I had had enough. On reaching the office, I went straight to my desk and began to draft my resignation. I had never written one before as this was the only job I'd had, and I suddenly realised I wasn't sure what you were supposed to write.

Andrew entered the office, looking rather dejected, as I sat pen in hand and an empty sheet in front of me.

'Andrew. Any ideas on how you should write a resignation letter?'

He frowned, said nothing and sat at his desk. He plonked his papers down and sat back in his chair with his shoulders dropped.

'Why? Are you thinking of leaving?'

'Sure am. You can have my job if you like.' I said it jokingly but then realised Andrew would probably take that seriously and jump at the chance.

Andrew exhaled deeply. 'Not particularly.'

His comment made me drop my pen. I was surprised I didn't fall off my chair.

As it turned out, I never wrote that letter of resignation. Things took a dramatic turn not long after that meeting, and suddenly all hands were to the pump. Ironically, Andrew did hand his notice in. I heard he had switched careers entirely, working in retail or something bizarre like that. At first, I was jealous that he had got the quieter life, but as soon as I was back in the fold, the thrill and exhilaration returned, and I realised the quieter life was not for me.

CHAPTER THIRTY-SIX

I knew she was here well before the knock on the door came. I had sensed her presence. It had become a useful skill that I had once found disturbing but now I found quite pleasing. Only two nights ago, someone thought they could sneak onto my property late at night and burgle me. They were barely on my property for more than two minutes before I sent them packing with their tail between their legs and quite possibly with a broken arm. I am fairly sure I heard something snap when I tackled him to the floor. His wailing as I dispensed him from my house certainly implied I had caused him considerable harm.

It wasn't the first time I had broken someone else's bones. My own tai chi instructor has been in plaster for the last month, courtesy of my overzealousness. We had been training together and I just hit him too hard. It was a complete accident and I don't know how I managed to do it. It felt to me like I barely touched him. He had already warned me about the ferocity I was putting into some of my moves. I had done my best to tame them down. Sometimes, I barely felt like I was putting any effort in at all, and I wondered if there was any real point in going to these training sessions. I genuinely felt like the trainer didn't want to be there anymore. I am not sure if he was even becoming frightened of me. He certainly appeared quite nervous.

Something was definitely going on. At first, I explained things away as just purely natural occurrences, maybe a fluke or just luck happening to be on my side. When I first started noticing I was under some kind of surveillance, I remember having that feeling of being watched. I assumed the reason I had detected them hiding was because I must have subconsciously heard or seen something that had alerted me to them. When my tai chi training sessions became so easy for me that I barely had to try and it had got to the point that they were boring, I assumed it was just because I had been such a good dedicated student and had mastered the skill. But as time progressed, what I was experiencing could not possibly constitute normal human behaviour.

I must have been part of the JAHL project. No matter what Lisa had said, I no longer believed it. It drove me almost to insanity knowing that again I had been lied to and completely taken in.

I had intended to contact Lisa myself and confront her about it, but before I had the chance she unexpectedly contacted me and asked to come and visit. She sounded quite desperate, and I got the impression she would have come anyway, even if I had refused.

The knock on the door finally came, and I readied myself for what was going to be a difficult conversation. As it turned out, nothing could have prepared me for what Lisa was about to say.

'Hi,' I said, with an air of sarcasm.

'Hi, Emma. We need to talk.'

'We do. Better come in then.'

I sat down but Lisa remained standing, and I was in no mood to play the kind host so didn't bother offering her a seat.

Lisa appeared agitated and also not in the mood for any small talk. Instead, she got straight to the point.

'We have a bit of a situation and we need your help.'

She looked at me in a way that suggested she knew she was being cheeky with such a request but at the same time was being perfectly serious.

'With what?'

'Unit 74.' It was at that point she decided to take a seat, as if she was giving me some time to digest it. I gave her a frown. 'It wouldn't be the first time you have been there now, would it?'

I'd long suspected that she had known about my second visit to Roseville, but this was the first time I had heard her admit it. I remember being suspicious of so many people potentially watching me and following me, but I had convinced myself it was just paranoia. While some were indubitably perfectly innocent people going about their daily lives, I am sure some were rogue and had been sent to follow me by Lisa.

'To do what?'

'To go on a reconnaissance mission.'

'And why do you want me specifically?'

She swayed her head a couple of times from side to side, looking up to the ceiling as if she was trying to find the right words.

'Well, how can I put it? We need someone who has unique abilities.'

'What kind of unique abilities?'

'Hmmph,' murmured Lisa with a wry smile, 'the kind that you possess.'

'And where did I get these unique abilities from exactly? I mean, it couldn't have been from the JAHL project because you told me I wasn't anything to do with that.' I was trying to stay calm, but I could feel the anger rising and hear the tension in my own voice.

I could see Lisa squirming in her seat, trying to find a more comfortable spot. Eventually, she settled on perching on the very edge of the seat, leaning forward, her hands wildly gesturing as she spoke.

'Look, Emma, I know this is difficult. I know I may not have handled all this too well at times. But the bottom line is. We have a situation. It might be serious but then again it might not be anything. I think it's probably just something that has been blown way out of proportion, but we obviously can't risk it and need to make sure. I am asking you. Please can you help us, because you are the best-placed person to help us with this.'

'You've got some serious gall.'

'Yeh, well, you don't get if you don't ask.'

My initial reaction was to throw her out. But as I sat and thought about it, I did begin to wonder.

I clearly was no ordinary person. In fact, I was something special. I had been born into this world unwanted. My life up until all this saga began had been unworthy and insignificant. But all that had now changed. I was desperately wanted. Needed. Invaluable. It made me feel invigorated. Was I really just going to sit here and live my life out in this isolated and unassuming existence? Lisa was giving me an opportunity to make a real purpose of my life and I was going to seize it. I could feel the fire igniting in my belly and a new lease of life forming. First, though, before agreeing to anything, I wanted answers.

'Let's just say I do agree to help you.'

Lisa's eyes suddenly perked up and she looked quite shocked. I think she thought the only thing she would get from me was a full-on rant. To be honest, that's probably all she deserved.

'I first want to know exactly how I came to get these so-called unique abilities. And I don't want any crap. You tell me the truth. Otherwise, you can just get lost and leave me alone.'

For a moment, I think I stunned Lisa into silence. She was not used to me being so blunt and taking such a hardline approach. It was completely out of character for me. At least my old character.

'OK,' she finally replied.

'Any chance of a drink first? I am a bit parched.'

'No.'

Another period of stunned silence.

'OK.'

I was really beginning to enjoy being the one in control for a change.

'I know you think I lied about you not being part of the JAHL project. But I was telling the truth.'

'Right. Fine. You can get out of my house now,' I said angrily, jumping to my feet and pointing to the door.

'Wait. Just hear me out,' she replied resolutely.

I dubiously returned to my seat.

'Let me rephrase that. You were not part of the *initial* stage of the JAHL project.'

'What?' I was not sure how that was supposed to make it any clearer.

'OK. So the JAHL project all started in 1975 and you were not anything to do with that, and the story I told you about the cover-up of Emma Stanton dying at the care home and the identity switch with you is all true.'

'Is it?' I said, not believing a word.

'Yes,' she replied firmly. 'I know it was a bit vague. Honestly, we did quite an extensive investigation around it because we didn't quite believe it at first, either, and it was difficult to establish all the evidence. Certainly, we don't know where Emma Stanton's body is buried, but there is overwhelming evidence that the switch between you two definitely happened. We have no doubt on that matter.'

She sounded very definite.

'But, during the second stage of JAHL when we brought you back to Roseville to run some tests, well, we did more than just run tests.'

Her admission, although it shouldn't have been a real surprise to me, still felt like a bombshell.

'I was injected with this stuff, wasn't I? Something extra ordinary that ended up giving me these superhuman abilities.'

'Yes. But it wasn't my doing. In fact, I tried to stop it. I thought I had stopped it.'

'So how did it happen?'

'I was overruled and it was done without my prior knowledge.'

'Was I injected with it on that first day at Roseville, when I blacked out and awoke the next day with a sore arm?'

'No. Only the tests were being run then. It was later on.'

I nodded casually. It mattered very little when I was injected with it; a few days here or there was beside the point. The point was, Lisa had gone to great lengths to persuade me I had never been a part of this experiment. Not ever. Not in the initial stage. Not in the second stage. Even though I had recently realised she must have lied, it still hurt to hear her confession.

We sat in silence for several minutes as I allowed my heartbeat to slow and I could reach back to a state of calm. It had been a long time since I had any discussions about what happened on that trip to Roseville, and I had barely thought about it in recent months. But now the mention of it again had triggered the long-distant memory, and I was becoming acutely aware of my interest in the place being sparked once again.

'So that first day when we arrived and you disappeared down that secret rabbit hole in our cabin …' Lisa looked taken aback by my comment. I think she thought the conversation about Roseville was over and was not expecting me to probe further. 'What was that all about?'

She huffed, sounding almost embarrassed.

‘It was all a bit of a disaster. I messed up. I was supposed to administer a drug in your drink that would put you to sleep so the tests could be conducted that evening. We weren’t even supposed to get as far as going to dinner.’

‘So what went wrong?’

‘I failed to put it in your first drink. Partly because I forgot and then by the time I was halfway through pouring it, you were standing right over me and I couldn’t do it then. Then trying to get you to have a second one was a nightmare. You kept saying no until then eventually I managed to persuade you. By then, I think I was in a bit of a panic, but I did manage to get the drug into the glass out of your sight.

‘It was only after I had given you yours and I had drunk a fair bit of mine that I began to question if I had given you the right one. I was fairly sure I hadn’t. That meant not only had I failed to give you the drug, it was now in my system instead.’

I couldn’t help but give a snort of laughter. That was Lisa through and through. I was surprised she would be entrusted with doing something like that. Sometimes, I wondered if she could tie her own shoelaces.

‘It wasn’t funny. I got into a lot of trouble for that. Anyway, I had no choice. I had to quickly get to the labs and sort my mess out because I wasn’t sure how long I had before the drug took effect. They gave me something to combat its effects … an antidote or something. They disguised it in a drink that looked roughly the colour of the wine and sent me back up with it as they wanted me back up there as quickly as possible in case you noticed I was gone.’

‘You weren’t quick enough. I also remember you coming back in with what looked like another glass of wine, because I was confused when I knew I had seen the bottle and glass in your room and they were both empty.’

‘Yep, I know. I never knew you were so observant. Anyway, we felt we had got away with it, but now we had to proceed with dinner and find some other way to give you the drug.’

‘So when was I slipped the drug? At dinner?’

‘No. Although I was expecting it to be then. I don’t know what was going on. They were trying to tell me that they were going to have to suspend it for a different day. I was getting quite wound up about it. In the end, we managed to spike one of the cocktails you had later.'

'Just after that, you disappeared for a bit. It took me ages to find you.'

'I was annoyed, not to mention exhausted, with how the night had gone. They told me the drug wouldn't take long to take effect, so I thought I was OK to just leave you in there. I assumed within minutes the deed would be done and my part would be over. As it turned out, you were able to resist the effects for a lot longer, so I was surprised to see you up and about at the point you found me outside, on the bench.'

'So when did I finally conk out?'

'Not too long after that, thankfully.'

'Did we not go to a club after?'

'Yes. But the drug had already started to take effect, and it wasn't long before you were taken straight to a lab to have the tests.'

'And that's when you found I didn't have any of the stuff in me?'

'Yes, but I didn't know that till first thing the next day. The eight of you that were the only remaining survivors from the original experiment were all tested that evening and, apart from you, everyone had traces of it to varying degrees in their blood.'

'So it had somehow regenerated?'

'Yes, in a way. We think, after initial injection, it managed to put itself into some kind of dormant state and camouflage itself in a way that our tests could no longer detect it. Then, at some point years later, it reawakened.'

'OK, so that still doesn't explain how I came to have this stuff in me?'

'No, it doesn't. Although the JAHL project did shut down after its failed attempt, there was still a group of scientists very much in favour of continuing with the research. They lobbied the government to continue with the project but they were refused. This, however, did not stop them, and they privately carried on. In the early eighties, they approached the government, lobbying them again, but this time presenting them with some very promising findings from the further research they had conducted. The government was impressed and agreed to fund a small team to run a legitimate project. Fast-forward another twenty years and they now had a new improved dose. The only issue now was to find subjects who would be injected with it.'

The penny then dropped.

'So you thought you would use the very same people from the first round.'

'Yes, although they only selected three of you. The ones who had the lowest reading of the original injected matter and who also seemed the most mentally stable. They picked you, for obvious reasons, Blake Riley and Zoe Abbot.'

I hadn't heard those names for a long time, and it stung me to hear them now.

'They both died,' I stated emphatically, 'not long after. Blake in a car accident and Zoe committed suicide.'

'Yes. In hindsight, our judgement of their mental stability was probably a bit off. When I think of it now, Blake was clearly out of control, and Zoe apparently had actually been showing signs of depression and struggling to cope with family life.'

'So it was the first shot that killed them rather than the second?'

'Yes, we think so. They just hadn't succumbed to the initial shot yet but were already well on the way.'

'So I have had the second dose but not the first.'

'Exactly.'

'And it is this second improved shot that has given me these abilities.'

Lisa nodded.

'And my anger problem?'

'Yes. But the behavioural problems associated with the first dose appear to be less severe and more easily controlled.'

'And I suppose this second dose was administered when I went for my spa treatment.'

'Yes. Although I wasn't aware that you had been given the second dose at that time. My suspicions had been aroused as soon as they said you had none of the stuff present, and as I knew you quite well, I was well aware of your gentle temperament and placid nature. This did not seem to fit the bill and so I strongly suggested they hold off injecting you with the second dose. Instead, just run some more tests to check if the original negative test was correct and let me investigate your background and ensure you were actually one of the subjects from the original experiment. I thought I had persuaded them to do just that.'

'But I had been given the second dose.'

'Yes. While I was off busy with the investigation, someone much higher than me overruled me. I think they already knew that Blake and Zoe were probably not going to make it, and you were their last hope to at least have one potential successful candidate.'

'So at what point did you know I had actually been injected with it?'

'When you tried to kill Amelia. Up until then, I thought the only problem I had to deal with was the memory purge had not worked and you were trying to uncover the truth about Roseville. I had to keep an eye on you and make sure you weren't going to cause us any grief. I thought we had succeeded when you finally seemed to run out of steam and give up on your pursuit. My superiors asked for regular updates on you, which I keenly obliged. What I didn't realise was they were not just interested in your quest to find Roseville and discover what JAHL was all about. They kept insisting I include reports about your behaviour and anything that might be deemed untoward. I should have realised why. As soon as the incident with Amelia happened, the penny finally dropped. I asked them outright and they instantly admitted it.'

'So whose idea was it to move me to Scotland?'

'Mine. They wanted to keep you at a facility. But I managed to persuade them to let you live in relative solitude in a remote place while we waited to see the results of this second dose. I hoped for out of sight, out of mind. As long as the reports did not show up anything of significance, maybe eventually they would abandon their pursuit and you would be left alone.'

'But something significant did happen?'

'At first, it was sporadic. The odd glimmer of suspicion. Nothing I couldn't explain away as hearsay or desperate wishful thinking. But then it got too regular and more obvious, and the evidence just got too strong.'

I wasn't sure if she was expecting me to be grateful for doing her utmost to protect me and keep me away from all this. I didn't feel grateful. I felt resentment. But … I was also curious. Curious to know what was happening in Unit 74 right now. I was more than ready for my third visit to Roseville.

THE FINAL CHAPTER

It was strange being here again. I remember the last time I had come I was shocked by the state the place had fallen into, but now it was almost unrecognisable. I felt sadness at the dilapidated state it had become. The security fencing was the only thing that looked sturdy and intact. The rest, in view of my eyes at least, was so badly neglected and falling apart. I was shocked to see some of the buildings in the main square had now partially collapsed. The place had also noticeably lost its colour as most of the flowers that once paraded here had been overrun and long since died. There was only one eye-catching piece left: a beautiful magnolia that was in full bloom and stood proudly, high above the havoc. Curiously, it was not a tree I could remember from either of my previous visits, and I supposed it was because it was a different time of year, when it would not be in flower.

As I stood gazing up at its beauty, I became acutely aware of someone's presence. I had come with four other people – one scientist and three armed guards – but I knew there was someone else here too that was not from our party.

'What's wrong?' asked Felix, the guy who seemed to at least think he was in charge.

'There's someone else here.'

'Where?' he demanded.

'Not far.' I scanned the area, trying to sense the location. I could feel they were hiding in a partially collapsed building just across from us.

'In there,' I replied, pointing.

Felix indicated to his other two comrades to conduct a search. I did not like Felix nor was I too fussed by his two army associates, but at least they were efficient in military-style operations. It took them a matter of a very few minutes to wheedle him out.

'Any more?' Felix asked me as they brought him over.

I shook my head. 'No, that's it.'

'What are you doing here?' Felix demanded from him.

'It's OK,' I said, raising my hand, gesturing Felix to leave him alone. 'I know him and I know why he is here.'

Felix looked at me in bemusement but questioned him no further and instructed his men to back away.

'Hi, Danny. Long time, no see.'

'Hi. Nice to see you again,' Danny replied.

'Have you found him?'

'No, not yet.'

'You're confident he is down there then?'

'I know there is definitely *something* down there.'

Danny took us into the building where he had set himself up. It used to be the main reception, although it resembled nothing of that now. In one corner were his living quarters where he had a camp bed, a portable gas stove and a few other bits and pieces. In another corner he had set up a makeshift desk that was covered in drawings and other paperwork. It was a keen reminder of the time we spent at his flat in London when we first tried to search for the existence of this place.

'Are those drawings maps of Unit 74?'

'Yes, well, parts of it at least. It is vast. You would not believe how far it extends. The cave system branches off into so many separate tunnels and extends for miles underground. It is so hard to navigate and find your way around. I have got lost on many occasions and feared I would not be able to find my way back to the surface. I am trying to map it all out. It is no easy task, and it has taken me months just to get this far. There is still a lot of the cave system I have not yet reached.'

'And have you found anything?'

'Oh yes. For the most part, I am not sure what I have found. But it is enough to know there is something very strange going on deep inside those caves.'

'And you still believe your dad is down there?'

He didn't answer straight away and looked very unsure of himself.

'I don't know. I think there is a chance. Someone is down there, but whether it is him or not, I don't know.'

'Well. Let's find out, shall we?'

Danny nodded with vigour and I sensed he was relieved to have some help. I glanced around the room at everyone else, and they did not look as enthusiastic.

We entered the cave system from a concealed entrance just round the back of the reception building. It amused me to think that there had been an entrance here all along and to think we traipsed all the way to the lodge I stayed at in order to gain entrance the last time.

I was impressed by Danny's ability to navigate us so easily to the Unit 74 entrance. He clearly had spent a lot of time down here and had familiarised himself with the intricate layout of the tunnels. I instantly recognised the large cavern and remembered vividly the red glow that shone from the Unit 74 corridor. The black iron gates stood wide open, just as they did when I was here last, when I had been terrified at what might have been allowed to escape and potentially attack us. This time, it was different. This time, I had no fear at all, only a strong compelling feeling to enter. I barely hesitated. Ignoring the beauty of the caverns that last time had captured my gaze, I went straight in. Even Danny seemed surprised but did follow, choosing to keep close by me. Felix was certainly taken aback but did eventually follow with his comrades, guns raised and poised to fire, while Larry, the nerdy scientist, nervously took the rear.

I am not sure how long we had been walking. Certainly, hours had passed and we had exhausted Danny's maps and were now purely following my intuition. Danny had become nervous at this point and was not keen to rely on me for directions. He couldn't understand how I seemed so sure on which way to go. I guess I had changed a lot since the last time he had seen me. Once so careful and unconfident and yet now bold and decisive. He had mentioned several times turning back, but for me that was not an option. We were to keep going at all costs. I had little regard for other people's weaknesses. I was not turning back now. For the most part, there were only cave walls and crevices and caverns. Occasionally, there were odd rooms or areas Larry was insistent on searching but I refused. I knew they were of little significance, to me at least. I wanted to keep going and find who it was that was down here. The deeper we got, the stronger I could feel their presence. I knew we were closing in, and I knew there was more than one of them. In fact, I could feel the presence of many.

'Welcome, Emma. So, finally, you made it!'

I stood defiantly as I carefully appraised the situation. We had arrived at what I can only describe as some sort of large metal hexagon-shaped structure. It looked very alien and futuristic to this world. There was some odd equipment dotted about and several computerised control panels in the walls.

Two people stood before us, although one looked only part human.

Danny collapsed onto the floor, clearly in shock at seeing what his father had become.

Although he was still recognisable as the man he once was, it was obvious he had metamorphosed into something quite different.

I studied the woman standing next to him, trying to figure out who it was, but I couldn't place her. She was unfamiliar to me. She looked very human and there was nothing obvious to suggest she was anything else.

Danny was sobbing on the floor, and Felix and his two men had guns raised, trained on Gerald, while Larry was stood shaking in the background. Gerald did not seem worried by the guns, and I doubted how much effect they would really have on him anyway. He did not take much interest even in his son. His interest seemed to lie with me.

'It's taken you a long time to get here, Emma, but I knew you would come eventually.'

If I had closed my eyes and heard only his voice, I would not picture the creature that stood before me, because his weedy human-sounding voice did not match the strong powerful and unhuman stature.

'What made you so sure I would come?'

'Because you are one of us. You belong with us.'

'And who is us?' I asked, looking directly at his companion.

'Why, this is Emma Stanton,' he replied proudly.

I remained calm and stoic but inside I was reeling with shock.

'I was told Emma Stanton died a long time ago at the care home.'

'You were told wrong, my dear. As you can see, she is very much alive.'

I looked at her with great suspicion. It was plausible, I suppose. She looked about the right age, and Lisa had told me they never actually found her body.

Presumably sensing my distrust, he elaborated.

'I took her and brought her back home. Emma was always a special one and should never have been put in that home in the first place. They couldn't cope with her at all. Even with their callous attitude, they still failed to exert any kind of control. If I hadn't taken her, they would probably have got rid of her somehow. I know they pushed her down the stairs once, no doubt in the hope of finishing her off and ending their misery. I did them a favour, although I did not do it for their benefit. They chose to cover up the kidnapping by swapping you in her place. I didn't have anything to do with that but, unknowingly to them, it actually made it all the more easier for me.'

Lisa had told me she had done a thorough investigation on all this, and yet it was obvious that some details had been missed. I was now also beginning to wonder about the legitimacy of Gerald's part in the JAHL project.

'What do you mean, she was special?'

It was an eerie feeling hearing him talk about her in such high esteem. It was as if he was completely besotted with her and worshipped her as some sort of god.

'She was always my favourite. She stood out as being superior to the rest of them. By far, the strongest and boldest. I remember her arming herself with a kitchen knife when she was a toddler at Roseville and the threat she posed even at that young age. Yes, she was my prodigy. So I treated her differently to the rest.'

'Differently?'

'She had extra-special attention when she was initiated into the project and received extra medicine to the others.'

'Medicine? You mean the injection of alien matter?'

He shrugged, as if he did not like me using that particular terminology. I remained frustrated that no one was willing to confirm to me the exact nature of what this stuff actually was.

'Did you stage your own disappearance?'

He smiled. I could tell something was amiss here. Danny had stopped sobbing and was listening very closely.

'Yes.'

Danny's head dropped. I wasn't sure if his heart could take any more.

'They didn't know what they were doing. There was so much potential, but it was run by people who were too careful and not willing to open their eyes to the possibilities. I told them over and over again what was possible. They just kept pushing back. Holding me back from making amazing discoveries. Then they wanted to close the whole project down. Unbelievable. Little did they know the progress I was making and the relationships I was forging with the creatures they held down here. What we were building together.'

It was alarming to hear him talk. He sounded like a complete lunatic or borderline megalomaniac. I wondered if that was something he was born with as a human trait or if he had acquired it from whatever his non-human side was.

'For a while, I continued leading a double life. Feigning the work for the government but secretly doing the real work down here. I was forced to because of their short-sightedness. It wasn't my intention to break away, but it soon became clear to me which group I truly belonged with. When the incident happened with the break-out, they were killing them. I couldn't stand by and just let that happen. So I made my choice.'

'And how did you become ... whatever it is you have become? Did you inject the stuff into yourself as well?'

'Of course. In fact, I was the very first person to receive it. I had already injected myself with it before the main experiment had even started.'

Judging by the obvious and stark comparisons you could make between the supposed real Emma Stanton and Gerald, I strongly suspected Gerald had a good many extra doses injected into him than her.

'I am confused, Gerald. What is the purpose of all this?'

'To create a superior race, of course. To eliminate the weak-minded people of this world who order us around and whom we have to follow like puppets.'

He spoke with real venom in his voice.

'You mean the government?'

'They are one good example, yes.'

'But you just live hidden underground in these caves.'

'For now. But not forever. Many of the creatures down here had an aversion to sunlight. But I have found ways to alter and enhance them, and they have adapted.'

He then raised his arms high into the air with his fists clenched and shouted, 'Soon we shall rise and become glorious!'

It was at this point it obviously became too much for Larry, who had so far spent the time cowering at the back. I could hear him scuffling about. I turned to look at him and he was clumsily trying to make his escape by retreating back up the tunnel from where we had come. From out of nowhere, two creatures flew right past me, one on each side. They flew so close I swear I felt them brush against my ears. I had no time to react as they moved like lightning. One of them took him by the jugular as he swooped past and took him off down the tunnel, while the other followed closely behind. I could hear Larry screaming some way off in the distance, but after a few seconds it subsided and there was only deathly silence. The creatures returned, flying breathtakingly fast past me and disappearing as mysteriously as they had emerged.

Felix then opened fire on Gerald, and his two guards subsequently copied. It was pointless. Gerald was impervious to it. The two creatures imminently returned, each attacking one of the guards. They killed them almost instantly on the very spot where they once stood but now lay crumpled on the floor. Emma had gone straight for Felix. I tried to intervene to defend him by getting in between them, but she was also amazingly quick and got to him first. She knocked him to the floor, and it looked like she may have killed him in just one blow. I grabbed at her and managed to pull her away from him. She pushed me away but did not attack me and simply returned to Gerald's side. I bent down to Felix to check for signs of life. He was not breathing and I could find no pulse.

I looked to Gerald and Emma and they were just watching me with no emotion. I then suddenly remembered Danny, but when I turned to look at him he was clearly dead, his body also crumpled on the floor and blood frothing from his mouth. I did not see how he came to die, but I could see Gerald had bloodstained hands, and I shuddered at the thought that he may very well have killed his own son.

I stood back up on my feet, disbelieving that four people's lives could be taken in what must have been less than two minutes. I no longer felt so bold and confident. I remembered what it was like to feel fear.

'Why did you kill them?' I asked despairingly.

'They are weak. They are no one. They are not one of us.'

'He is your son!' I shouted as I pointed to Danny's body.

'He is not one of us. He does not belong here.'

I stared at them both as I contemplated the horrific events I had just witnessed and had been unable to prevent. I realised that they had spared my life because they counted me as one of them and that I did belong here. They regarded me as part of their superior race.

I refound my confidence and strode over to Danny. I picked up his broken body and lifted him up onto my shoulder.

I took one last look at Gerald.

'You are not superior. You are a monstrosity.'

'You are one of us,' he replied as he sneered back.

'I am nothing like you,' I snapped back, although deep inside I knew there was some truth in what he said.

I turned my back on them and started walking back down the tunnel, carrying Danny on my shoulder with me. I had no idea if they would allow me to leave, but I knew I had to get back to Lisa and warn her about the terrible atrocities that were down here. There was no telling what would happen to the world if I did not succeed.

www.ingramcontent.com/pod-product-compliance
Ingram Content Group UK Ltd.
Pitfield, Milton Keynes, MK11 3LW, UK
UKHW012047071025
8281UKWH00002B/186